# THE HAMMER OF THE SMITH

Enjoy!

# The Hammer of the Smith

J.T. Sibley

| Library of Congress Control Number: | | 2008906087 |
|---|---|---|
| ISBN: | Hardcover | 978-1-4363-5572-8 |
| | Softcover | 978-1-4363-5571-1 |



This is a work of fiction. Names, characters, places and incidents either are the product of the author's imagination or are used fictitiously, and any resemblance to any actual persons, living or dead, events, or locales is entirely coincidental.

This book was printed in the United States of America.

**To order additional copies of this book, contact:**
Xlibris Corporation
1-888-795-4274
www.Xlibris.com
Orders@Xlibris.com
49264

# PREFACE

Not too many folks write novels set in pre-Viking period Scandinavia during what we call "The Dark Ages." There are, however, rich archaeological and epigraphic records from that time, upon which I drew extensively. Several characters herein were actual people; Muha and Asugisalas are mentioned on the Kragehul spearshaft (Denmark), and Beowulf (here, Biornulf) has his own saga. The Spear's head is also an actual item, the Kowel spearhead, found in the Ukraine. The regional variants of god-names ( for example, Thor to the Norse, Thunor to the Danes, Donar to the Continental Germanics) have been preserved. Traditional smithcraft, as well as Norse medical, runological, magical, herbal, and marine lore and folklore have been incorporated into this tale, although my purist friends will remind me that the counterweighted bellows apparently came into use during medieval times, that charcoal was pretty much the exclusive fuel used by smiths in pre-industrial Norway, and that aseptic surgical technique was essentially unknown before the 19th century. They might also mention that the Norse names used are modern forms, whereas those of the Danes and the Continental Germanics are closer to the original forms used in period. Very few Dark Ages Norse names are known, and it's simply easier to use more recognizable names. Please note that the patronymic is divided, i.e. "Sverre's son" rather than "Sverresson," as was the usage in earlier times. The main protagonist, Diccon, has an Anglo-Saxon name; to be explained in a second volume.

This book is a work of fiction, so liberties were taken. It is entirely possible that a skilled healer might have had the knowledge set down in these pages; ditto various aspects of the other disciplines. It's my thought that maybe we simply haven't yet found any surviving supporting documentation or examples for some of my more speculative interpretations.

I want to thank Virginia Fair Richards-Taylor, who painted the great cover art, Karen MacLeod, who cheerfully and skillfully copy-edited the manuscript; Kevin Hall, upon whom I partially modeled the smith Thorgrim, and who taught me much about smithcraft and forge-lore; the late Nicholas Taylor (Count Sir Ælfwine), a battle tactician and warrior; and my friends in the SCA and Reindeer Clan who egged me on to get this done, published, and in bookstores ASAP. I also wish to thank my family, which wonders if I'll ever stop playing with four or five half-finished manuscripts at one time.

# Chapter 1

The black and white cat, which we would call a tuxedo cat, sat huddled close to the warm forge, staring sourly out at the weather. No hunting this evening. No mouse in its right mind would be out and abroad, which meant that there'd be no supper tonight. The heat of the forge's stone walls warmed the cat's fur, which was one blessing, at least.

The forge itself was a large stone and brick structure, with the wide opening of the chimney above it. To one side was an oak tree trunk which had an anvil seated on its broad flat surface. The six-foot-long stump was sunk some four feet into the earth, and the anvil was securely bolted in place so that it couldn't be jarred off its resting place and mash the smith's toes. A heavy work table, next to the long wall away from the smithy door, held a variety of tools, none of which interested the cat. To one side of the forge was a mighty bellows, whose snout rested in a hole piercing the stonework, ready to breathe on the fire when the smith's apprentice pulled the counterweighted rope.

The smith was snug in bed, as was the apprentice. The only one awake was the cat, curled into a legless ball as close to the warm stones as she could get. Even the smithcrafter's magic was quiet. That magic only sang when the smith was at work, taming the fire and ruling the metal. But tonight, the great and small hammers rested quietly on the scarred work table, sleeping until tomorrow's work began.

The cat was used to the magic. Even though it raised her fur, she reveled in the whirl and tingle of the Power when the smith was at work. In her own way, she could channel bits of it; mostly to keep warm and to bring luck into her home. Soon it would be called upon to bring forth kittens, new life which she would nurse and teach and send out into the world. But now, she only wrapped the faint whispers of it around herself, keeping the gusty wind away from her cozy little spot. Before long, she dozed off, purring faintly to herself, singing her cozy sleep-song to the forge and the anvil.

When dawn arrived, the cat slowly began to awaken. It was a languorous awakening, with occasional backslidings into brief naps. Soon the apprentice would come, bringing her some milk still warm from the cow, and maybe a bit of leftovers from the night's meal. The cat hummed a purr around herself and the forge and the room, making a welcoming song to the morning and to the soon-to-appear, long-awaited meal. Last night's rain had slackened to a drizzle, and the cat knew that soon even that would go away and she could go outside for her morning stroll.

Breakfast arrived on schedule, and the cat was content. The apprentice, a lanky teenager with ash-blond hair tied back in a neat ponytail, bustled about, getting the forge ready for the day's work. He went over to the corner where the great bins of coal sat, and began cracking lumps of it into acorn-sized bits. The forge patiently awaited its own breakfast, which the apprentice would see to when he had enough small coal to feed it. The forge magic was quietly awake, too, waiting its turn to be fed and then to rouse into action. But it was the smith who would do that; the apprentice was as yet unskilled in its use and care. The smith was the magician, and he alone could call on the full Powers. The apprentice swept the room, careful to start at the back and sweep towards the door, pushing out any bad luck which might have sneaked in past the threshold wards and the cat.

The threshold wards were well set, and the busy broom found nothing more than dust and ashes. The cat finished her breakfast and sauntered to the wide-open door, ready to face the world. She felt the comforting, strong touch of the threshold wards in front of her, and was glad that her smith was skilled enough in his Power to make them strong and durable. Threshold magic sang a deep note, almost too low for the cat to hear. The Power cradled her as it recognized her, stroking her head and flanks with a reassuring touch. Once the cat walked out the door, she would be on her own, but here, just inside the door, the threshold kept all evil at bay. The cat decided that she'd wait until the last of the drizzle had finished its visit and had moved on.

The threshold magic was very strong today, the cat thought to herself. Much stronger than usual, it seemed. Was there something Out There which challenged it? The cat flicked her ears and looked back over her shoulder to see if the apprentice had noticed anything unusual. But that fellow was busy at his own chores, oblivious to the cat and the strong thummm of the threshold magic. The cat couldn't understand why he couldn't hear the magic, when it was so clear to her. Maybe it was because he was newly come, and hadn't been exposed to it since kittenhood, as she had been.

It seemed like forever before the cat heard the smith's heavy tread on the path leading toward the smithy. Thorgrim, the smith, slept in another building close by, which was off limits to the cat. She was a smithy cat, not a house cat, and she knew her responsibilities in that regard. Thorgrim, a tall, broad man with a short red beard and big gentle hands, came to the door of the smithy, smiling at the cat who stared up at him with round yellow eyes. Look at me, the cat thought at the man, I'm worried about the Outside. Listen to the wards, they're saying something to us! Thorgrim stooped and reached a wide callused hand to the cat's head, rumpling her ears and stroking her back. The cat didn't purr this time, as she tried to thought-punch her message through to the smith.

Some of her message seemed to get through. Thorgrim straightened up and looked back over his shoulder at the forest beyond the small smithy yard. He grunted deep in his chest and then stepped over the threshold into the smithy, into the protection of the place. He grunted again as he walked over to the forge, checking it and the anvil, making sure that all was in order for the day's work. The cat remained at the door, staring outwards, trying to sense what had aroused the threshold wards. Whatever it was, it wasn't close by. Everything looked to be as it should be. But the cat didn't relax her watch.

Behind her, Thorgrim reached for his heavy leather apron. He murmured as he donned it, settling the bib against his broad chest and tying the leather straps around his waist. The cat felt the forge magic move, anticipating its new work day. The apprentice was tending the fire, waking it up and feeding it bits of small coal and charcoal. The smith, standing between the table and the anvil, laid his hands on the black surface of the metal, still whispering something under his breath. The cat saw the anvil wake up, heard the songs of the hammers and pliers and other tools on the bench as they, too, awakened. It was Time.

The smith picked up his Great Hammer, the one with the deeply-carved symbol on its head. He tapped it lightly three times on the flat surface of the anvil, making it sing with bell tones, sanctifying the smithy and all within it. The cat felt the surge of forge magic sweep over her back and blend with the threshold magic, blanking out the faint stirrings of whatever was Outside which bothered her. She tried to hold onto it, but the song of the anvil was too strong and soon she forgot and slept, a black and white ball near the door.

"What shall we make today, do you think?" Thorgrim asked the anvil, "We're going to have to shoe old Butterball this afternoon, which means we'll have to make a special shoe for the crooked hoof on his right fore." The apprentice looked up, and then selected a couple of bars of iron for the smith to choose from. The smith looked the pieces over, and then pointed to another piece lying on the floor next to the coal.

"That one, I think," he said, "The others don't want to be horseshoes." The apprentice looked curiously at the apparently identical bars, trying to see why the smith had rejected the ones he'd picked.

"Look, lad, you have to listen to the metal," Thorgrim rumbled. "Iron knows what it wants to do. The right piece will bend to the hammer's will the way a wrong piece won't. Come, feel this piece and think of Butterball's right fore hoof. Feel how the metal will be shaped to be wed to it. Think of the hoof and the shoe as one."

The apprentice obediently held each of the various bars briefly, and shook his head. "They all look alike to me," he said, "They're just bars of iron."

"Look, Diccon, the metal *is* different. That piece you're holding wants to be a wheel rim. Those others will make good spikes. Close your eyes and try to *see* what the iron wants to do. It will tell you, every time." Diccon scrunched his eyes shut and tried hard to connect with the metal, but nothing came to him. He *wanted* to feel the metal, sense the magic, but it was if he were deaf. The bar lay in his hands, not saying anything that the apprentice could hear.

Thorgrim sighed. "Diccon, you're trying too hard. Relax and let the metal speak. It sort of whispers; it doesn't shout." The apprentice tried hard to relax, but still nothing. "Oh, well, maybe next time we'll try you on a piece of metal with a louder voice," grunted the smith, as he waved to the lad to man the bellows.

The chosen bar was thrust into the heart of the fire, warmed by the breath of the slowly pumping bellows. Thorgrim waited while it heated, listening to the tiny crackles and snaps of the burning nuggets of coal. The pungent smoke coiled up into the maw of the chimney on its way to the sky, passing the chimney wards as it went. Chimney wards let things out, but don't permit anything of the Outside to go down past them into the room below. There was nothing in the flow of the smoke to tell the smith that those wards, too, were unusually alert and on guard.

The first blow of the hammer on the white-hot bar woke the cat, who had been dreaming about a terrible giant mouse which had been chasing her. Gratefully, she welcomed the normal, homey sounds of the hammer on the soft metal, beating it into Butterball's new shoe. She relaxed and slept again. The clamor of the hammer drowned out the deep bass of the threshold wards, which were getting more insistent. Something was not as it should be, and whatever it was, was going to happen soon.

The smith worked on the shoe, carefully explaining his every move to the apprentice, who stood at the far side of the forge, keeping a stream of air flowing onto the coals. The forge fire danced and laughed, staccato grace notes to the song of the hammer. When the shoe was finished, Thorgrim carried it in his tongs over to the large oaken barrel in which thunder-water was kept. The very best water for quenching iron was that gathered during a thunderstorm on a Thor's day; the thunder god himself sent the water, and it was full of his lightning power. The horseshoe spat and sizzled in the water, drinking in the magic as it cooled. With such shoes, Butterball would be protected from any evil lurking in the ground; he would walk on iron touched by the Thor himself!

The cat awoke with a start. The threshold wards were glowing to the cat's sight, and the fur raised on her back. She sprang to her feet, facing out the door, and spat loudly. Thorgrim looked over at her, and then quickly grabbed his Great Hammer. Diccon, still pumping the bellows, had been looking at the fire and hadn't seen either the cat or the smith alerting to an as-yet unrevealed danger. It was only when the smith spoke that he noticed that something was up.

"Thor, aid us!" yelled the smith as he laid the Hammer down on the threshold, barring the way with the symbol of the god. The cat had backed away from the smith, deeper into the safety of the smithy. Her dark coat blended with the shadows until all anyone could see of her was her white triangle of nose, white bib, white gloves, and wide yellow eyes. The hammer's Power mated with that of the threshold, growling as it ramped up, sending glowing lines of magic around the smithy, netting it in a protective tapestry which shimmered faintly in the grey light. Thorgrim wheeled and snatched a small flask of rowan mead from the workbench, hastily unstoppered it, and splashed a swallow of the golden liquid onto the forge fire.

"Thor, come to us and protect us from what comes!" he chanted, as the liquid boiled away, adding its sweet fumes to the smoke arising from the forge and going up the chimney. It was well known that the thunder god liked his mead, and calling him with Hammer and mead would surely bring his active attention to the smithy and its occupants. Diccon looked wildly about, trying to see what had brought all this on, as the smith pulled him over to the anvil.

"Put your hands on that anvil and don't take them off until I tell you!" the smith commanded. "The magic will protect you there! Think only of the anvil and the forge magic wrapping around you, like a coat of steel!" Diccon's hands trembled on the anvil as he tried to follow the smith's directions and still see what was going on.

The smith took a double handful of the thunder-water and splashed it on his head. He then wetted his apron and carried a handful over to the Hammer at the door. Outside, the sky was darkening suddenly, and the sound of thunder burst upon the eardrums of the humans and the cat. The latter wedged herself into as small a ball as she could, dipping her head to hide the white parts, and closing her eyes. She willed herself to invisibility, a catly talent, disappearing in the gloom of the far corner where she'd fetched up.

Thorgrim hurried to the work table and took up a large single-edged knife which was made of star-metal and hilted with amber. This knife was a scramasax, and had certain runes made of silver wire embedded in grooves etched into the blade. It was a very special knife, not to be used for ordinary purposes. Holding the scramasax in front of his chest, the grim-faced smith strode to the door, ready to face whatever danger was about to strike.

Thunder crashed and jagged spears of lightning thrust themselves from the sky, smashing into the ground around the smithy and the small cottage which was the smith's home. The god was there in person, striking out with his divine thunderweapon at whatever it was that threatened his followers. The anvil hummed, sending vibrations up Diccon's arms, which made the apprentice shiver even more violently. He could *feel* the magic now; even a dead cow could have felt the magic. Diccon shuddered as the anvil's Power crested over him, shielding and protecting him from the as-yet unseen menace without.

Thorgrim stood with legs apart, facing the door. The gleaming blade of the bright-metal scramasax was aimed toward the open doorway in front of the smith, whose steady hands gripped the rune-inscribed amber hilt with both hands. He chanted and channeled the Power, feeling it surge up his legs and down his arms, making his hair and beard stand out stiffly like the bristles on a hairbrush.

A sudden swirl of the air near his ankles marked where the good gnomes of the land scampered into the safe haven offered by the smithy. Thorgrim noted their passage, recognizing that anything that spooked the *vettir* wouldn't be your usual werewolf or walking-deadman-with-an-agenda. He hoped that the other Talents in the area were on guard as well; a multilayered defense was much better than only one smith standing in the way of the incoming threat or threats.

Thor's lightning still sought for the enemy, but apparently wasn't finding any discrete targets. Thorgrim knew that in a bit the thunder god would tire of this and go off somewhere else, leaving the smithy and the land about it unprotected by the gods. One could only stay at top alert for so long . . . and before that edge wore off, the enemy had to reveal itself. Or so the smith hoped in sort of a dreading way.

The air seemed to get heavier and there was a kind of droning noise off in the forest, a humming as of many swarms of bees flying rapidly toward the smithy, away from the not-so-distant river which fed into a short fjord leading to the sea. Thorgrim stiffened in place, holding the now-glowing scramasax straight-armed in front of him, willing that the smithy and its occupants be invisible to whatever was flying toward them. The droning noise got louder and louder, and seemed to be broadening out as it approached.

A flickering smoky-dark wall swept over and through the trees toward the small buildings nestled in the little clearing. It was mindless, roaring along on a fixed path, seeking any life it might meet. There was a glowing spark directly in front of it, white-hot in its intensity, but the Dark paid it no heed. Where there was no mind, there was no judgement.

The Darkness surged over the smithy, avoiding the bright web of magic which enclosed the small building and the bright spear of energy which lanced out at it from the smith's knife-tip. The droning sound got so loud that it drowned out the thunder, and the apprentice, eyes tightly shut, hung onto the anvil for dear life. The smith, calling on the chthonic Earth-Fire, fed Power to the knife, whose coruscating beam swept back and forth as he moved his hands, pushing the Darkness away from his home and workplace.

And then, as suddenly as it came, the Dark was gone, scudding past them. The Power had kept it clear of the smithy and cottage, but only a smallish hole had been punched in the tidal wave of malignant energy as it mindlessly swept on, broadening even wider in its path as it went.

Thorgrim dropped his arms, the knife hilt still clutched in his shaking hands. He had stood firm, and none of the Darkness had managed to touch what he and the Power had protected. He looked up at the now-blue sky; obviously the thunder god had followed the onrushing threat and taken his cloud-wagon with him. Shaking his head and blowing out a huge breath, the smith flexed his shoulders and turned away from the now-innocent light streaming through the door.

"You can let go now, Diccon," he said in a low voice, "We should be safe now."

"W-what was that?"

"I have heard of such curses before, but never have I had to face such a one," the smith replied, "Someone out there on or near the river wants to knock out the land defenses. He's probably landing his boats now. He has a worker of magic with him . . . someone who knows well the Powers of the Dark . . . someone who could strip away the land's defenses and chase off the *vettir*, leaving us helpless, confused, and at his mercy.

"Learn this, Diccon. There are people Out There who don't care how they get rich, don't care how they gain land. You've just survived a mighty spell, one designed to bring madness and terror to whoever lives in the way of its wielder.

"Part of the smith's lore is how to make horseshoes. But by far, the most important is the forgecraft, the magic which permits him to tame the metal and fire. We appear to be simple craftsmen to the villagers, but we're actually far more than that. The Smithcrafters' Way is both a Warrior and Mage's Way, and only a few are selected to follow this path. You're one, in spite of the fact that you haven't been able to hear magic at all so far. You can, you know."

Diccon looked up at the smith, who towered over him. All the years of his parents and older brothers telling him that he was a nerdy little twerp who'd never amount to a hill of beans . . . and here, Thorgrim himself thought that he was actually worth something! The smith's broad right hand clasped warmly and firmly on the apprentice's shoulder.

"Lad, you'll surprise them all someday," he said with a smile, "I've walked in your shoes, and now look at me! I had a good teacher, and I only hope to be as good a teacher to you as he was to me. And I could tell that you finally felt the forge magic when you linked with the anvil!

"But enough of this! We must see what faces us on the river, and see if any others have managed to divert the Dark curse. Marit should be fine; she's seen and dealt with more evil than I have bits of coal . . . and I'd bet that old Sven Bluemouth wouldn't bow to it, either."

"B-but Marit, she's a witch, isn't she? And Sven hasn't been sober since I was playing with wooden horses!"

Thorgrim chuckled and said, "Marit *is* a witch, sure enough. She knows a lot of magic that only the womenfolk can learn, and is one of the Clan. Sven . . . do you know why they call him 'Bluemouth'? That's because he knows every swear word there ever was, and no curse can confound him! Even drunk as a weasel, that man knows his curses! But we've gotta move, lad; ordinary folks Out There have probably been caught by the Darkness, and can't defend themselves! Grab that sword over there; I'll just take my scramasax and my trusty axe!" And with that, the now-armed smith stepped over the Great Hammer lying on the threshold. Without a glance backward, he and Diccon strode forth, leaving the smithy in the nominal charge of one hard-to-see tuxedo cat.

# CHAPTER 2

The smith and his apprentice cautiously approached the village. The smithy lay about fifteen minutes' walk to the north from the riverbank settlement, since the fumes of the forge and the din of the hammers disturbed folks who preferred peace and quiet to honest industry. Sven Bluemouth should be hereabouts, the smith opined; he was never far from Jan Sverre's son's brewery. And sure enough, as the two approached the large shed which housed the beer-works, there was Sven. The old boozer was a scrawny bucktoothed specimen, something that no female in her right mind would take a second glance at. His scraggly grey hair stuck out at right angles from his skull, and he was wearing the most disreputable tunic and trousers that Diccon had ever seen. The fellow probably even attracted flies!

Thorgrim courteously greeted Sven, who opened one bleary eye and hiccuped loudly. Diccon was surprised to see his master so respectful of the old bum. He was even more surprised when the smith knelt down so that his eyes were level with those of the man, who was sort of propped up against the brewery wall.

"So, how did *you* deal with the Dark sending?" asked the smith, "Do you have any idea where it came from?"

"Urrrrrrrp . . . reshited a poem my Maw taught me. Hic. Sheemed to work OK, so I kept shaying it over an' over. Din't want annnnnything to happen to the brewery! Hic!" Sven waved a hand vaguely around as he continued, "An' shure enough, the wordsh kept the bad shtuff away! Had to check out the buuurrrp . . . beer afterwardsh, though. Hic."

"Sven, get your sorry ass up out of the street and go for help! I'm going down to the riverbank, where I think this all came from. Diccon, you come with me!" Thorgrim got to his feet and headed towards the water, his bright-bladed scramasax still held in one capable hand. He dodged around buildings, darting and pausing from one house to another. Diccon followed, sword in hand, copying the smith's moves. He was scared, but didn't want the smith to see his fear. Magic in general scared the apprentice, who had been raised by a non-magical family out in the boonies. Thorgrim reached the last building and cautiously peeked around it at the river.

Sure enough, a twelve-oar boat was pulled up onto the sloping mud and pebble beach. Most of the crew had disembarked and were forming up on the beach, swords and shields at the ready. A tallish lean man with medium brown hair and beard, obviously the skipper, was helping a shorter, stocky man toward dry land.

Thorgrim, whose keen-bladed axe was thrust in his belt, held his bright-metal knife in his right hand, pointing downwards toward the earth in front of him. He leaned back out of sight of the invaders and began to weave a pattern in the air with the gleaming blade, muttering under his breath in time to his movements. Diccon crouched next to the building, watching what the smith did. The hair on his arms stood straight up and, for the first time, he could feel the powerful summoning magic tingle in the air.

The smith finished his pattern with a flourish and then stabbed the earth in front of him. The glowing blade sizzled as it sank into the earth, and the earth actually howled back.

There were shouts from the beach, and the clattering sound of running armed men coming toward them, but Thorgrim remained in his stooping position, holding the blade steady as it bucked and twisted in the dirt. There was a kind of indrawing feeling, and then the earth moved under their feet. Diccon heard the sound of screams and curses as the earth magic reached the invaders, and then he ducked as an answering blast of freezing air loaded with hail shook the building behind which the two of them were hiding. Thorgrim wasn't the only one with Power there; the invaders had apparently brought a worker of magic along with them.

More shouts came from the direction of the brewery as the knot of men rousted by Sven came tearing down toward the river, intent on protecting their homes and livestock. Old Sven was among them, somehow keeping on his feet as he lurched along, cursing a blue streak. As the smith continued to summon the earth to his bidding, Sven screeched to a halt, raised his hands into the air, and spat out a sequence of words . . . Diccon presumed that they were words . . . and a great blue smoky serpent shot out from his mouth. That creature sped straight towards the invaders, strengthened by the torrent of words pouring from the old drunk's mouth. When Old Sven pronounced a curse, it was a dilly!

The land shuddered under their feet, but the smith held steady. This wasn't an "aim and fire" type of magic; it had to be kept up until it wasn't needed any more. There were more screams, and the sounds of men frantically trying to push the boat off the beach in their effort to escape. Diccon peered around the shed just as the short stocky man got off one last spell. A greasy dark ball of Something shot toward the apprentice, who tried to duck back before it hit him. He would have made it if he hadn't stumbled back and then bounced forward off the rock-steady body of the smith. The ball hit Diccon on the side of his face, flowed over his head, and seemed to soak into his pores. He fell to the ground, screaming as the Darkness flowed into his mind, overwhelming his feeble defenses. He didn't see Thorgrim hastily hop to the side, still holding his blade sunk into the earth. Diccon's body lay there, trembling on the ground, and then it began to writhe slowly in place.

Sven's smoky blue serpent tried to reach out over the water to the fleeing boat, but the craft was now too far from the shore. The serpent's ropy figure hung there, slowly dissipating as the gentle breeze pulled it apart. Sven's curse was a good one, but only effective on or over land. The boat pulled jerkily away, with only four rowers at work. The rest of the crew never made it back to the boat; Thorgrim's earth magic and Sven's snake had pulled them down, smashing and crushing them. Even their swords were warped and twisted, as if partially melted by a great heat.

Thorgrim, satisfied that the threat was retreating, pulled his blade from the earth and straightened up, staying well clear of the rocking, shuddering body of his apprentice. The village men went to help Diccon, but the smith stuck out one thick arm, fending them off.

"Stay back! That's a Contagion spell he's under, and anyone who touches him will catch it in turn!" The smith quickly scribed a circle with his scramasax on the ground around the boy, fencing in the evil so that it could not spread further. He didn't know the healing magics, but he could at least contain the danger until Gytha, the village Wise Woman, arrived on the scene.

As one of the men ran off to fetch Gytha, the others watched the fleeing boat until it was lost to sight. "I wonder what brought *that* on?" asked one, "We're not a rich village and we certainly don't have any treasure hidden hereabouts!" "Yeah, an' that was some kinda serious magic that fella threw at us, too! Never seen anything like that in my life!" "Hey, let's check out the bodies, see if they have any silver on 'em!" "Uuuunh, look, Ulf, they got pretty messed up from our magic; wouldn't doubt that Sven's curse was still riding 'em! You wouldn't want to catch one of Sven's spells now, wouldja?" "Damn, forgot about that! Let's get Sven to check the bodies!" "Hey, Sven, c'mere! Ya wanna check out the stiffs for us, see if they have anything worthwhile on 'em?"

"Rather not, fellas, hic! Leave 'em there until the water getsh to 'em, hic, cleans the spellsh off 'em! When I curshes something, they gets *curshed*! Hic!"

It took a while before Gytha came. In the meantime, Diccon tried to crawl out of the circle, driven by the Contagion spell to seek out new victims. The smith's circle held, in spite of the apprentice's repeated attempts to cross the faintly-glowing line scratched in the earth. More of the villagers appeared, drawn by the commotion and curious to see what was happening. Rubbernecking is a part of human makeup, and these folks didn't normally lead terribly exciting lives. The apprentice, drawn to the body heat of the villagers, redoubled his efforts to reach them. His conscious mind, walled into a seething black prison, tried to hold his body back, but it was like spitting inside a tornado. He made strange mewing sounds as he scrabbled at the invisible hemisphere of force penning him in. Thorgrim hoped that Gytha would hurry up; he'd been pretty exhausted when he drew that circle, and he didn't know how long it would last.

# Chapter 3

Diccon was lost. All around him it was dark and swirling, with sticky gooey black tendrils of hate fencing him in. His consciousness had contracted into a tiny nutshell . . . he thought of it as a hazel nut with a hard shell protecting the essence, the life-force that was himself. Trapped but still there, still himself. He only hoped that his master, who knew so much, would be able to shatter the bonds that imprisoned him. He couldn't feel his body at all. Vision and hearing were denied him, too. He tried not to scream there in the Darkness; tried to hold that last desperate shell protecting him intact, tried not to go mad.

Time was endless; Diccon had no concept of it. A minute? Could have been an hour or a day or a week. He thought of the forge, of the white-hot heart of it that glowed and drove away the darkness. If he could become the forge, become the glowing bed of coals that tamed the metal, then maybe he could drive the cold away bit by bit. In his mind, he drew on the memory of the Power that whispered in the bellows that he had so carefully pumped at his master's command. Carefully, so as not to crack his shell, he blew the tiniest wisp of that Power on the glowing core that was himself. Carefully . . . mustn't blow too hard, lest the metal burn.

Eons passed as he breathed life into his tiny world. He was glad that he'd paid such close attention to what the smith had taught him. The Darkness retreated slightly from the fiery coal that was Diccon, but he didn't let his concentration slip. Carefully, carefully . . . slowly pump the bellows, slowly add a tiny bit more coal to the flame . . . time was immaterial to him as he gradually expanded the nutshell, slowly heated his forge fire. He couldn't make a mistake now. That would lead to disaster; the Dark's cold winds would swoosh in and kill the flame, kill the life-force that was Diccon.

The dreadful Darkness retreated slowly as Diccon worked. He didn't need his eyes or ears for this, nor his legs or arms. With all his mind, he fed the slowly-growing flame, felt its hunger and need for more coal. He could use slightly bigger bits now . . . where he found them he hadn't a clue, but somehow they were there as he needed them. He was unaware of the people standing around him, of his body struggling to escape the force-field set by the smith, of Time itself.

The fire grew larger and more insistent, requiring more fuel. Diccon had to be careful not to let it grow too fast lest some flaw in the firing give the Darkness a crack to creep in. He felt as if he *was* the forge itself, cradling the fire, calling the smithcrafter's Power to do his bidding. Patiently, carefully, he kept at his task.

Outside his prison, in the world of people, the villagers stared at the wildly thrashing boy, fearful that he would escape. The smith stood silently with his eyes closed, feeding his Power into that shimmering force-field, knowing that he had to stand firm as long as he could lest the Contagion escape. If Diccon managed to touch anyone, his curse would instantly infect the second person, and then both of them would continue to seek other victims. A curse like this could wipe out the whole village. Old Sven lurched over to the smith and added what Power he could, but carefully, so as to not set up a frequency beat interfering with Thorgrim's Working. All they could do was to play a waiting game until Gytha came.

Gytha was the Wise Woman of the village. She helped would-be mothers call the souls of children so that they could conceive. It wasn't simply the mating of the man's seed with the woman's; the child's spirit had to be brought from wherever it had been waiting. Gytha had called many lives into waiting wombs, and then taught the mothers how to protect themselves from those supernatural beings who wanted to swap their own horrible offspring for the human baby. Birthing magic was a lot more than simply helping the mother have a baby. Gytha knew the herbs to use, the charms and amulets to carry, and the tricksy ways of the trolls, bears, and other beings which followed the expectant mother, hoping for a chance at the child. It was also Gytha who eased the dying person's spirit into the path to the Beautiful Lands; that path was fraught with its own dangers. And when a person was wounded or sick, Gytha was summoned to sing away death, sing the cells of the body into fighting the injury or illness, sing the Power of growing things and the Earth into the patient. A Wise Woman was very important to the life and health of her village, and Gytha was one of the best.

She came, with hastily-grabbed healer's bag in hand, her kerchief flying behind her as she ran. She was a smallish woman with a rosy-apple face and well-fed figure; her greying dark hair was coiled around her head in a long braid. If you didn't look into her eyes, you'd think that she was just somebody's grandmother, but once you made eye contact, you saw the Power within her soul. People on the outskirts of the crowd made way for her as she approached; the amulets around her neck and the keys and small tools at her belt tinkled and clattered as she slowed to a walk. She halted next to the smith, feeling the Power of the force-field around the smith's apprentice. She nodded once, and then set her bag on the ground so that she could fetch out what was needed to face this new enemy.

This was going to be dangerous. Somehow, Gytha had to get inside that force-field so that she could work. But if the apprentice touched her before she was ready, she would face his terrible fate herself. Drawing an ancient obsidian knife from her bag, she faced the crowd, making pushing motions with her hands so that they would draw back, away from the force-field, Thorgrim, and Old Sven. The crowd hastily obeyed, retreating well out of range. The smith and the drunkard took no notice; their attention was elsewhere. As she raised the knife to the sun, Gytha noticed Marit, the dairy witch, running towards the crowd. A grey bird flew above Marit's head, twittering as it flew. Gytha was glad to see her; she would need all the Power she could summon to deal with this case.

Marit was young, tall and leggy, with long wheat-blonde braids that reached to her waist. She had obviously been with her cows, judging from the mire on her boots and the friendly smell of manure surrounding her. Milk and dairy magic were Marit's specialties, although she made love potions and told fortunes on the side. Some people feared her power, and none dared insult her, lest their cows run dry and their chickens lay no eggs. Marit came up to Gytha, and the two women seemed to have a quick, voiceless conference. The dairy witch pulled a ripe stalk of barley from her hair, whispering to it as she did so. Then the two women turned to face Diccon, and as one they raised their respective Tools to the sun. Gytha then began scribing a larger circle on the ground around the two men and the apprentice, walking sunwise and singing a shapeless low tune as she moved. Marit followed on her tracks, brushing the line cut by the obsidian knife with the beard of the grain-head; her song interweaving with that of the birthing-woman as the magic entwined in the new, larger circle.

When the two women came around to their original starting point, Gytha drove the knife hard into the ground to seal the circle; made it a solid ring with no breaks in it. Marit's barley stalk was placed beside it, lying in the shallow groove of the earth with the grain end to the right of the knife, and the root end on the other side. The women whispered something to the knife and barley, and then raised their eyes heavenward. Calling on its Power to feed the magic, the women saluted the sun. The faint line which they had made glowed a sudden greenish gold, and then faded almost to invisibility. Those villagers who had a bit of Talent could see the energy flowing around it, but to most folks, it appeared like a simple circle scribed on the ground with a stick, such as those drawn by children playing a game.

Gytha moved up to stand by Thorgrim's right side, and Marit took her place to the left of Sven. In a low voice, each spoke to the man next to her, quietly so as not to startle him When the smith turned his head slightly toward her, Gytha knew that he heard what she said. A nod from Marit indicated that Sven was also paying attention. It was time for the men to drop their inner circle; free the captive so that the women could work. Thorgrim took a small handful of forged nails from his apron pocket and struck them with a piece of flint which had also been in that pocket. A shower of sparks answered him; the smith then blew gently on the nails as if they were alight. He then moved sunwise around the force-field containing his apprentice, driving a nail into the ground every foot or so just outside of the shimmering hemisphere. Old Sven swayed where he stood; fortunately his type of magic didn't seem to mind hiccups or burps in the Power-chant he mumbled.

The smith's star-metal blade flashed in the sun as he cut across the line he had originally drawn, severing the Power that maintained the circle. He then leaped backward as the shimmering dome vanished like a popped soap bubble. Diccon was now hemmed in by only a simple picket fence of nails, but the smithcraft magic in them kept the apprentice corralled. He couldn't pass beyond the nail-fence, although his arms could reach out above it. The dome was down, which meant that the women could work directly on the cursed boy.

Gytha swayed where she stood, raising her hands towards the sky. Marit's hands reached down toward the good earth. Thorgrim, trembling with exhaustion, stood behind the ladies. Sven merely slid to the ground and began snoring gently. The two women, minds linked, surveyed the patient . . . that's what Diccon was to them, a patient . . . and scanned the nature of the curse which had struck him. It was a really nasty one; but like most curses, it had its limits, and couldn't act to defend itself against a creative attack, being mindless evil and contagion. With a simultaneous nod, the two set to work. Marit was the ground; she would channel the Darkness into a pebble near her feet which could then be burnt and destroyed. Her dairy magic, which helped her bring down the milk, could be used to milk off the spell, transferring it to another container. Gytha's task was to slip between the coils of the unraveling spell, searching for Diccon's life force, and birthing it from the terrible womb which imprisoned him.

As Marit worked, Thorgrim could see the curse being pulled out of Diccon's pores, ears, nose, mouth, and eyes. Most of the villagers weren't Talented, so all they saw was Marit making stroking motions in the air. Gytha stood still; her hands outstretched toward the boy, calling quietly with her mind, building a silvery rope of Power which she snaked in past the uncoiling spell. The smith's eyes closed; he called upon the good *vettir* of the place to help the women and to protect them from any backlash or traps. Sven merely slept.

Diccon's forge fire had expanded to the size of an apple. He noticed that it suddenly seemed to be easier to push the Dark fog away, and he added more fuel to his fire. He was still cautious; this could be a trap. But then he thought he heard a faint voice calling his name . . . summoning the essence that was Diccon. He moved slightly toward it, and the Darkness gave way in front of him. A tiny patch in front of him seemed to glow from the outside, like a candle seen through a piece of linen. The glow brightened, and Diccon moved toward it. This was not the Dark; it was something of the Light!

"Grab on!" it seemed to say, "Hold fast to the lifeline!" Diccon moved his forge-fire self as close to it as he could. A sort of tingle touched his shell as the silvery thread made contact. Its end opened up like a flower, engulfing the apple-sized forge fire, and the sense of release was almost dizzying to the boy. He was still scared of traps, and kept his shell as hard as he could make it. There was sort of a pulling, swaying sensation and the Darkness around him seemed to be getting lighter and lighter. "Keep fighting!" the silvery thread said, "Don't relax yet!"

Suddenly, he was vigorously rotated around like a top spun by a small child. He fell to the ground . . . and felt himself hit the earth. His eyes opened groggily as Marit milked the last of the curse from him into the pebble at her feet. His mouth tasted like the floor of the hencoop and his ears rang, but he could see and feel and hear and smell and taste and touch again! It was *wonderful.*

# CHAPTER 4

Diccon felt the strong hands of his master clasp his shoulders where he lay. Thorgrim's keen eyes scanned the youth for any damage, and finding none, he breathed out a gusty sigh of relief as he rose to his feet, smiling down at his apprentice.

"Good job!" said the smith, "You *have* learned well! And you could feel the Power, couldn't you?"

"Y-yes . . . it came when I needed it! That curse-spell was *awful*! I didn't think I could get free . . . how did you do it?"

"I had some very good help." Thorgrim waved one hand toward Sven, Marit, and Gytha. The ladies had broken their outer circle and reclaimed their Tools, and were now beaming at the limp boy half-sitting on the ground. "Let's get you back to the smithy and to bed!"

"*I'll* drink to that!" exclaimed Sven, suddenly sitting up in mid-snore. How he managed to do magic while drunk was a hot topic of discussion, but nobody had ever managed to sober him up to see if he could still work in a non-inebriated state. It was said that Sven could magic a drink out of thin air if he was thirsty.

The smith reclaimed his nails, and tucked his star-metal scramasax in his broad belt next to his unused axe. He effortlessly picked up his apprentice, cradling him in his arms to carry him home. As he turned to leave, he told the villagers to set a watch; that boat might come back, and he wanted to have more warning the next time.

Marit carefully nudged the shiny black pebble which now contained Diccon's curse into a small leather bag, using a smallish twig which she then dropped into the bag after the stone. Holding the bag suspended by its drawstring, she headed off to the nearest fire in order to burn the pouch, stone, and twig. Fire was the best way to destroy that kind of spell.

As Thorgrim finished his speech, Soti, the village chieftain finally showed up. He'd been deep in conversation with a passing trader, who had news as well as bronze pins in stock. That worthy had told him that a band of armed men from somewhere down south were searching for someone or something, and even the non-Talented knew that these men weren't simply innocent travelers. They were a bit too creepy for that. Anyway, these men had been working their way up the coast, casually quizzing each settlement in their path. Any person who seemed to be of interest was grilled further, with a short, stocky, intense man supervising each session. The strangers seemed to be inordinately interested in any orphaned or fosterling young boys, and in anyone who was gifted with the Talent. If a person lied, the short stocky man would make a funny gesture in the air and the liar would stiffen, his eyes glaze over, and he'd spill his guts. The trader wanted to stay well clear of those folks. It was nobody's business how much he'd paid for his stock compared to how much he was selling it for.

Thorgrim, still cradling Diccon in his arms, frowned at this. Folks were always shifting around, getting married and moving to the next valley, or coming to this one in search of employment or marriage. What was it that brought those men here, he wondered. Why are they looking for certain very young boys? And what was this fascination with the Talented?

The crowd started breaking up. There was nothing more to see here, and chores were waiting. Gytha had left, and Marit headed back to her home and pastures. Sven had vanished into the brewery, no doubt to see if the beer within had suffered during the recent happenings. Jan Sverre's son, the brewmaster, would welcome Sven with open arms; Sven had the fortuitous Talent of making sure that anything containing alcohol would be acceptable to his finely-tuned taste buds. Thorgrim wanted to get home too; he needed a quiet place in which to examine Diccon more carefully to see if there was anything lingering in him that the ladies had missed.

Diccon, exhausted from his battle, fell asleep in the smith's arms. Before he knew it, he was back in the smithy, being laid on the floor next to the forge. Thorgrim decided to leave his Great Hammer on the threshold as an additional ward . . . there might be another attack, and he didn't want to get caught short. The forge fire was still burning, hunkered deep in its bed of coke and ashes. The smith added some coal and stirred the fire so that sparks went up the chimney. He wanted the smithcraft magic fully awake, and the fire was the heart of that magic.

It was time to do a Seeing. There were many techniques for this, but the one he would use was part of the Power of this place. He went over to his work table, and pulled a small oaken box from a pile of scrap metal bits and odd pieces of wire. In that box were a few small chunks of precious star-metal, fallen from the sky and never worked by the hand of Man. Thorgrim closed his eyes and let his hands hover over the open top of the box, waiting for the proper piece to announce itself.

There! A small nugget, no larger than the end of his thumb . . . that was the one! Thorgrim picked it up and carried it over to the forge. With a pair of tongs, he inserted the nugget into the heart of the flames. Whispering under his breath, he went to the bellows and slowly began pumping air to the forge fire. In one corner, the tuxedo cat felt the magic come, and her fur bristled. She heard the smith asking the Powers to reveal what he wanted to learn and, wide-eyed, she crept close to the warm forge box in the hopes of better seeing what was going on. The smith pumped the bellows harder, causing the fire to sparkle and leap upwards. Occasionally, he added some more bits of coal, still whispering, still asking.

Diccon roused himself. His master was doing the apprentice's work; Diccon should have been working the bellows. Supporting himself with one hand on the hot stone of the forge box, he pulled himself to his feet.

"I should be doing that," he croaked, "I'm OK now!"

Thorgrim grunted and kept whispering. The top of the huge bellows rose and fell, creaking as it breathed air on the fire. Then the smith took up his tongs and pulled the white-hot nugget forth. It glowed like a tiny star in the grip of the iron jaws as he carried it to the anvil.

"Don't disturb me now!" he said to his apprentice, "I need all my concentration for this. Watch carefully what I do, so that you can tell me later what happens." Pulling his star-metal scramasax from his belt and holding it vertically with both hands, he carefully touched its tip to the white-hot nugget.

"Powers of Iron, Powers of Fire! Powers of Gods above! Grant me to See, grant me to Know, grant me to learn what lies Hid!" Thorgrim slowly chanted those words, head upraised toward the chimney, his eyes closed. For a minute he stood there; the tip of his blade barely touching the incandescent nugget. Diccon stared as a smoky cloud seemed to arise from that contact point, and shadowy figures moved within it. A man and a woman dressed in rich clothes, holding a baby high in the air. The mouths of the couple were moving, but Diccon couldn't hear what they said. The smoke-cloud dissipated and swept up the chimney, and the vision was gone.

When he looked down again, Thorgrim had pulled his blade away from the rapidly-cooling nugget. The smith was breathing deeply as he put the scramasax away, as if he had run a race. Almost delicately, he picked up the nugget with his tongs and carried it to the barrel of thunder-water in order to quench it. The cooling star-metal was no longer a nugget-shaped mass; it was now twisted into an odd formation. Thorgrim juggled the wet metal in his hands, and then carried it over to the doorway to examine it more closely in the sunlight.

"Diccon, lad, the Power came and worked this lump into a clue for us. What did you see when I called?"

Diccon related his vision, describing the dress and demeanor of the couple and the baby as best he could. Then the smith held out the star-metal piece, asking Diccon to take it in his hands. The youth's eyes widened as the metal warmed in his hands. It got hotter and hotter, until he was forced to drop it onto the floor.

"War! I see armed men and terrible magic!" he stammered, "Men dying, some by the sword and others by unclean spells! The man in the dream . . . he was there! The woman, too! Both of them were dead! I didn't see the baby, though."

"I saw some of the same things you did. Those raiders will be back, with more terrible spells and many more men. And somehow we're both going to be at the heart of what's coming!

"The time for making horseshoes is now past, Diccon," the smith continued, "We'll have to forge weapons to meet those raiders. This piece of star-metal . . . you must carry this with you, even to bathe and to bed. I think that it was shaped by the Powers to protect you in some fashion. It heats up in *your* hands, not in mine."

Diccon stooped and picked up the nugget. Again, it started warming in his hands, and he hastily put it on the edge of the forge. "I can't hold it next to my skin; it burns!" he exclaimed, "Do you think it'll be OK in a pouch?"

Thorgrim grunted and rummaged around for a small elk-skin leather pouch. He had all sorts of miscellaneous things on his great work table, and sure enough, he found what he was looking for. Not touching the star-metal bit with his hands now that it was attuned to Diccon, he nudged it into the pouch with his scramasax, and pulled the drawstrings tight.

"Now see if you can hold it!" And sure enough, Diccon didn't feel it heat up in its new home. The smith handed him a thong, and Diccon looped it through the drawstrings so that it could hang around his neck, with the pouch lying on his chest. In her corner, the tuxedo cat purred, feeling the good magic wrap itself around the boy who brought her such nice breakfasts.

# CHAPTER 5

The night was uneventful, and both smith and apprentice slept well, as did the tuxedo cat. When the sun peeped over the trees, Diccon brought her milk and began his morning chores in the smithy. He was also thinking hard about yesterday's events and the strange metal amulet that he now bore in a pouch around his neck. Going over toward the threshold, which was still protected by its wards and the smith's Great Hammer, he opened the pouch carefully and peeked within. The lump of star-metal lay there, and Diccon tried to angle the mouth of the pouch so that the sun would shine in and he could study the metal more closely.

The star-metal now looked like a kind of bug. It had leggy protrusions on both sides of a central elongated nubbin, and those metal legs looked as if they had been twisted. Diccon had seen the smith twist metal to form decorative shanks for harness fittings and knife handles, but those twists were looser. These metal legs were wrung very tightly, so that their surface was almost smooth.

Thorgrim's shadow darkened the door and Diccon looked up. "What do you see there?" the smith asked quietly, "Close your eyes and look." The boy scrunched his eyes shut and tried to reach out with his mind, as he did when he was trapped in the Contagion spell.

Minutes passed, and Thorgrim stood patiently, willing his apprentice to see. Not everybody had that Talent; but from the events of yesterday, it was possible that Diccon did, in fact, have the latent ability to learn about an object which he held or touched. It was a valuable skill for a smith to have. A true smith could, by touching a cart wheel, detect any flaws in its metal rim. He would know what a piece of metal wanted to be, and also how worn or broken metal tools could be recycled into new items. It was a kind of "awakeness," a way of seeing superimposed on sight. The smith could guide his apprentice, but it was up to Diccon himself to discover and grow his own Talents.

"Fire," said the apprentice at last, "But not the usual kind of fire. This is more like what lightning is made of. Fire in the air." His voice petered out uncertainly.

"Hmmmm . . . we *did* call on the thunder god yesterday, and he did come, striking out with his hammer all around the smithy. And the star-metal was cooled by rain given by the god. Also, remember that this bit of metal came from the sky, and was not pulled from the earth. Let me feel the pouch; see what I can learn."

Thorgrim balanced the pouch, still hung on its thong around Diccon's neck, in his right palm, and bowed his head. He had the Seeing Talent in full, and the star-metal repeated its message to the smith.

"You're right. This is a powerful thunderbolt amulet. It will keep sudden disaster from you, since lightning cannot strike twice in the same spot. Since it was forged by the Powers for you, only you can call upon it. And I think that this will act as more than a ward, which shields a person or building like magical armor. If I'm right, this amulet will let you call on the divine thunderbolt itself! It's not something to use lightly. You'll know when you need its Power."

"You mean that I can throw lightning like Thor?"

"Something like that, I think. But you *must* keep this amulet secret! And don't go out and test it out on some helpless tree or rock in the forest! It's not meant for things like that! This is a gift of the Gods!"

The apprentice, who had been thinking of doing just that, looked up at the smith's face with round eyes. "I can try to use it if those men come again, though, can't I?"

"Yes, that would be an appropriate use. Be sure, however, that the first person you aim the Power at is the magic-worker among them. If you go knocking off some warrior with a sword, the magician will nail you before you can re-target your spell. I fear that we may be seeing this talisman in use sooner than we'd hope to!

"Now, let's get busy with today's work. We've got to arm everyone in the village. Today, I think we shall make arrowheads. I'll show you what to do, and then I want you to try your hand at some. We'll need to make many, many dozens of them!"

They took turns on the bellows and at the forge. By the day's end, Diccon was turning out arrowheads almost as well and as fast as the smith. The next day, they made spearheads, and the day after that, shield rims. Shield bosses were more difficult; they had to be hammered into bowl shapes in a heavy oaken block with a concave hemisphere in its center. It was easy to crack them or make the metal uneven, so Diccon worked especially hard to get them right. Shield bosses also had to have flat rims on them, so that they could be riveted to the wooden shields. It was an intensive few days; the apprentice learned more about the craft of the smith than he'd thought possible.

Marit showed up at the smithy on the fifth day, bringing freshly-baked loaves of bread, a bucket of buttermilk, and new cheese. The smith and apprentice didn't notice her at first, but the wonderful yeasty smell of that bread sneaked through the fumes of the coal-fed forge fire. First Diccon, and then Thorgrim looked up. The tuxedo cat, of course, was winding around Marit's ankles, insisting that yes, she liked cheese, and that she would really, *really* like to have some.

"I guess we can take a break now," the smith said, wiping his sweaty forehead with a well-used rag. "May the Gods bless you, Marit, for bringing us such a nice treat!" Diccon nodded vigorously; Thorgrim wasn't much of a cook, and neither was he. While they sat and ate, the smith asked Marit how things were going in the village, and whether anything unusual or untoward had happened since the raid.

"Nothing in the village yet," said Marit, "But my birds tell me that something is coming. They smell it, sort of like the way the air smells before a storm. People are getting ready for a new attack, and Old Sven has laid some dandy traps on the beach. But somehow I think that the next time they won't come over the water."

"Diccon, I think we'd better start making you a mail shirt right now. I have one, but you're unprotected. Marit, could you help us with your weaving magic, enchant the rings so that they knit together? Diccon and I will make the rings, and if you help, we might even be able to get this shirt done in one afternoon!"

"Why . . . I hadn't thought of using the Power that way . . . mmmm . . . . it *would* work, I think! Let's see if it does!"

The smith took his station by the forge, and Diccon manned the bellows. They had plenty of drawn wire of the proper gauge, which the apprentice had learned to make as another facet of the smith's trade. Since speed was required, Thorgrim did all the forge work himself. The drawn wire was wound around a foot-long dowel clamped in a vise, and the smith muttered under his breath as he worked. Each time the dowel was full, he pulled the coiled spring of metal off it, and cut the coil so that a shower of rings fell into a wooden bowl on the floor.

Marit had a short wand which looked rather like a crochet hook, and she used her Power to link the rings together and then to fuse the cuts in each ring. Her hands hovered over the bowl of newly-made rings, making weaving motions. A faint greenish glow surrounded her hands and the wand as she worked, eddying around the rapidly growing length of mail. She made sure to provide deep gussets under the arms, so that Diccon would be able to raise his arms over his head if he wanted, and she also made slits fore and aft, so that Diccon could ride a horse without the shirt binding on his thighs.

The work went so quickly that Thorgrim decided that he had time to make a helmet for his apprentice before the sun set. He took a piece of wire and fitted it as a circlet around Diccon's head, so that he had a model for the rim, making allowance for the padded cap which would protect Diccon's head underneath the helm. He also made cross-pieces of wire over Diccon's head, front to back and side-to-side, including the nasal guard which would protect Diccon's nose. This would be the model for the frame of the helm. Marit, fascinated, watched as the man and boy worked, each seeming to know without words what the other was doing. As the triangular sheets of metal were shaped to fit the heavier frame, she realized that this was sort of like making a hat, and that meant that she could lend her Power to that, too. When the sun set, Diccon tried on his new mail shirt and helmet.

"You look just like a warrior in the sagas!" exclaimed Marit, "All you need is a sword and shield, and you would look just like Sigurd Fafnir's Bane, the hero who slew the dragon and won all that treasure!" Diccon tried to strut a little, but since a mail shirt weighs some forty pounds and the helm about four more, his strut was nowhere near as perky as he wanted.

"Now, lad, you have to learn how to move in that shirt! That means that you'll sleep in it, work in it, and live in it until it becomes as a second skin to you. You can only take it off when you take your Saturday bath. It's going to be tough at first, but the muscles will come, and someday you'll thank me for making you do this!"

Diccon groaned. He hadn't realized how heavy the shirt would be. He also knew that he had to do this. His muscles had grown a lot since he began his apprenticeship, but now he had to learn to move while weighing much more than he was used to. It wasn't going to be easy. Marit grinned at him and winked flirtatiously. That cheered the boy up some; hey, if women liked the way he looked in this shirt, maybe learning to live in it wouldn't be such a bad thing after all!

The smith grinned, too. He knew that after a few days, he'd start Diccon on cutting trees for the next year's charcoal supply. Trees had to be felled one year, and left to season for the next. Chopping wood would strengthen the side-to-side hewing muscles. Then there'd be last year's wood to be cut into lengths and piled just so for the village charcoal-burner's attentions. But he didn't tell Diccon about this part yet. Better to break it to him gradually. Thorgrim, who was used to swinging his hammer all day, had no problems doing two hundred strokes on a dead tree with a seven-pound broadsword, fully armored, carrying a twelve-pound shield, and with a hundred-pound backpack strapped on. Lad had to start somewhere . . . and if nothing happened, all this would make him strong as an ox. Smiths were not, as a rule, weedy fellows.

# Chapter 6

The days passed slowly at first for Diccon. The first three were spent merely in manning the bellows and trying his hand at the forge under the smith's supervision. Working at a hot forge clad in a mail shirt and helmet was tough, even with a heavy leather apron over the mail shirt and elbow-length leather gauntlets. The metal dragged earthwards, pulling down on Diccon's arms as he hauled on the bellows rope or swung a two-pound hammer. The smith, in order to encourage the lad, also donned his own mail shirt. Diccon was awed by Thorgrim's strength. He swung a five-pound hammer, and seemed to strike as easily as if he were clad in his usual working attire. Trying not to get discouraged by this display, Diccon doggedly kept at his tasks.

Then came the day when Diccon was sent into the woods to chop trees. He wanted to impress his master, so he picked a big old beech. He finally managed to fell it by mid-afternoon. Sweat poured off him, and his whole body ached. Even with frequent rests, it seemed to take forever before the tree swayed, crackled, and fell. Diccon was too tired to cheer his success . . . he nearly followed the tree to the ground, but realized just in time that getting up from the ground while wearing a forty-pound mail shirt wasn't going to be easy, especially since he was so tired.

Thorgrim, who had heard the tree fall, came out of the smithy, carrying a bucket of cold water in one hand and a hunk of Marit's bread and a big piece of bacon in the other. He grinned broadly as he surveyed his dead-tired apprentice and the fallen tree.

"*Well* done!" he exclaimed, "When I cut my first tree while wearing a mail shirt and helm, it took me all day! And what a monster you picked! Here, I brought you something to eat; you'll need your strength if you're going to get a second tree today!"

Diccon moaned faintly, and sort of plopped onto a nearby stump. Thorgrim lifted the helm from his apprentice's head and then slowly poured half the bucket of water over Diccon's head. It felt absolutely *wonderful.* The water tasted wonderful, too, and the bread and bacon awoke Diccon's appetite. He wolfed them down, and took another great drink of water.

They sat there, the smith and his apprentice, admiring the felled tree and the not-too-badly-mangled trunk where Diccon had wielded his axe. A forester would have made a clean cut, but that didn't take any of the pleasure away from Diccon as he rested and breathed the clear autumn air.

Eventually the smith arose, clapped Diccon on the shoulder as a man does who approves the work of another man, and headed back to the forge. The sun was now rapidly angling down toward the west, so Diccon groaningly stood up, tried to stretch, and then staggered off to find another suitable tree. This time, he'd pick one with a *much* smaller girth!

The days melted into weeks, and the apprentice began to grow new muscles. His arms filled out, as did his chest, and the mail shirt seemed to be less and less noticeable as the days went on. Before the first snows came, Diccon was able to cut more than a dozen trees a day. He also had to haul last year's wood to the charcoal-place, where he chopped it into suitable lengths. Under the direction of the itinerant charcoal burner, he carefully stacked the wood into a sort of layered haystack shape around the motty peg, which was comprised of two vertical logs, one seated in a notch in the other. Small twigs and chips around the chimney pole would act as tinder. When the stack was ready to be lit, the top half of the motty peg would be pulled out, leaving a hollow chimney down to the bottom half, which supported the base wood.

The charcoal burner had Diccon bring many buckets full of dirt and ashes, and then watched as the youth packed it over the mound of wood, which had been covered in a straw and ash sheath. When all was ready, the charcoal-burner asked the smith for the fire to kindle the wood.

Thorgrim brought out a pine torch lit from the forge, and the charcoal burner thrust it into the motty hole, igniting the tinder. A few hours later, after the wood had caught and the kiln was well alight, Diccon climbed up a ladder laid against the warm mound in order to plug the chimney hole. It was important for the wood to char, not burn. The pile would smolder for days, and the charcoal burner would stay with it, on the watch for any stray sparks. Thorgrim made sure that the man had plenty of ale and food to see him through the long nights.

The mail shirt had become second nature to Diccon by the time the first snows fell. When he removed it prior to taking his weekly bath, he felt eerily light, as if he would simply float up into the air. Clean clothes and a light padded tunic, and then the mail shirt settled on top of that made Diccon feel like a new man. The lanky youth was gone; in his place stood a tallish, muscular young man. To cap things off, his mustache had begun to grow, and the first thin beginnings of a beard were making themselves at home on his chin and cheeks. Diccon felt very manly as he hauled water, pumped the bellows, and wielded the hammer at the anvil. The smith approved of the changes, and took pains to teach him the deeper intricacies of the smithcrafter's Way.

The days grew shorter and darker. Soon it would be the Winter Solstice and the time of the New Fire. Marit came by the smithy more and more frequently with bread, butter, cheese, and the local gossip . . . she also approved of the new, improved, well-muscled Diccon. Her birds were great spies, and told her the most outrageous things. There was, however, no news at all of the strangers, of the stocky short man who threw the curse at Diccon, or of anything threatening the quiet, small village. The three of them discussed plans as to how to deal with the invaders when . . . not if, but *when* . . . they came again. Thorgrim was concerned, but Diccon seemed to be more interested in having Marit notice him than worrying about some inchoate threat. It was clear that the boy had become a man, and that meant that the feminine side took on a whole new meaning.

The day of the Solstice dawned cold and crisp, with clouds hiding the sky and threatening snow. Thorgrim woke his apprentice while it was still dark, as it would take all day to create the New Fire. Now, in those days, all the fires in the village would have to be quenched and only the smith could make the New Fire. He might use flint and steel or a fire-drill, but by far the best New Fire was made from cold iron. This could be accomplished by either striking flint on the anvil for sparks, or by repeatedly beating on a strip of iron until it became red-hot and could ignite the tinder. Only a master smith might hope to accomplish this last way of kindling the New Fire.

Charcoal made from a lightning-struck oak was arranged in the forge box, with strips of char-cloth woven among the lumps. The char-cloth had been made from virgin linen strips which had been placed in a thick-walled iron tube which then had both ends sealed shut. There was a small hole drilled in the center of one end-cap, so that a minute amount of air and fumes could escape. The loaded tube was placed in the forge fire after the previous day's work so that the cloth would char, just like the wood charred to make charcoal. Such char-cloth made wonderful tinder, and would catch sparks eagerly.

Thorgrim also had bits of well-dried mistletoe handy. Gytha had harvested this mistletoe on Midsummer Eve from a lightning-struck oak which was also a bee tree. She had used her obsidian knife to cut several branches of the clump free of its host tree, taking care to not let the mistletoe touch the ground, since that would drain off all its all magic. Gytha wasn't rich enough to have a gold knife like those used by the ancient Druid folk, and an iron knife would not do. She had carried the mistletoe to the smithy in a new linen bag, and hung it above the forge where it would dry.

Very early in the morning on Solstice day, the smith and his apprentice had a hearty breakfast of ale, bread, comb honey, cheese, and smoked ham. As a special treat, Diccon was allowed to shed his mail shirt and helm for the day. It was still dark when the two made their way to the smithy, awakening the tuxedo cat. Diccon gave her a saucer of cream . . . not milk, but real heavy cream! To her great delight, she also got some bits of ham and cheese. Purring thunderously, she settled into the business of devouring the best breakfast ever, while the men prepared to make the New Fire.

The forge was dark; the old fire had been raked out and let die. It was freezingly cold in the smithy, but exercise would take care of that little problem. The smith awoke the anvil, and then placed a strip of iron on it and clamped one end down. Then he and Diccon, swinging their hammers in alternating blows, began beating on the cold metal. Thorgrim used his Great Hammer, but Diccon had to use an ordinary three-pounder. The blows had to be kept constant, and had to be continued until the metal was hot enough to light the tinder which was close at hand.

It would take much of the day, the smith opined; that metal had begun the day somewhere below the freezing temperature of water. Having the two of them beat on the metal meant that it might take only a few hours instead of most of the day to bring the metal to the desired temperature. Diccon, who had applied himself to his lessons, knew his way about a forge by now, so the proprieties were observed. Two smiths halved the work.

The cat finished her breakfast and began the elaborate washing-up ritual. She didn't like the cold, but she had good, thick fur and she knew that soon the smithy would be warm again and she could sleep next to a newly-awakened forge. The even beat of the hammers rang in the air, and before long, Marit showed up with some spiced mead and a basket of honey buns. The smith had Diccon drop out of the pattern so that he could get a bite of Marit's gift. The apprentice was not at all averse to this, and he sat with Marit, sipping the mead and nibbling on a bun and admiring the sheen of Marit's newly-washed fragrant hair. Thorgrim grinned at the two young people as he worked, keeping the beat, heating the metal with the might of his muscles and his symbol-engraved Great Hammer.

Much too soon, it was time for Diccon to rise and take up his hammer. Thorgrim welcomed him into the pattern of sound, into the rhythm of the beat. When Diccon was well and truly meshed with the metal and hammer, the smith dropped out of the pattern and strolled over to the mead. Nobody said a thing, since only the hammers should speak until the New Fire was kindled. Even the tuxedo cat held her voice still, but that didn't stop her purring. No voice goes into a purr, and a cat who is wanting a good head-rub and yes, maybe another nice bit or two of cheese, tends to purr without even thinking of it. Thorgrim thanked Marit with his eyes and uplifted wooden cup, and she smiled back. He grinned again as he noted that Marit's eyes tended to stray to the muscular figure of his apprentice, who was oblivious to all but the beat of his hammer on the warming strip of metal on the anvil in front of him.

Marit rose to go, and the smith rejoined his apprentice. He knew that she would report to Soti, the chieftain, and that before long, some of the menfolk of the village would start showing up, unlit pine torches in hand. He hoped that some of them would also bring some ale . . . it was thirsty work, pounding metal. He also hoped that Old Sven would be late or not show up at all, because if Old Sven was in the same room with a bucket full of ale, soon that ale would be snugly tucked behind Old Sven's bellybutton and the smith would still be thirsty.

It seemed like forever before the metal heated to the desired temperature. Both smith and apprentice were sweating profusely as they kept up their tireless beat. The villagers came as predicted, and so did the ale, which was very welcome. The smith and the apprentice took turns dropping out of the pattern to wet their parched throats. Diccon, noticing Sven approaching, hastily gulped down about a quart of the brew, and got a coughing fit when some of it went down the wrong way. Everybody had a good laugh except for Sven, who had been hoping for a full bucket, not a scant pint.

There! The metal was reddening into orange where the hammers had been pounding it. Thorgrim raised his Hammer ceremonially, and Diccon followed suit. The smith then took a wisp of char-cloth and laid it on the hot metal, blowing ever so softly on it. Everybody (except the cat) held their breaths, waiting for the New Fire to be born. As the Sun would be reborn in the sky and rise higher and higher each day, this rebirth was echoed on the anvil.

A tiny wisp of smoke arose from the char-cloth, and Thorgrim cupped his hands around it, still blowing gently. A bit more . . . and the first little flame poked its head up. The smith, midwife to the flame, nursed it to life, feeding it tiny bits of dried mistletoe and fluff pulled from the undersides of dried bracket fungus that one finds on birch trees. The flame grew stronger, and Diccon held a long splinter of wood daubed with pine pitch on one end into its heart. The sweet smell of scorching pine resin curled up, and then the little flame on the anvil gave of itself to the splinter in Diccon's hand. From there to the forge, and from the forge to the torches. The New Fire grew and shared itself with the villagers, who would carry it back to their own homes and to the homes of those who hadn't been there at the smithy when the fire was born.

The metal which had been used to kindle the New Fire was now sacred. Thorgrim placed it on the edge of the forge, where it would watch over its child, the Fire, protecting it from all evil. It could be re-used again the next year for another New Fire, but not for making horseshoes or nails. The smith and his apprentice, their work done, were escorted with much singing and laughing to the great feast in the chieftain's hall. It was a grand party, with plenty of food, marvelous stories and songs, and too much ale for even Old Sven to finish.

Gytha set a bowl of hot porridge with a great lump of butter in it outside the door for the *vettir* of the village, so that they might come and celebrate the coming of the New Fire, as well as bring good luck for the coming year.

The last thing to be done was to perform the auguries for the new year. The chieftain had a small supply of lead that he'd liberated during a raid in the soft lands of the south, and that was melted in a long-handled crucible on the hearth. Marit, who was the best fortune-teller in the village, placed a large circular sheet of stiff rye flat-bread over a bucket of cold water. This bread had a hole in its middle, so that it sort of looked like a wheel. She then grasped the handle of the crucible with a thick pot holder, and raised the crucible high. All eyes went to it, and all minds wished for the auguries to predict a good year. Marit then poured a thin stream of lead through the hole in the bread. Steam puffed out of the hole as the metal spat and cooled in the water. Then she raised up the flat-bread and looked into the depths of the bucket. Not only were the shapes of the congealed metal important, but also where they lay in the bucket in relationship to each other.

She took a long time, longer than past Midwinter auguries. When she raised her head, her face was grim. "They will come again, the invaders . . . I see murder and fire, bloodshed and evil, pain and misery!"

The audience gasped, round-eyed. Someone started crying softly.

Marit continued in a whisper, "I also see great magic, wonderful things . . . and . . . and . . . I see *you*, Diccon, in the heart of it all!"

# CHAPTER 7

The gods of snow and wind put on quite a show during the weeks following the feast of the New Fire. Blizzard followed blizzard, and Diccon spent a lot of time shoveling snow, still clad in his mail shirt. Of course, he had a thick padded tunic underneath it and a skin-side-out fur parka over it to keep him somewhat warm. His exertions developed his lifting muscles even more, and between that and hauling in wood for the smith's hearth and charcoal for the forge, his strength had grown to nearly rival that of the smith. Diccon was thrilled with his new muscles, and sometimes when nobody was looking, he'd flex his arms and strike poses so that he could admire them.

Marit's summer birds had flown south for the winter, and all she could call on was a phlegmatic barn owl who lived in her dairy barn where the mice had conveniently taken shelter from the cold. The owl was a night bird, so any news of daytime events had to come to Marit by word-of-mouth from the occasional villager whose cattle she doctored.

She still came to the smithy now and then, mostly to bring freshly-baked bread and buttermilk, and to watch Diccon at the forge. Of course, she didn't up and *tell* Diccon that he was one of the main reasons for her to trudge all the way from her holdings to the smithy. Thorgrim, wise in studying faces, knew the reason, though, and approved.

Diccon was now a rather good-looking young man. His beard had begun to grow in earnest, and Marit loved to watch his muscles ripple as he pumped the bellows or pounded metal on the anvil. It was sometimes hard to carry on a conversation over the din, but Marit persisted. Diccon was always glad when she came; she was strong and wise, skilled in Hearth and Home magic. Her witcheries tended to frighten off most of the eligible young men in the village, but Diccon had Talent and valued Talent in others. Sometimes, as he worked on an orange-hot bar of iron, his mind would wander and he'd dream of Marit's white arms around his neck.

A distracted smith is not a good smith, so the master had to gently steer the apprentice's mind back to his task now and then. He taught Diccon how to make bear and wolf traps, those fearsomely toothed jaws that waited in the snow for any imprudent beast which dared to come too close to the village. Set along paths, these might also snap shut on the ankle of a traveler, so the hunters of the village made sure that everyone knew just where the traps were laid. The chieftain hadn't forgotten Marit's warning that the invaders might come over land, so he made sure that Thorgrim and Diccon got plenty of practice making bear and wolf traps.

The weeks passed uneventfully, and the villagers began to relax a bit. Who in their right mind would face a cold, hard journey over the mountains to their little hamlet? Marit's owl edited out the mouse population in her barn, and was forced to fly out into the night in hopes of getting a decent meal. Marit would question him when he returned, but the owl wasn't much for conversation. Marit named all her furred and feathered friends, so he became "Greyman." Getting a proper name pleased the owl, who began to look for anything Marit might want to know so that she would call him by his fine new name. Generally, it was the movements of deer and grouse and pheasants and wolves, with the occasional fox or squirrel thrown in. And, of course, where the tastiest, plumpest mice were hiding. Marit praised his hunting skills and his reports, which made Greyman fluff out his feathers and make low warbling noises in his chest. If an owl could smile, Greyman would have.

The owl ranged farther and farther from Marit's home in search of small rodents as the winter wore on. Sometimes he followed Marit to the smithy, but he took care to stay well out of the reach of the tuxedo cat. There wasn't much profit, mouse-wise, at the smithy, but the woods beyond had promise. When Marit entered the smithy or the cottage, Greyman would glide off on silent wings, his large golden eyes and keen ears missing nothing.

Diccon would sometimes go out into the night, partly on patrol, and mostly to enjoy the still, clear nights with dancing curtains of the aurora borealis flickering among the stars. Occasionally, he would slip away to visit Marit when the smith didn't need him. He marveled at Marit's ability to talk to animals, but anytime he tried talking to Greyman or to the smithy cat, nothing would happen. Marit tried to explain to him that there were many different types of Talent, and that not every Talented person could communicate with the furred and feathered ones. Diccon had seen Thorgrim listen to the cat on occasion, so maybe in time, he could, too. He'd haul and split firewood for her, fetch buckets of water from the small half-frozen brook, do any number of useful chores if she could teach him this skill. Marit was perfectly happy with that arrangement.

One day he brought a haunch of a small deer which had fallen afoul of one of the traps. Meat was rare these days, and Marit was thrilled to see such bounty. Diccon had, of course, left the bulk of the meat with the smith as was his due. Thorgrim didn't begrudge Diccon taking some of the meat to the dairy witch, since she would surely send some cheese, butter, and a loaf of that glorious bread back to the smithy in return. Marit bedded the meat in a soapstone pot on a layer of onions, garlic cloves, carrots, herbs, a dusting of sea salt, and a good measure of ale, and set it in the coals at the edge of the fire, covering the pot with a slate disk. While the meat baked, she and Diccon shared a partial loaf of bread with good yellow cheese, and more of the ale. Greyman was out hunting, so there could be no lesson until he returned.

He still hadn't come back when the venison was ready, so Diccon and Marit had a hearty meal. There was plenty of meat left over, which Marit placed in a large soapstone tub set just inside the outer door of her cottage. Marit's home featured an inner and outer door, with a small entry-way between them. This served the dual purpose of helping keep the house warm during the winter, and providing a relatively cool area in which to store perishables. The soapstone tub had a heavy slate cover which fitted snugly on the rim of the tub, so anything within was safe from hungry owls or other beings. During the winter, meat could be kept in that tub for weeks without spoiling.

Eventually, Diccon had to leave. It would be a busy day tomorrow in the smithy; they were going to start making chain for the boatmen, who would soon begin to get their craft ready for the first fishing of the early spring. Greyman must have had to travel far to find dinner tonight, Diccon mused to himself as he shrugged his parka over his chain mail shirt. After he had stuck his feet into the bindings of his skis, Marit handed him a full basket of goodies to take back to the smithy. She also shyly kissed Diccon on the cheek, which led to Diccon nearly dropping the basket, which led to Marit giggling, which led to Diccon carefully setting the basket on the ground and then putting his arms around her and kissing her back. Marit chuckled deep and low in her throat as she kissed him back, this time on the mouth. Diccon's breath came in gasps as she put her arms around his neck . . . just like in his daydreams, except in his daydreams, he wasn't all bundled up like that.

He was frantically trying to think of any excuse to rectify that situation when Marit laughingly reminded him that the smith was waiting for him. If he didn't get going, the cheese would freeze and then go all crumbly when it thawed, and the smith might not like that. Maybe Diccon could come back in a day or two with the empty basket, she hinted with a little smile. Ever so reluctantly, the young man agreed. They kissed again, and both Marit and Diccon knew that the next time they met, the mail shirt would spend some time alone on the floor near the fireplace.

# CHAPTER 8

Diccon barely remembered setting off on his journey home. His eyes were full of stars, and his heart pounded as if he were doing heavy labor. There was a silly grin on his face as he set off for the smithy, with a long ski pole in one hand and the basket in the other. He glanced back just before he vanished into the woods, and saw Marit clutching a fur cloak around herself, watching him ski into the night. He trembled with joy, daydreaming ahead to the return trip with the basket. Of course, it was bad luck to return an empty container, so tomorrow he'd make something nice for her . . . maybe a sweet sounding cow bell . . . after he'd finished his chores.

There was no moon that night, but the dancing northern lights provided enough light for Diccon to navigate along the well-known route back to the smithy. As he came into a small clearing, he saw an odd-looking smallish pile of something in his path. Coming closer, he saw that whatever it was had an arrow sticking up from it . . . and when he reached it, he discovered that the something was Greyman. That snapped Diccon out of his reverie. He quickly stooped to pick up the stiffening body from the snow just as another arrow zinged past where his head would have been, had he still been standing. Startled, the young man pushed hard on his pole, still hunched over and clinging to owl and basket. He shot into a small copse of fir trees, chased by a shower of arrows, some of which struck him in the side and back. The mail shirt prevented the arrows from penetrating Diccon's skin, but the impacts stung. Now there were shouts behind him as he fled. Whoever had murdered Greyman was out for him, now . . . and these wouldn't be the village hunters who knew him! Diccon prayed that he'd remember where all the wolf and bear traps were laid as he zigzagged deeper into the forest. He could hear the pursuit behind him; his skis left a clear trail in the snow for the marauders to follow.

Diccon had absolutely no intention of dropping either Greyman or the basket. These items encumbered him as he fought to keep ahead of the outlaws, and he struggled to gain ground and reach safety. He had no sword or spear; all he was armed with was one long pole, a dead owl, and a basket full of cheese, butter, and bread.

The harsh panting sounds of the band of men chasing him and the crunching, hissing noises of their skis on the snow were not dropping back. Diccon tried not to gasp or grunt as he pushed himself harder, exerting all his strength to ski faster. If there was some way he could ambush them . . . somehow he had to stop them. He was heading away from the smithy now, deep into the woods where nobody lived. If those men caught him, nobody would hear his death-scream, nobody would know where he was . . . and maybe his body wouldn't be found until the spring when the snow melted. He dodged around a rocky outcrop, and suddenly remembered that there was a string of traps laid between it and the old oak tree some ten feet away. A game trail! He was going far too fast to stop now. Diccon prayed to the *vettir* and to Thor that he'd run his skis between where the traps on the line were set. If a trap snapped shut on one of his skis, he'd be at the mercy of the pursuing outlaws.

Diccon's heart was in his mouth as he shot toward the trap line . . . and nothing grabbed his skis. He'd made it! Breathing thanks to the Powers, he took a quick right angle . . . there was a small down-slope there . . . and he sped through the low-branched trees, hunched way down on his skis so that he could duck under the snow-laden boughs. He was moving as quietly as he could; fortunately, the parka muffled any sounds generated by the metal rings of his byrnie.

A snap and a scream. One of the outlaws didn't miss one of the traps! Diccon grinned briefly, and kept going. Ahead, he knew, there was a boulder field, huge stones thrown by the ancient giants when they fought. If he could lose the rest of the outlaws in that . . . he would have to quickly kick off his skis and carry them as he climbed into the rock garden; he'd need them again on the far side of the boulder field.

Well it was, that Diccon had built up his strength and endurance! Some of the outlaws were obviously dropping back, but he could hear two or three still hot on his tracks. Diccon tried to climb as quietly as he could, blessing the fact that the surface of his parka was light in color, as were his winter leggings.

Sometimes the gods ignore people, and sometimes they take an active hand in things. Diccon heard a loud crack as of lightning striking something . . . but the sky was clear, except for the myriad points of starlight and the colored, weaving curtains of the northern lights. Suddenly it came to him . . . his amulet!

The star-metal lightning-bolt! Diccon ducked down behind a jagged boulder, dropping his skis and basket just as three outlaws came out of the woods in a bunch. Movement would attract their eyes, Diccon knew. But the hand which whipped to the pouch hanging from a thong around his neck was hidden from them.

Not knowing whether the thunderbolt amulet would work from inside the pouch, Diccon frantically stripped off the mitten of his right hand. His fingers pulled open the pouch as the outlaws hesitated just beyond where the rocks began. One of them kicked off his skis, and then the others did, too. Two of them had bows, and one a spear. Diccon's breath caught between his teeth as the cold metal amulet tumbled into his bare hand.

Focusing his will on the twisted, leggy piece of star-metal, Diccon silently called upon Thor, willing the god's lightning to strike the outlaws dead. The metal warmed quickly in Diccon's hand, getting hotter and hotter. He mustn't drop it, no matter how hot it got . . . his eyes swivelled back to the outlaws . . . they were beginning to climb into the rock field . . . and suddenly, there was a deep drawing sensation in his body. Time seemed to slow. Then, it was as if Something was filling him with incredible energy . . . so quickly that his vision blurred and he felt as if he were a sun about to explode. As his consciousness dimmed, he heard a tremendous crashing noise. He screamed as the Power streamed from him in a fat blue-white ribbon of fire, lashing out at the men who were closing in on him, ready for the kill. The blast knocked him backward, and he lay three-quarters stunned on the snow, still holding the white-hot bit of metal.

The young man fought his way back to consciousness just as the remaining outlaws came bursting out of the woods. One was on foot, thanks to a bear trap which had snapped one of his skis. Diccon's hand clenched on the scorchingly hot star-metal, sure that it was going to burn his hand off, but knowing that if he dropped it, he would be dead in seconds. Again he focused his will, struggling not to black out. It was a lot harder this time. His body had been pummeled by that first blast, and it was all he could do to call upon the lightning again to loose destruction on the rest of the bandits.

Once again that incredible heat and energy built up in his body, and was suddenly and violently discharged. This time, Diccon did black out, falling back among the rocks, one mittened hand flung wide and the other hand, naked, clenched on a slowly-cooling bit of star metal. When he finally opened his eyes again, the sun had risen high in the sky, and he felt as if he'd been trampled by one of the giants. At first, he didn't know where he was, what he was doing there, or what had happened. Slowly and painfully, the realization came, and he remembered. He had survived! Groaning, he turned his head to look at his right hand, sure that it would have been burned off at the wrist from the two mighty bolts he'd called up. To his surprise, he still had a hand. It felt as if he'd dipped it into boiling tar, but it was still attached to his wrist.

Suddenly mindful of the outlaws, Diccon managed to turn over and carefully and quietly pull himself up on the jagged boulder. There was no sound from in front of him where the men had been. Very slowly and cautiously, he poked his head up over the boulder so that he could see what had happened to them. His eyes widened as he focused on two deep oval craters with slagged-down rock spewing backward from them. The snow was melted for easily six feet around each crater, and the inside walls of those craters glistened like glassy ice. There were no traces of the men, except for one half-burned ski about twenty feet back from the far lip of one of the craters.

Diccon slumped back to the ground. He could barely move. He had to get his amulet back into its pouch. The fingers of his right hand had to be pried open, which meant shedding his left mitten. Fearing that he would see char and burnt bone when he got the hand open, Diccon scrunched his eyes shut as he gritted his teeth and one by one, managed to get his fingers bent back from the star-metal.

His left hand brushed against the amulet, which was hot but not unbearably so. Diccon opened his eyes and saw that his right hand seemed to be fine . . . it had a white-ish powder all over it, though. With his left hand, he returned the amulet to its pouch, and then raised his right palm up for a closer inspection. The powder was like fine ash, as if his hand had been flash-exposed to great heat. He couldn't move the fingers, and the hand still felt as if it were on fire.

The young man fell in and out of consciousness for most of the short day, but as the shadows started to lengthen, he willed himself to awaken. If he lay there motionless during the coming night, he would surely freeze to death. He realized that he was ravenous, and then he thought of the basket. Without a second thought, he wolfed down the bread and cheese and most of the butter. Strength flowed into his body as he ate, and he gratefully blessed the *vettir* and Thor . . . and Marit . . . for having aided him and for having saved his life. It was beginning to get colder as the sun began to set, and Diccon tenderly placed Greyman's stiff body into the nearly empty basket. It was awkward working with only one hand; he had to take several trips back and forth to flat ground carrying the basket, the pole, and the skis. Somehow he managed to loop his belt through the handle of the basket, which he slid around so that it hung behind him where it would not interfere with his skiing. He got his mittens back on with the help of his teeth, and set out once again for home.

# CHAPTER 9

Thorgrim was mightily relieved to see Diccon return. He'd been worried when his apprentice hadn't come home the night before, and was most interested in the tale Diccon had to tell about his adventures. Diccon didn't tell the smith about the kisses and his feelings about Marit, but the news about the star-metal amulet and how it destroyed the outlaws was compelling information in of itself. Diccon's right hand was still useless, and the smith was of the opinion that they should go to the village and see if Gytha, the Wise Woman, might know how to restore its strength.

Before they went to the village, however, Thorgrim insisted that the chain be made so that it could be delivered to the boatmen. Diccon could work the bellows one-handed, and did so while the smith worked at the anvil.

"If that hand can't be healed, you'll have to learn to use your left hand to wield the hammer," the smith said, "And even if it can be healed, it would be good for you to learn to use both hands for what needs to be done." Diccon's hand still felt as if it were on fire, and he couldn't move his fingers to his command. He devoutly hoped that this was a transitory effect, and that Gytha could fix him up.

"I promised to make Marit a cow bell," said Diccon slowly, "Her bread and cheese saved my life out there, and I should repay her. But with my right hand out of commission, I don't see how I can do this!"

"You work the bellows, lad, and I'll work on the bell. You watch what I do so that you can make a good cow bell in the future. Deal?"

Diccon nodded agreement and began pulling on the counterweighted rope for the bellows, alert to Thorgrim's needs as the latter set to work. First, a flat plate of metal had to be thinned and formed into a roughly rectangular shape with one long side shorter than the other. A notched tab was then shaped, extending from the shorter "long side." That was the piece that would eventually be folded over to make the top of the bell. The clapper, a simple iron knob on the end of a strip of metal, was then attached to an eye made in another strip of metal, which had first been hammer-welded into the tab's notch. The smith carefully bent first the tab, and then the metal sheet into the shape of the bell, making sure that the clapper would swing freely within its body. The protruding end of the welded strip extending from the top of the bell was then curled over into a wide loop so that it could be attached to a leather collar to be worn around the cow's neck. Diccon was grateful to the smith for his help, even though all his master had gotten from Marit's basket was a smallish knob of butter.

When the bell was quenched, Diccon left the bellows, eager to hear its sound. Thorgrim lifted it from the barrel of thunder-water and shook it gently. Even wet, the sound of the bell was pure and sweet. Marit would be pleased. Diccon could hardly wait to take it to her, though he dreaded bringing her the stiff body of Greyman and telling what had happened. Marit loved her friends in fur and feather, and Greyman's death would be hard for her to take. But it had to be done, and so the smith and Diccon, bearing the basket with its sad burden, set off for Marit's place.

Marit was glad to see Diccon, though the presence of the smith prevented her from flying into Diccon's arms and kissing him the way she wanted to. She was thrilled with the bell, which would grace the neck of her Mama Cow, leader of the small herd. When Diccon brought forth Greyman's body, Marit gasped with horror, and then wept and cradled the small corpse in her arms.

"He was a good friend!" she sobbed, "I'm *glad* you killed his murderers! I wonder what made them shoot at him? Greyman wouldn't harm anyone . . . except maybe a mouse! Why did they target *him*?"

Diccon had been wondering the same thing. What was it about this particular owl that made it dangerous to those men? Did they sense that Greyman was Marit's spy? Could they tell that this owl spoke to someone with Talent? Diccon shivered as he remembered the force of the thunderbolts he'd called, and how they had so thoroughly destroyed all of the outlaws. Or did they? Did all of the outlaws emerge from the woods in pursuit of him? Might there have been one who had lagged behind and escaped? The news of his supernatural defense would be of great interest to someone, he knew. The short, stocky man who had cast the curse on him? Was there any connection between these outlaws and the invaders who had come last fall?

They held a simple funeral for Greyman. Since the ground was frozen solid, Marit had to wrap him in a clean linen cloth and place him next to the soapstone tub in her entryway. Then the three set off for town; Thorgrim to deliver his chain, Diccon to see if Gytha could bring strength back to his right hand, and Marit to ask Gytha to ease Greyman's soul into the Beautiful Lands.

When they reached the village, the smith insisted that the chieftain be told about the outlaws, first thing. This was something that might impact the entire village. If outlaws were abroad, the hunters should know about it. Who knows, maybe this was only one independent band, but again, maybe not. The next stop was the head boatman's house. Arngrim the Lucky was the best fisherman in the village, and he had ordered the chain for his boat. He was pleased with the smith's work, and paid him with a large pile of dried fish. Thorgrim and Diccon had to share the bounty, as there was too much for one person to carry, even in an oversized back pack.

At last, it was time to visit Gytha. Marit led the way, and greeted the older woman warmly. Gytha welcomed them into her home . . . the fish had to stay outdoors, though. Over steaming cups of rose-hip tea sweetened with honey, Marit told her about Greyman and Diccon told her about his hand. Gytha was sad about the owl; the loss of any life grieved her. Since owls were especial friends of midwives, Gytha would do her best for Greyman's last journey.

They sat around the Wise Woman's fireplace as she sank into trance, linking to the lost and wandering soul of the owl. It had been roaming in the Other Place, sort of a nowhere world, with no guide to help it to freedom. As she had done for Diccon when she had pulled him free of the Dark curse, Gytha called to Greyman, asking him to follow her to his new home. Thorgrim and Diccon were silent during this séance, hardly daring to breathe lest they disturb Gytha's contact with Greyman. Marit was able to follow Gytha in trance, since her Talent, useful for helping cows and sheep birth their young, permitted her the use of some of the midwife's magic.

Finally, Gytha sighed and leaned back in her chair. "Greyman is safe in the Beautiful Lands now," she said to Marit, "He will have many friends there, and will be waiting for you when you finally pass the Last Gate. Greyman was a good friend to you, Marit, and I think that he will be watching out for you on the Other Side. Listen for him!" Marit thanked the Wise Woman, who then turned to the problem of Diccon's hand.

Diccon's hand was a more difficult case. Gytha examined it closely, turning it over in her hands and prodding at it with gentle fingertips. She then cupped the hand in both hands and entered it with her mind, feeling the tendons and muscles as if they were a part of her. Scalding heat enveloped her as she studied the internal structure of the hand, and she moaned with the pain. That didn't stop her from pulling the fire out of the hand and transferring that fire into a smallish piece of kindling wood which she had laid upon Diccon's open palm. The wood burst into flame as Gytha sent the last of Diccon's pain into it, and she made haste to push it into the hearth-fire, where the pain would burn away and be gone. Then Gytha stroked Diccon's hand, calling the strength of his body back into it, teaching the hand how to move to Diccon's command. She manipulated the fingers and thumb, telling them to remember how they should work. Diccon sort of followed what she was doing, but was unable to perceive the finer details of her working.

Eventually Gytha released Diccon's hand, telling him that it was up to him to exercise it and re-teach it its job. Diccon gratefully flexed his now pain-free fingers, which felt stiff and weak . . . but he could move them! Gytha gave him a small firm ball of yarn to clench in his hand in order to build up its strength. Diccon promised her that he'd come and do chores for her in repayment when the smith didn't need his services. Gytha, who lived alone, was pleased with this arrangement, and immediately set to writing out a job list for him on a scrap of birch bark, which she placed on the mantel over the fireplace.

They could relax now, and Gytha poured a round of ale for all. As they were sipping the nut-brown brew, Gytha filled them in on the gossip of the village. It seemed that Old Sven had laid off the booze. His wife had been nagging him about his perennial stupor, and had decided that enough was enough. Now that he was sober, he seemed to have lost his Talent, and was mightily annoyed with that situation. He apparently begged and pleaded to have a drink, but his wife was adamant. Not a happy situation. Jan Sverre's son, the brewer, also regretted Sven's new sobriety; the old man's special kind of magic had ensured that anything he brewed would be first-rate. Of course, though Sven would have to liberally test each batch, it was certainly worth it to Jan. Gytha gave Sven maybe a week before he'd be back at the brewery getting his Talent back.

The next piece of news was that Arngrim the Lucky's wife was pregnant again. This was no surprise to the listeners; Sigyn was always either pregnant or giving birth. In nine years of marriage, they'd had nine children, all girls. Arngrim was hoping for a boy this time, and Gytha didn't have the heart to tell him that his tenth daughter would be born in early summer. Arngrim was called "the Lucky" for more reasons than his fishing skills, it seemed.

Then, there was news about Odd and Ulfgeir, the sons of the chieftain. They were supposed to be going out each day to hunt, but someone had spied them at Aun's place. Aun lived with four other women, and seemed to be *very* popular with the menfolk of the village. Soti was annoyed that his sons weren't bringing home any game, and their weak explanations and lame excuses had finally been bared for what they were. That meant that the chieftain himself had to take his boys out on the hunt, which made all three grumpy and twitchy. His wife had words with Aun, who merely laughed at her fervor.

Finally, there was the tale of Halfdan and Berit. They'd just announced their engagement, and then Berit had fallen ill. Gytha had done all she could for the girl, but even her great skills couldn't combat the tumor which was silently invading Berit's spine. Halfdan spent all his time with her, even though he should have been making his boat ready for the spring fishing. Gytha made sure that Berit took the pain-numbing potion she'd prepared from the gum of opium poppy seed-cases which had come from the south. Opium was hideously expensive, but since Berit wasn't rich, Gytha didn't charge her. After all, she'd gotten many of her drugs as gifts or in trade from those villagers who had voyaged to the south's Golden Lands to barter for silk, wine, and luxury goods. Those traders, when they returned, needed Gytha's services now and then, and were willing to pay well for them. Gytha had told Halfdan about Berit's condition, and it was agreed that they would be married the next Thor's day so that they could truly be together for whatever time remained to her.

It was time to leave, time to head home. Thorgrim, who had known Berit since she was a child, was silent as he glided along on his skis, the heavy pack of dried fish on his back. Marit followed in his tracks, wishing that there was something she could do for the doomed bride, but her Talent didn't work in that way. She also wished that she wasn't downwind of the fish on the smith's back, but that couldn't be helped either. Diccon brought up the rear, carrying a second pack of dried fish, and glorying in the fact that he could now use his right hand.

When they got to Marit's place, Diccon suggested that the smith might want to go ahead and that he'd catch up later, but Thorgrim sternly told him that there was danger in traveling alone at night . . . remember the night before last? . . . and that they'd be a lot safer traveling together. Diccon could only look yearningly at Marit and wish her a good night, promising to come again soon. Marit's eyes followed Diccon as he and the smith headed out toward their home.

A romance was dying, and one was being born. All too soon, Gytha would have to guide Berit to the Beautiful Lands, where there was no more pain. And soon Diccon would return to Marit, where her arms would finally encircle his neck . . . or so he hoped!

# CHAPTER 10

The weeks fled, one crystal-cold day after another. Diccon worked hard to regain the strength of his right hand, and continued to wear his mail shirt. It was second nature to him now, and he felt half-naked without its comforting weight on his back. Plowshares had to be repaired, metal fittings for the boats made, and there was also the need to forge arrowheads and other weaponry against the time the raiders would return. The tuxedo cat, hearing the lustful yowling of a sudden influx of tomcats, knew that it was finally time to find a mate. Eagerly, she went out into the woods to meet the father of her kittens-to-come, and just as eagerly a bevy of suitors greeted her. The smithy was a hotbed of activity, punctuated by Marit's visits and those of the village horses which needed to be shod. Gytha and Marit did what they could for Berit, but everybody knew that the young woman would not see the next Yule.

The days grew longer and warmer, and the tuxedo cat grew round about her middle. She could feel the little ones inside her, moving gently in the warmth of her womb. She purred long lullabies and Power songs to them, teaching them as they grew aware inside her. And slowly, Diccon's right hand regained its old strength and skills.

One morning, as the sun was melting the long icicles which hung from the roof-edges of the smithy, a runner came from the village with news. The chieftain was calling a war council to plan the village's defenses against the raiders, who were sure to return. The first of Marit's summer birds had come back from the south, twittering about the wonderful things they had seen, and bringing their own little ones into the world. They told Marit about far-away battles, which had been attended by unusual numbers of ravens and other scavengers.

The chieftain wasn't going to take any chances; and he certainly didn't want the ravens to pick over the bodies of *his* people. To that end, he had, months ago, sent a messenger to the south to find an *erilaz*, a trained adept who could lay powerful spells on weapons and men. The messenger finally located one who agreed to come to the northlands, thanks to some freaky good luck, as well as the fact that the *erilaz* in question was one of his cousin's cousins. The *erilaz*, a long-bearded old man clad in blue, had arrived in due course, and the council was called to take advantage of his knowledge. Thorgrim, Diccon, Marit, Gytha, and Sven were urgently invited to attend. Sven had regained his Talent, much to the disgust of his long-suffering wife, and he was quiveringly eager to help defend the village and to prove to his wife that his Talent was, indeed, necessary for their survival.

The council met, and the chieftain's longhouse was filled almost to capacity. Muha, the *erilaz*, carefully examined the sheaves of arrows, stacks of bows, mounds of axes, and piles of swords and daggers. On some of the best arrow shafts, he carved good luck runes, which he called "ale runes." The three-rune sequence "alu" meant "ale." The person who owned the inscribed arrows would have great good luck, and be prosperous enough to have plenty of ale and, by extension, bread. That meant that he and his family wouldn't starve.

Muha also incised a number of bone amulets with the triple-Týr rune, which brought courage and Power to the wearer. When he met the smith, Muha instantly recognized that this tall, muscular red-bearded man was more than a simple metal-pounder. The *erilaz* drew Thorgrim to one side and described a very special spearhead which had to be forged, one that would ensure victory to a group of fighters if they had to face a band of well-armed invaders. The *erilaz* had scanned the smith, and recognized that he had mastered the high-level skills and smithcraft Powers needed for such a task. Thorgrim listened gravely as Muha explained the symbols which should be engraved on the spearhead. One was a crescent, which had to appear on both sides of the blade. In Muha's homeland, it was common knowledge that the knapped flint crescents which folks sometimes found on the ground after thunderstorms were actually left behind by Thor's hammer when it brought fire from the sky. Placing a crescent on each side of the blade designated that spearhead as such a core. A spear so equipped, when thrown with intent, would thus be magically transformed into an in-flight supernatural thunderbolt. Good spellcraft required that clear specifications had to be made. Muha grinned as he remembered some of his own apprentice mistakes . . . his father-in-law never *did* find out why his best cow suddenly and persistently insisted on mooing at the full moon!

Another symbol was a dot surrounded by one or two concentric circles. This stood for *hagall*, the supernatural hail, the projectile weapons of the gods. Spears, arrows, and slingshot were human analogs of the irresistible missiles of the gods. A third glyph resembled a short broadly-fletched dart. That would ensure that the spear, both head and shaft, would fly swiftly and truly to the intended target and purpose. The fourth sigil was a two-part symbol which looked like a short zigzag (two zigs with only one zag in the middle) which had curled ends bending away from the zag; one half-symbol to be placed on one side of the spearhead and the other half, a mirror image, on the other side. This was sort of a repetition of the crescent and the *hagall* circles, further defining the iron spearhead as the core of a supernatural missile. Three times made the charm. Each half-symbol represented half of the magical side-flares that propelled the god's thunderbolt to its target. A short sequence of runes, yet to be determined, would spell out the spear's name and mission. Finally, there was a *fylfot*, the ancient sun and good luck symbol.

Diccon, looking at the *erilaz'* sketches, suddenly thought about his thunderbolt amulet. The paired symbol somewhat resembled the legs of his amulet, but he didn't really understand why only half of the symbol would appear on each side of the blade of the spearhead. Muha asked to see Diccon's amulet, and the young man tipped it out of its leather bag onto a table. People crowded around to see it; they'd heard about the thunderbolt magic that Diccon had called upon that winter. The *erilaz* leaned close, holding his hands above the oddly-shaped bit of star-metal.

"Now this . . . this has *real* Power!" he exclaimed, "Young man, you must have a singular Talent indeed to be able to wield such a thing properly! *You* must be the one to bear the Spear which shall be made, and *you* must have a hand in its forging!"

"But I'm not a real smith yet!" Diccon blurted, "I'm just an apprentice!"

"No, I see *you* with the Spear. Your Talent lies not only in the craft of the forge, but also in the craft of battle! If you were able to call that amulet of yours to life as I've been told, you can call upon the spells and symbols which we shall set on the Spear's head and on its shaft. I'm old and no longer nimble; my strength would fail me if I tried to wield the Spear as it should be wielded. You'll have to take it south to the very heart of the evil, and use it there. Destroy the source before it gets even stronger . . . it will, you know! If nobody does anything, the raiders will just get bolder and bolder. Inaction, to them, means weakness. And they will first target the weak; they're less costly to conquer.

"You should have a companion or two with you, especially ones with wild or unusual Talents, when you head south looking for the invaders' headquarters. You know the enemy as simply 'the invaders' or 'the raiders.' Let me tell you now that these are Black Agnold and his men. He's power-hungry, ruthless, greedy, the works. He's got more than one *erilaz* working for him, wizards who have turned away from the path of the Light and who dabble with the Dark magics. Wiegand *erilaz*, who is the most powerful one of the lot, is one to be feared!"

"Can't you just send a knockout spell against him?" asked Marit, who had edged into the conversation. "Yesh, an' I got a wonnnnerfull cursh that jusht came to me. Hic." suggested Sven, who had been helping himself liberally to the chieftain's pitcher of ale. "Dicconnn, hic, can I come, too?"

"Lady, Wiegand *erilaz* knows what I can do, and has defenses set against us of the Light. But Diccon here is a new factor. Wiegand doesn't know about him . . . yet. Very few have the Talent to call upon the supernatural thunderbolt, and Diccon has proved that he has that Talent." Muha then studied Sven, who had picked up the pitcher and was making sure that it was quite empty. "And you, whose Power seems to ride on ale, yes, you should be there, too. I don't even have to carve you an 'alu' pendant; you carry your ale-luck with you as a basic part of your Power! The more wild magic and unexpected Talents that we can throw at Agnold and his men, the better! That misbegotten son of a fleabitten rat has plagued too many decent landholders of late, and he's *got* to be stopped! When I heard that your chieftain was looking for an *erilaz* to help you save your village, I *had* to come. His messenger, Thorgeir Arn's son, is distant kin to me."

And so it was decided. Muha accompanied the smith and Diccon to the smithy, nodding his head as he crossed the threshold and felt the wards set thereon. The smith placed Muha's sketches on his work table, and pulled out his box of star-metal. In the corner of the room, the tuxedo cat suddenly realized that something wonderful was about to happen . . . actually, six somethings. As Diccon busied himself with the forge, she gave birth to her first kitten.

"Muha, place your hands on mine as we seek the proper metal to make the Spear's head," the smith muttered, "Diccon, you get the forge fire ready for a Working. Be sure to use some of the charred wood you harvested from that lightning-struck oak last week!" As the apprentice approached the forge fire, Muha did as Thorgrim bade, watching as the smith's Talent sought out just the perfect piece of star-metal. The Master Smithcrafter's Way was not his, but the old *erilaz* could sense a great part of what the smith was doing.

Muha also noticed the kitten's arrival; the swirl of mother's magic ushering a new life into the world was unmistakable. He smiled; that a mother was giving birth while the Spear was being forged was doubly auspicious. The *erilaz* then excused himself; he had to go into the woods to select the proper wood for the Spear's shaft. Both shaft and head were to have their own magics laid on them, and the weapon had to be made as a unit. He needed a straight length of ash, one that wouldn't warp as it dried. It took him almost a half hour to find what he wanted, and he hurried back to the smithy with his prize.

Thorgrim was waiting for him. The forge magic was awake, and two more kittens lay beside the first, squeaking their first milk-calls. The smith handed the chosen piece of star-metal to Muha, who weighed it in his hands and pronounced it worthy. The smith then called Diccon over, and the three of them cupped their hands around the metal, telling it why it had been selected, and why it was so important that it hold the true Power. The cat, giving birth to her fourth kitten, felt the threshold and chimney wards ramp up, and she was glad to be having her babies in such a safe, warm place. Each kitten, as it drew its first breath, drew in some of the Power that simmered in the room, Seeing even though its eyes were still closed. The tuxedo cat hummed a song of joy as she readied herself for number five.

The forge was ready. Thorgrim poured a sip of rowan mead on the coals, saluting the forge fire. He then took his symbol-engraved Great Hammer and struck the anvil three times, calling upon Týr, Thor, and Frey to aid him. Next, he sprinkled rowan mead and thunder water around the edges of the room and then some on his Hammer, the anvil, and lastly, on the tuxedo cat and her growing family. Instead of objecting to the droplets as most cats would have done, she welcomed them, knowing what was intended. Yes, her kittens would be special indeed!

It was Time. The smith grasped the star-metal in his tongs and thrust it into the heart of the fire. Diccon worked the bellows so that it provided just the proper amount of air, and Muha linked all three humans and the cat family into a single mind, a single gestalt being. It was this Unit, not the smith, who watched the metal warm; it was the Unit, not the cat, who gave birth to the sixth and last kitten. It was the Unit, not just the metal, which heated in the forge fire, and it was the Unit which called on the smithcraft magic to manifest itself in their Working.

The metal glowed brilliant orange in the fire. Thorgrim pulled it out with his long-handled tongs and laid it on the anvil. Muttering under his breath, he and the Linkage struck the first blow. The star-metal, knowing what it had to do, began to shape itself into its new form. The Unit poured Power into each stroke of the smith's Great Hammer, feeling itself strike and be struck. When the metal began to stiffen, it was returned to the heart of the forge fire and heated anew. Not a word was spoken; the Unit had no need of words. The only sounds were those of the Hammer beating on metal, the crackling of the coals, the creak of the bellows, and the faint purring . . . she couldn't help it . . . of the tuxedo cat, who was giving her newborn children their first meal.

It took most of the afternoon to forge the Spearhead. Before it was quenched, Muha drew the symbols on the hot metal, one at a time, with a pin of mistletoe wood dipped in rowan mead. The liquid boiled right off, but Thorgrim could see the Power lines in the metal as the old wizard sang them into life. Taking his engraving tools, the smith bade Diccon hold the Spearhead steady while he carved the symbols into the still-soft metal. When one side of the blade was finished, Muha drew the symbols on the other side, and the smith finished the engraving. The Unit knew that the job was well done, and that the Spearhead could now be quenched. Muha then asked the smith to place the Spearhead on the anvil, and told Diccon to lay his thunderbolt amulet on top of it.

"One half of the thunderbolt's flares of its power are engraved on one side; that's what that sort of zigzag line with curled ends is. The other half is on the other side. Thus, the Spear's head itself is the core of the god's thunderbolt. When this Spear is thrown over the heads of an group of enemy warriors, those warriors will instantly be made magically vulnerable to the weapons of you and your men, both the physical ones and the magical ones," said Muha, "I have named this spear '*Tilarids*,' 'target-seeker,' so that it will bring the wrath of the Gods directly and unerringly upon any foe it faces." The old man then drew a small roll of silver wire from his pouch. "This must be hammered into the engraved symbols," he continued, "Silver has its own magic, and will add to the Spear's Power."

Thorgrim did as the old man bade, after which he re-heated the Spearhead slightly so that the silver would set fast in the grooves. He then carried the Spearhead over to the barrel of thunder water in order to quench it for the last time. Muha turned and picked up the ash shaft which he had been carving while the forging was going on. It had a long line of runes on it, triply-carved to give them more power. The three humans fitted the shaft to the Spearhead, and the ferrule of the star-metal instinctively grasped the wood thrust deep within it. The Spear was made, but now it was time to finish it. The *erilaz* placed the Spear horizontally in Diccon's outstretched hands, and then took out a small obsidian knife.

"This is the last part which must be done," he said quietly, "It is my Power which is bound in this spear as well as yours." He then nicked a vein in his wrist and, dipping his mistletoe splinter into the blood, drew over each rune and symbol, muttering under his breath as he did so, uniting the wood and metal to one purpose. The tuxedo cat and all six kittens felt their fur rise as the Power swirled and entered the Spear. The Power grew and grew as this last step was carried out, and one could swear that the entire smithy glowed from it. When the final stroke was completed, Muha shouted a string of archaic syllables, and the Power crested and coalesced into the Spear. The Unit cried out the same syllables along with Muha, being linked with him . . . and even the cat mewed and kittens squeaked in tempo.

It was done. The Unit dissolved into its component parts. Exhausted, Muha sought out a bench and applied a rag to his wound, not minding the ashes on the cloth. Diccon carefully placed the Spear on the edge of the forge, and then pulled a bench over, while Thorgrim thanked the forge, the anvil, and his Great Hammer for their work. He then relaxed visibly, and hunted up some ale, cheese, and a half loaf of Marit's bread. Diccon asked Muha what the runes on the shaft said.

"Ah, those. They say 'I, Asugisalas' *erilaz*' . . . oh, I do a lot of work for a fellow named Asugisalas; pays really well and it's nice to have a home base, especially during the winter. Plus that, anyone reading the runes on this spear shaft will see who made them, and I don't mind a little bit of advertising on my work. Folks in my home country all know where Asugisalas lives! OK, 'I, Asugisalas' *erilaz*, am called Muha. Go! Go! Go! The supernatural chaos-hail I hallow as this spear!' You see those bind-runes forming 'Go, Go, Go'? A triple bind-rune triply-carved is thrice three; that makes the spell have far more power than simply writing the runes out once. I put the action verb three times, because it's the shaft that carries the star-metal Spearhead to its target. Without the shaft, you'd do just as well by throwing rocks at the enemy, not a good move unless you're really desperate. The spell hallows the supernatural hail . . . that's the thunderbolt itself, the star-metal Spearhead which we all just forged, dooming the spirit-strength or *megin* of all who are touched by this spell to spin away into the chaotic Otherworld. That's what *ginunga* means. Hard place to find one's way around in or even out of; it's totally wild. My spell also sends any spells or lesser Powers protecting the enemy straight to Ginunga Gap. Even the higher gods don't like to find themselves suddenly transported to the Gap and tossed in to sink or swim."

Diccon whistled a long, low note before saying "Wow, that must be *some* spell!"

"Yep, that it is. I don't usually go explaining what I do, but you're different from most folks I have to deal with. Who knows? Maybe you might even be able to study the Way of the *erilaz*! There are so few of us left these days, and those who are still active are mostly grandparents now. We who follow the Path of the *erilaz* have great learning, but that makes us great targets, too. Any half-baked wizard with too much man-juice running fire in his blood wants to take us on. That's why most of us move around a lot. I got lucky. Asugisalas likes me, and *nobody* around those parts messes with Asugisalas!"

"But I'm apprenticed to be a smith!" exclaimed the young man, "If I work hard, maybe in a few years I'll be able to set up my own smithy! I've always dreamed of being a smith!"

"Smithcraft is only one part of an *erilaz*' training, lad. We must cross-class in many disciplines; learn the magics and Powers of many trades. Where do you think many of your spells come from? Not out of thin air! The *erilaz* must be absolutely familiar with *many* kinds of magic, so that he or she can explore new ways of doing things. We do the research, we perform experimental magic and, since some of the stuff we play with is more than slightly dangerous, we have to be masters of warding and protection. It's not enough to simply possess the raw Talent needed to become an *erilaz*. One also has to have raw courage, an unstoppable need to succeed, and most important of all, be aware."

"Uhhh . . . aware?"

"Aware. Awake. Seeing not only the world around you, but also the magic in the world around you. Lots of folks are walking around in this world who aren't aware. Colors . . . the *erilaz* sees the differences in how the vibrations in colors move, as well as the hue. We see the slow eddies of Power in rocks, the joyful Power of a tree waking up in spring . . . all of Life and the world is bathed in Power currents. You have been learning how to see the Power in metals. But metals are only one thing. To be an *erilaz*, you have to be constantly aware of the Power in all things."

"You think I might become an *erilaz*? And not a smith?"

"You could be both, lad! No reason why you cannot shoe horses and make nails! You'll marry and have a family; that requires money. An *erilaz* can earn a lot from a patron, but if you would be free of a patron and his or her demands, having a trade is a very good idea."

"You'll make a good smith, Diccon," said his master, "You're a natural at it. But I agree with Muha. I think you can be a smith and something more. If Muha wishes to take you on as his student, I won't stand in your way. I don't want to lose you; finding a good apprentice is harder than you might think. But it would be criminal of me if I insisted you stay here if your fate is elsewhere."

Diccon was faced with a terrible, frightening decision. He was comfortable and accepted as the smith's apprentice. Muha held Knowledge, something that Diccon thirsted after. On one hand, if he stayed in the village with the smith, he'd get to see Marit regularly. On the other hand, if he followed Muha, he'd be in a foreign land, far from Marit and the smith and the simple life he'd led at the snug smithy. Muha and Thorgrim traded an amused glance. Both Craftmasters knew very well what the state of Diccon's mind must be like. The old *erilaz*, who'd had to make that same decision some forty-five-odd years earlier, said that Diccon didn't have to decide on the spot. But if Diccon ever decided to follow the path of the *erilaz* while Muha was still alive, the latter would gladly welcome him as his student.

# CHAPTER 11

Under Muha's instruction, Diccon made a simple birchbark casing for the Spear. This casing was a long hollow tube with a short cap fitting snugly over its top, so that the Spear could be retrieved quickly from its protective sheath. It was padded at both ends with reindeer moss, which kept the butt and tip of the weapon from piercing through the bark. He laced the tube with linen string well lubricated with melted beeswax, and then sealed over the holes and seams with more wax so that water and dirt would not get in. The seam between the cap and the main tube also got its coating of wax, so that the Spear was sealed and safe. Next, Diccon took a longish strap of leather and looped each end around the casing, about three hands apart, and stitched the pieces together so that the tube could be slung across his back like a quiver. While this work was being done, Muha continued to instruct the youth in various aspects of battle magic, teaching him spells to blunt swords, cause arrows and spears to fly wide of their intended targets, and to confuse the enemy. Diccon listened intently, soaking up this new lore which was so different from that of the smithcrafter's Way.

The evening meal, eaten around the firepit in the smith's cottage, was simple and good. Thorgrim, an indifferent brewer, served his version of nut-brown ale. Muha politely drank it, although he was used to far better. There was some of Marit's bread and cheese, three fat rabbits roasted on a spit over the fire, and oatmeal porridge laced with bits of dried apple and hazelnuts with a swirl of honey in it. Diccon set a double handful of roast rabbit and cheese aside for the tuxedo cat's breakfast, knowing that she would be ravenous after her ordeal and the present necessity of feeding six milk-hungry mouths.

They chatted then, sitting around the fire, listening to the wood sizzle and pop as it burned. Muha told stories of the south, and of the flat land he called home. He reminisced about battles long gone, folk customs, traditions, and how people dressed and spoke. There were tales of the gods and goddesses, and a long description of the great Spring procession to bring the goddess Nerthus to the waters so that the land would be fertile and the springs not run dry. Asugisalas kept an ornate wagon for this, as well as the *lur* players, drummers, acrobats, and sun dancers who would accompany the goddess from her shrine to the lake. Diccon sat enthralled, listening to the old man's voice rise and fall in the firelit room. The smith also paid close attention, hoping that Muha might let fall some tidbits of useful information, such as what weapons and armor were used in those lands. He hadn't forgotten about Marit's warning, and didn't want to come up short. The villagers were counting on his smithcraft skills to produce the very best weaponry possible.

Almost two weeks passed, and Diccon's education at the hands of the old man had him, on one occasion, spending hours observing a nest of ants. On another occasion, the youth was tasked with performing his smithy work with his legs bound together, so that he had to hop in order to get around. He learned the ways of the beasts and birds, bugs and people. Each night Muha had him recite or imitate what he'd seen. On one full-moon night, Diccon was told to take off his mail shirt and helm, and to go out into the forest, out of sight of the smithy. He then had to sneak back to the smithy, get inside, and lay his hands on the anvil without being seen or heard. The smith and the *erilaz*, who would try to trap the lad, entered into this game with vigor. It wasn't until dawn that Diccon was finally able to silently creep up to the back of the smithy undetected, climb barefooted and barehanded up to the great chimney and, without disturbing the chimney wards or soot, edge down the chimney to land spraddle-legged and noiselessly, with both feet on the edges of the warm forge box. In one smooth motion, he continued his controlled fall to the floor, and when his hands smacked down on the anvil, Thorgrim (who had been nodding beside it) and Muha (who had been looking out the door) jumped in unison.

"You're *darn* good, lad!" beamed the old man, "Clever of you to strip naked and rub yourself down with streaks of soot! Breaks up the human outline! You avoided the rustle of clothing, too! Well done!" The tuxedo cat, who had been snoozing with her family in the corner, had also been startled by the sudden noise. She looked sourly up at Diccon, sniffed with disdain, and put her head back down. She was asleep again within thirty seconds. The kittens, of course, were past masters at sleeping, and never stirred a whisker.

The next morning, Muha announced that he had to leave. The journey home was long and not without danger, and he was eager to get on his way. The old *erilaz* waved off an escort, although Diccon did see him safely on his way. Once out of sight of the smithy, Muha ducked under the down-swept branches of a large fir tree and slipped off his backpack. He dug around inside it, pulling out a disreputable tunic, a beaten old wide brimmed hat, and a small leather box which had bits of charcoal, white lead, red ocher, and other such oddments in it.

"I'll have to go in disguise," he muttered, "Diccon, here's an opportunity for you to learn another skill. Everybody around here knows what I look like, and what I am. If I change my appearance to that of a sick old beggar, I won't be a tempting target to lawless men. Let's see . . . what disease should I fake up? I could be insane, drooling and mumbling as I travel, or maybe I should be a leper. Leprosy always makes folks stand off."

"What's that?" asked the youth, "I've never seen a leper!"

"It's a terrible thing, leprosy. Folks who have it lose the feeling in their hands and feet, and pieces of their body fall off. It's quite contagious, so a leper must carry a bell or a rattle to warn folks away when he comes near. Nobody knows what causes the disease, but it is said that whoever gets it has wronged the gods, and that they have cursed him. The leper's spirit will never go to the Beautiful Lands when he dies; it will be snatched up and carried to the Pain Land far under-earth. It's a cold, grim land, a place where nothing grows and where poisonous snakes dwell in great numbers!"

"Um, how are you going to fake pieces of your body falling off?"

"Oh, that's easy. I don't have to actually *drop* a finger or nose on the ground. I just have to *smell* as if I were about to do so. That means that I'll have to be on the lookout for a dead squirrel or some other small animal; a good ripe long-dead smell will do the trick. I must wear a cloth mask with crude eye holes cut out, and wrap my hands and feet in old rags. Some of this red ocher . . . here, get some of that pitch from the tree over there; I can mix the ocher up in that to make it look like crusted blood. If I'm lucky, I'll also draw flies!"

It took Muha only a short time to transform himself from the wise blue-clad *erilaz* into a miserable specimen. He sprinkled little bits of white lead onto the shoulders of his patched, ragged dun tunic, to look like flakes of skin. His hands were swathed in tightly wrapped strips of dirty linen, with red ocher-pitch "blood" dabbled on his knuckles. The mask was a shapeless tube of dark cloth which hung loosely around his head, and the ragged eye holes revealed a pallid skin . . . white lead mixed with a little butter smeared around his eyes made the old man look truly ghastly. Diccon found him a suitable piece of wood for a staff, and Muha tied leather thongs around several smallish flat rocks so that they could dangle from the top of the staff and clack together. The transformation was complete, and Diccon, even though he'd seen the costume change, backed away from the "leper" in spite of himself.

"Yep, this'll do!" cackled the old man in an odd, breathy, scratchy voice. Diccon's eyes went round and he backed up even further, fearing that somehow he'd catch this horrible disease.

"Look, lad," said Muha in his normal voice, "I have to disguise my voice, too. I can't sound like a perfectly healthy man. I have to sound as if I were really *sick*! I'll have to move like a sick man, beg for scraps along the way, and pretend at all times that I *am* a leper! That way, *nobody* will dare attack me lest the disease-curse fly to them! You must learn to disguise yourself, too. Sometimes it's good to appear in another seeming. A healthy young lad like you will attract attention. Ruffians along the way will try to rob or even kill you. There's a lot of fear out there, fear of strangers, fear of Black Agnold and his men, fear that you might be one of his spies. The farther south you go, the more careful you must be. If folks find out that you have Talent, your life will be in serious jeopardy. Only in places like this remote village or the lands ruled by Asugisalas will it be safe for you to appear as you are now. Practice your shielding! You must be able to hide your Talent from over-curious strangers!

"Now, you'd better go home. Tell nobody about my new appearance! It must be secret, even from the smith! If only you and I know what I look like now, I will be able to travel in safety. Lad, if ever you come south to the flat lands, ask where Asugisalas lives. I'll be waiting for you there!" With that, the old man turned and shambled off, leaving Diccon with much to think about.

# Chapter 12

Thorgrim breathed a deep sigh of relief when his apprentice returned to the smithy. He'd half thought that Diccon might have decided on the spur of the moment to go with Muha to the southern lands. It was clear to the smith that this young man's path would not be limited to the smith's craft alone, and that he would have to finish his training under another Master . . . . or Masters. In the meantime, however, there were horseshoes to be made, and Diccon would have to begin forging his own smith's tools. He had mastered the apprentice's skills, and it was time for him to become a journeyman, one who could operate a smithy of his own. Thorgrim would also have to think about finding a new apprentice.

Diccon was really happy that he didn't have to make his own anvil. Wrestling a huge block of iron wasn't something he needed to do right now. He did have to make his long-handled tongs, some with flat square jaws and others with shaped jaws that could hold round or square rods. Hammers, too, he had to forge, as well as files, a coal raking tool, and a small pierced container which swivelled on a long-handled Y-bracket so that he could wet down the coals as needed. He traded a double handful of arrowheads for the leather to make his apron and gauntlets, and learned how to manufacture a variety of vises and clamps. Finally, he had to forge his own symbol-engraved Great Hammer, following the careful instructions of the smith. This all took time, and Diccon's work was closely supervised by the smith, the tuxedo cat, and her six curious kittens.

Weeks passed, and the village was left in peace. The fishermen caught shoals of cod and salmon, which they either dried on willow racks or took to the smokehouse. Some fish was salted down in barrels, but the livers and tongues had to be eaten immediately, as they didn't take to being preserved very well. Marit and Inga, her little sister, took their cows and goats up to the high plateau, where their family had a rustic summer cottage. The grass there was lush and tasty, and before long a swarm of small brown calves and long-legged kids came into the world. There was plenty of milk to go around, and Marit and Inga made tubs of butter and stacks of good yellow and white cheeses. Inga had the Talent for goats, so she watched over them, milked them, and made sturdy little blocks of their tawny cheese. Marit blended wild thyme in some of the cheeses, and gathered bags and bags of reindeer moss for Gytha's herb room.

Gytha herself was out and about, teaching some of the younger girls how to find, harvest, and preserve the healing herbs, roots, barks, berries, and suchlike for the coming year. Diccon, when he was working off his jobs list, was included in this schooling. Angelica, which she called *kvann*, was tended in a small garden; that herb was worth its weight in gold. She also grew dill, thyme, sage, caraway, garlic, onions, plantain (Gytha called it *groblad*, "grow-leaf"), and comfrey (*valurt*, "battle-dead wort"), which was supposed to be so effective a wound-healing plant that it was said that one leaf placed into a stew pot would heal all the stew meat together! There were herbs, seeds, fungi, lichens, roots, and berries for all kinds of ailments, and Gytha made sure that Diccon learned the uses and powers of each one that she put into a travelling bag for him, as well as the charms to recite while preparing and administering them.

"It's one thing getting a sword slash," she told him, "Often that slash becomes red and hot, and pus comes out of it. You have to treat a wound right away, *before* the Red Wolf begins gnawing at it! If he is ignored, he will take your arm or leg, and then your life! If you get a slash, let it bleed freely; the blood washes the Wolf away. Then stitch the wound closed with clean . . . and I mean *clean!* linen thread stroked on a piece of beeswax . . . I always keep several bone needles threaded just in case. I've also found that if I wrap them securely in a clean linen cloth and put the packet to steam in a grate over a boiling kettle of water for the afternoon, that the Wolf will not ride the thread when you sew yourself up. You only open the packet when you need it. The Wolf is everywhere, and if he sees the needle or thread before it's to be used, he will come to you. After your wound is closed, smear on some of this salve . . . (here, she pointed out a small willow container with a large beeswax plug) . . . which is made from *valurt* and the barks of white willow and oak. Then put a bruised *groblad* leaf or two, underside down, over the wound and tie it securely in place with linen strips. Keep the wound dry and clean, and change the dressing daily if you can."

There was much more advice, and Diccon soon became dizzy with plant names and charms to be learned. He was wondering if smiths really had to know all of this, but Gytha assured him that there would be times when he'd not have a handy herb-woman around to tend to him. "Your life may depend on what you learn from me here, so pay attention!" she repeated each time she saw the boy's eyes drift away or glaze. But she did allow breaks so that Diccon could fetch water for her, or do other jobs from her handy little birch bark "to do" list. Time was getting short . . . Gytha was surprised that there had been no move on the village by now . . . and she wanted to make sure that Diccon would be ready to face what she knew was out there.

It was high summer. Diccon realized that he would soon have to leave the village and follow his fate. The smith knew this, too, and spoke to the chieftain about the latter's sons. Perhaps one or both of them would benefit from some time at the forge? The chieftain's wife, Sigrun, was all for it; the boys hadn't stopped their visits to Aun's place, and Aun and her "sisters" were not the marrying kind. Sigrun wanted grandchildren.

Diccon decided to leave the smithy and the tuxedo cat and all he held dear on a Thor's day. That would be an auspicious time to depart on this journey to follow his fated path in life, he opined. Thorgrim was loath to let him go; knowing that he had to let him go. Diccon packed his newly forged tools and some clothing, and slung them onto the back of a rather disreputable gelding given him by the chieftain. He'd said his goodbyes to Marit the evening before. She'd held him close and wept on his shoulder. He'd tried to comfort her, and before long, the mail shirt had found itself all alone, puddled on Marit's hearth. Marit's featherbed supervised the next part, when the two young people became one at last. Diccon, awed at the miracle that had taken place, remained there the night, learning much about a great Mystery. When the sun rose . . . how soon it rose! Diccon gently kissed his sleeping Marit, and dressed as quietly as he could. If Marit woke, she would call him back to her, and he knew that he'd break down and stay. Diccon knew that he *had* to go. It was the hardest decision he'd ever had to make in his life.

He'd left her an arrowhead he'd made of star-metal, which had silver-inlaid dot-and-circle patterns on its blade. That item he placed where his mail shirt had spent the night, along with a tuft of hair hastily hacked from his head. Marit would recognize that the arrowhead held Power and would protect her, and he knew that she would cherish the hair, laying protective charms on it and, by extension, on its erstwhile owner. It had been the first time for Marit, too.

The smith watched Diccon go, wishing him well, wishing that he'd decide to stay but knowing that the youth's journey in life was not limited to the smithy. Soon enough, Thorgrim would have to deal with the chieftain's loutish offspring. He wasn't looking forward to that . . . well, actually, he was. Time to teach those fellows some life skills. Time to ride roughshod over them, rein them in, teach them some manners and also some skills which they would have to master, ones that would give them honest work and honest achievement.

The tuxedo cat had given Diccon her firstborn kitten to take on his travels. She gave of her heart, of the best she had to offer. Diccon solemnly thanked her, knowing that she was sending her beloved son into what could very well be harm's way. He promised her that Svarting, for so he'd named the little fellow, would eat if there was only enough for one, and that Svarting would drink if there was only a sip of water to be had. The tuxedo cat, content with this arrangement, purred at the young smith, wishing her magic on him, thanking him for his acknowledgment of her gift. Svarting, of course, could hardly wait for the Big Adventure to Begin.

Diccon, Svarting, and the disreputable gelding, which was now hitched to an equally disreputable wagon which had been tucked away behind Tosti the carpenter's shed, started on their way. Tosti was glad to get rid of the wagon; it was an eyesore. Not one of his best creations. But he'd always somehow been too busy to break it up for firewood, so it had sat there for years, its wood weathering to a silvery grey. A wagon was needed for the array of smith's tools, provisions, and other miscellanea that they would take with them on the trip south. Svarting rode proudly, seated next to Diccon. The kitten felt Very Masculine and Grown Up; his mother had herself chosen him to accompany the smith's apprentice, and had told him to watch out for the human. Humans sometimes got into serious trouble, and they only had one life. Svarting, at the beginning of his own first life, had plenty of wiggle room, as it were. It was a big responsibility, but Svarting's line was not comprised of your common, ordinary cats.

The wagon rattled through town toward Gytha's; he had to pick up various parcels of simples, roots, and barks from the Wise Woman not only for himself, but to be delivered to others of the Wise Folk that they would meet during their travels. Others in the village hailed Diccon as he and Svarting rumbled along, handing him various and sundry bundles and message-sticks of their own to be carried to distant friends, family, and trading associates. Anytime anyone went on a journey, it was customary for the voyager to deliver messages and packages along the way. Each bundle was labeled with the name of the recipient, so that Diccon wouldn't give the wrong item to someone. The last stop was the brewery. Old Sven Bluemouth was waiting for him, along with several casks of ale, all labeled "Sven owns me" in big runes carved on their tops. Sven hopped nimbly up onto the wagon, and helped the brewer's men position his precious casks just right on the bed of the wagon, between the axles. Then Jan Sverre's son, the brewer, came out of his long shed, carrying a smaller keg which he handed up to a pleased Sven.

"You'll need some mead on your trip, I think!" Jan chuckled, and Sven's eyes sparkled as he cradled the keg lovingly before securing it in the wagon. His eyes sparkled even more when the brewer's apprentice handed him a full tankard to cut the dust of the trail, even though the wagon hadn't moved yet. He carefully threaded the lip of the tankard past his whiskers to his lips, and began chugging. Sven's head tilted back as the tankard emptied, his Adam's apple bobbing rhythmically as the mead disappeared. It didn't take long for the old lush to empty the tankard, which he then held high in the air in a kind of salute.

"Aaaaaah! That hitsh the shpot-uuuuurrrp-erooney!" he declared. "I'm gonna mish you guysh!" It was obvious to all that Sven was about to launch into a long-winded farewell speech, hopefully punctuated by numerous refills, so Diccon flipped the reins and the gelding lurched forward. Sven merely swayed in place. A sober man would have lost his footing and tumbled down to the bottom of the wagon. The brewer and his crew watched them rattle down the road and out of sight; Sven still holding his tankard aloft and continuing with his speech.

# CHAPTER 13

Marit found out soon enough about Diccon's departure. She wasn't happy that he'd left so abruptly, but when she found the arrowhead and hank of hair, she realized that Diccon had, in fact, given her his heart. Marit's birds told her that Diccon whispered her name to the willow trees as he passed, so she dried her tears, knowing that he would not forget her, even though he was accompanied by Sven Bluemouth. The latter, who had taken good care to load their ancient wagon with as many casks as he could afford, was happy to have escaped his wife's "discussions," as she put it, about the Demon Mead.

Odd and Ulfgeir, the chieftain's sons, were almost literally dragged to the smithy by their mother, who had learned that they'd been goofing off at Aun's place instead of reporting to the smith as they'd agreed. Odd was well-named. He was kind of an odd sort of fellow. He had long freckled arms, a freckled face surrounded by a tangle of reddish brown hair, and an incipient mustache under his long nose, which he stroked continually. It was clear to all that this young man thought that he was Frey's gift to women. His younger brother, Ulfgeir, deferred to Odd even though he stood a hand's length taller. Not the sharpest knife in the drawer, thought the smith, as he looked the boys up and down. Ulfgeir looked strong, but his face was puffy and his hands showed little in the way of calluses.

"Look, you lot, I'll have no excuses from you! You are here to learn a trade, and how to be men. Right now, you're a pair of sniveling boys! If either of you want to inherit after your father, you must buckle down and learn how to follow directions. In order to command men, you must be worthy of that job. People won't follow a layabout!" The smith's voice rang clear and loud, like the sound of a hammer striking the anvil. The boys stood nonchalantly, waiting for the chance to escape, but their mother blocked the door. She smiled sweetly at their discomfiture as the smith continued.

"It's time for you boys to begin. This is the first step in your path to Knowledge. Come over here to the anvil; this is the soul of the smithy. The forge-fire, of course, is the heart. You must be introduced to both, so that they will work with you as you work with them!"

The youths cautiously approached the anvil. They weren't sure if it would bite or not. Thorgrim grinned in his beard, and then placed their hands flat on the cold surface of the metal and laid his symbol-engraved Great Hammer across the backs of their hands, cautioning the boys not to move. He murmured several words under his breath, laying a geas upon the new apprentices, binding them to the forge. This tie was simply a precaution; the smith didn't want to spend his mornings hunting down his new helpers. The geas would ensure that the boys would come to the smithy every morning at dawn, and that they'd put in honest work. As the boys' attitudes adjusted, the geas would imperceptibly weaken and before long, vanish. Most apprentices came willingly to the smithy, but these two needed a little extra help.

It was time to begin the first lesson. The smith nodded at the twain as he lifted his Hammer from their hands and replaced it on his work bench. He then told their mother that she could return home, adding that the boys were in his care now. After she left, the smith grunted and said, "Odd, you take those buckets over there and fill the cistern from the stream. I want the water up to the top of that cistern, and I want it filled by the time I get the forge fire ready. Ulfgeir, there's charcoal to be brought in. Make a stack as tall as you are over there in that corner. We have a lot of work to get done today. Don't even think of slipping away or slacking on the job! The village's safety depends on us! I expect no more of you than I expect of myself, and that's probably more than you're used to." He looked at Odd, who was looking around the smithy incuriously, and continued in a gentler tone, "Odd, if you want to attract women, you've got to put on some muscle. Right now, you're all legs and arms and attitude. Ulfgeir, you've got the build to do well; we just have to get some of that baby fat off you!"

Meanwhile, Diccon and Sven rattled along on their way. They slept under the wagon at night, with Svarting on guard. The kitten took his job seriously . . . well, there were the occasional crickets to chase and little naps to be taken. He was fully aware of the trust that his mother had laid upon him, that these two humans should travel in safety. It was a big job for a small kitten, but he approached his task with tail high.

Their path led up and down winding, narrow, rutted trails . . . one couldn't properly call them roads. The wagon lurched over rocks and tussocks, pulled by Diccon's patient gelding, which made it too unstable for Svarting to get a decent snooze if he rode on the seat. Diccon made room for him in the top of his backpack, which contained spare clothes and various essentials in case they had to make a run for it. The Spear in its case looked a lot like a stout hiking staff, thanks to a simple disguising spell which Muha had taught Diccon. A second spell masked the tingle of magic that emanated from it, and as long as the runes remained legible, the cloaking spells would continue to be effective.

Diccon and Sven had decided to pretend to be son and father, fleeing from a famine in the north. They did odd jobs along the way for hot meals and the chance to sleep in a barn when it rained. Sven could sing a startling repertoire of racy ditties in his cracked voice, which kept him in food, ale and mead. He didn't want to tap his own kegs if there was hooch to be gotten along the way. The miles melted away as they traveled south, and before long, they faced the sea. It was time to turn east, work their way up the coast, and then as the road bent around again to the south, to follow the coast toward Muha's land. Diccon tried to imitate the new accents he heard along the way. Folks didn't talk the same way as they did where he came from. Words bounced more, and consonants were softer. He listened much and spoke little when they were with other people. Sven's speech was naturally slurred and hiccupy, so folks didn't peg him as a stranger right off. Svarting's mews and purrs were in a universal language.

Back at the smithy, Odd and Ulfgeir spent long days, cursing their luck. The discipline, though hard, was not unbearable; and soon they were gaining new muscles and the beginnings of pride in each day's work. The tuxedo cat, whose remaining family was ready to move on, brought one tuxedo kitten to Marit and another to Gytha. A third kitten went to the chieftain; this was a sturdy long-haired tiger tom who got the name "Skogi," which meant "Forest." The fourth kitten chose Helga, Old Sven's wife, and the last one, a fluffy little grey female, came to Berit, the slowly-dying wife of Halfdan the fisherman. Berit was in almost constant pain now, and the soft, warm affection of her new companion soothed her. Gytha's poppy-syrup was needed less, thanks to the purring magic of little Mist. The tuxedo cat, alone again, returned to the smithy, content to see her children placed in good homes.

It was Mist who got the first warning. She was highly attuned to her mistress and, as a result, her sense of empathy was highly developed. The moon rode high in the summer sky as the shock of death rippled out toward her, shaking her awake and rough-furred. Nose-tip to Berit's nose, she saw that Berit was alive and resting comfortably. But not far away, a human had died suddenly. Mist leaped to the floor and streaked out the small hole that Halfdan had cut for her in the door. This hole had a swinging door on it, so that bugs and other animals wouldn't come into the small cottage. It let Mist come and go as she pleased, though, which is an important thing to a cat.

The echoes of death were fading rapidly. Mist followed it as far as she could, into the heart of the village. Then she smelled it, smelled blood on the air. Keeping to cover, she darted and paused to the chieftain's longhouse. There was no sound; and whoever had died had done so in silence. Only the kitten had noticed the event.

The body lay just outside the chieftain's door. Nobody was around, so Mist crept closer to the body, sniffing delicately. No, this wasn't anyone she knew, and whoever this was, he had come from someplace far away. His clothes didn't smell like those of the villagers. There was blood on the ground, coming from the man's nose and mouth, as well as from the wide gaping hole of his slit throat. The heavy smell of blood was almost overpowering, and the kitten drew back. She scanned for anyone who might be awake, anyone who she might be able to make follow her to the body, but all she picked up was scattered dreams. Whoever had killed this man was not nearby; she couldn't sense him or her.

Mist was young and inexperienced, so she didn't pick up the screened thoughts of the murderer, who wasn't far away at all. That wight watched her turn away, heading back to her home, where her human family slept. She hopped up onto the bed next to Berit and soon fell asleep, forgetting the corpse. The murderer nodded, smiled (but not with his eyes), and went on his way. Only the moon watched his victim now.

In the morning, there was quite a to-do about this mystery body. Odd and Ulfgeir discovered him as they barreled out of the longhouse to head over to the smithy. The man's blood had pooled into a congealed mass around him. Ulfgeir slipped in it, falling backwards in his eagerness to not come in contact with the stiff body. Bad luck came to those who touched the dead. The boys squalled and screamed hoarsely, which brought the thralls, and then the chieftain himself, to the scene. The geas was still strong on the boys, but they were able to fight it off long enough to gasp out their story before pelting on their way to the smithy. The chieftain sent a thrall to fetch Gytha; she might be able to learn what had happened, thanks to her magic.

That same morning, Diccon and Sven were making their way through a boggy area, trying to keep the wheels of the wagon on what passed for solid ground. A fog was rising, and Diccon was getting more and more uneasy. Nothing to point a finger at, just a rising sense of dread at the pit of his stomach. Sven, who had scored a large pitcher full of some rather strong mead the night before, was slower to pick up on this, thanks to his hangover. They didn't hear anything out of the ordinary . . . wait, there were no sounds at all, except for the ones they made themselves. Diccon brought the gelding to a halt and listened hard. The fog was getting thicker, which meant that they'd have to rely on their ears and special senses. Something plopped in the water off to the right, but it was probably only a frog. Or was it? Diccon's imagination began to spin up fantastic images of dragons and ogres about to attack them. Old Sven hiccuped gravely, hiccuped again, and then clambered off the wagon. He reeled forward to the gelding's head and poked his head underneath the horse's chin, peering out and forward through the reins. It was said that if one looked through a bridle, one could see unseen things and evil spirits. Diccon thought that the old man had gone crackers, but when he began to say so, Sven raised a hand sharply and hissed to him to be quiet. Svarting, who had been asleep in Diccon's pack, woke up with a start and echoed Sven's hiss. Cats can see the unseen, too.

Moving slowly, Sven pulled a small piece of clear quartz crystal from the pouch at his belt. Then he placed one hair from his head, one from the horse's head, and a third from Diccon's head on it, spat quietly on it, and then tied crystal and hairs with a bit of linen twine to a twig which he picked up from the path. He worked quickly and silently, with occasional peeks through the bridle. Svarting's eyes swivelled over to the right, where the plopping sound had come from, staring at the fog. Diccon, who couldn't see the kitten, was watching Sven work. The gelding moved uneasily, the last of the four of them to realize that there was Something out there that wished them no good. Sven finished his work, whispering a few words over the bundle, and then he reached for his throwing-stick, pulling it out of its sheath at his belt. The stick was about two feet long and had a cupped end, like a large wooden spoon. Sven could be mighty accurate with that; he could send a pebble the size of a walnut farther than most men could throw a spear.

The kitten and the horse screamed in unison. Diccon's hand whipped to his amulet, but Sven had placed his bundle in the cup of his throwing stick and launched his missile before Diccon could touch the leggy shape of metal at his throat. There was a tearing sound, as of a great sheet of linen being ripped, as the crystal/hair/twig missile sped through the air. A loud, snarling grunt and the scrabble of claws on rock gave Sven a vector for his curse, as the unseen Thing charged at what it thought was a madly-fleeing group of victims. Sven powered up, tapping into Diccon and Svarting, who gave willingly of their own Power. Diccon had to also hold the spooked horse, who was snorting, trying to turn around to bolt away from the threat.

Sven had a dandy curse for such an occasion, and he sent it on its way with a shout. He followed it up with another, and a third just to make sure. Diccon grabbed a piece of cloth with which to hood the horse in order to quiet him. Svarting launched himself from the wagon and disappeared forward in the dense fog, heading in the direction from which the grunt and scrabbling had come. Before he got there, he veered off to the left, hopping from tussock to tussock in an attempt to flank the unseen enemy. Kittens can sometimes be too bold for their own good.

Fortunately for Svarting, Old Sven's curses had hit their target squarely. Whatever it was that lurked in the fog was now the pursued, fleeing huge, slavering demonic shapes conjured up by the first curse. The second curse was a terror spell, and the third a confusion spell which projected one of Sven's more surrealistic drunken hallucinations into the dark mind of the bog-thing. Svarting flattened himself on a tussock, his fur bristling and his tail fluffed out like a bottle brush as the magic continued its work. The would-be attacker was fleeing for its life (or what passed for life), splashing through the water in a desperate attempt to escape. Old Sven had had some mighty strange hallucinations in his day, and this one was a real doozy. Diccon's gelding was plunging and thrashing in the harness, trying madly to get away from that spot, but the youth's soothing words and smith-strong grip on the reins and bridle quickly got him back under control. Sven straightened up, belched proudly, and returned his throwing stick to its scabbard with a flourish.

"Mushta been a water troll," the old lush said with relish, "None of 'em can shtand up to a decent curshe worth beans! Hic! But where there'sh one of 'em, there'sh likely more, so we'd better get a move on! Keep the horse blindfolded an' lead him; I'll jusht mosey on ahead an' shee if I can have shome more fun. As soon as the fog liftsh, we should be in the clear! Hic."

Diccon did as he was bid, and followed the faint sounds made by his companion. Svarting, relieved to be out of harm's way, headed back to his friend. His eyes were still round and his tail still bushed out, but the danger was truly past now. Diccon sent his senses out into the fog, feeling the tiny droplets of water hanging in the air, and willing them to move aside from the path. Before long, the fog thinned ahead of them, although it was still heavy on both sides of the trail they were following. Weather magic seemed to have come naturally to the youth; learning to call or send away the rains and thunderstorms when needed was a useful skill for a rural community to have. Diccon's Talent had been opened up by his experiences with the Dark curse, the desperate use of his amulet, and the teachings of his master, Gytha, and of Muha.

The chieftain stood by the body outside his door, keeping the gathering crowd at bay. Gytha came panting up, wiping breakfast crumbs from her mouth with one hand and clutching her tool bag with the other. She halted about six feet from the body, and in a commanding voice told everybody to get well back; she was going to see what information she could gather about the murder, and of the identity of the victim.

"That means *everybody*!" she said, looking the chieftain straight in the eyes, "In fact, I want each and every single one of you to go well away from here and leave me alone with the body! There are too many of you thinking loud thoughts! I need to have absolute silence and calm; this fellow has been dead for some hours, and I may have a hard time following his spirit!"

The chieftain gestured sharply at the crowd, which reluctantly began to give way. He gestured again, more vigorously, and then strode away from the dead man, shooing folks in front of him like a herd of geese. He brought them down to the boatyard, where they were well out of sight and earshot of the Wise Woman. Cautioning everybody to whisper if they wanted to talk, he began a quiet interrogation, asking if anyone had noticed anything out of the ordinary during the past few days, if anyone had heard the man die, if anyone had any knowledge of the victim's identity. This kept everybody busy while the Wise Woman worked.

Gytha took a peeled rune-inscribed alder wand from her bag as her tuxedo kitten, Moth, came around the corner of the longhouse at a flat run. The kitten slammed on the brakes, yellow eyes wide as she surveyed the scene. Gytha smiled, bent down and massaged her little friend's ears, and told her that she was going to learn a very important lesson today. "I must go Out and follow the man's spirit, but first, I must see backwards in time, from now to when the man was killed, and then before that. I must scan to see what happened. You, little Moth, must be my anchor. You've seen me work, but this will be a difficult task, and I must rely on you to be my link to the here-and-now. You must also watch so that I am not disturbed!"

Moth was a very bright kitten, and the Talent ran strongly in her. She understood what her mistress wanted her to do, so she settled down facing away from the corpse, tucking her legs underneath her, and wrapping her tail around her body. Gytha then muttered a few words as she anointed her wand with a few drops of golden liquid from a small stone jar, which was then carefully resealed and returned to her bag. Next, the Wise Woman drew a large sunwise circle on the ground around the victim, the kitten, and herself. Gytha and Moth saw the golden circle of energy shimmering in the morning light, arching over their heads in a dome as Gytha chanted. When the warding circle was set, Gytha settled on the front steps of the longhouse, which were just within the circle, easing her body into a comfortable position so that when she left it, it wouldn't fall over. She then closed her eyes and began her Clearing exercises, centering and focusing on the dead man, who lay sprawled in front of her. She saw the spark of life that was Moth, and the emptied corpse which had lost its spirit. There were some ants and earthworms within her scanning range, but she screened them out after making sure that they held no information of value. Deeper and deeper she sank into the trance, her body slumping against the doorpost.

Her spirit self rose from her body and floated over to the corpse. She hung there, reversing time in her trance, and saw Odd and Ulfgeir discover the body. It was clear that they were totally surprised by this, which meant that neither of them had slain the man. Back, back in time she went, and then she saw Mist's visit. The blood, black in her Vision, became warmer and warmer, flowing back into the body. Then she saw the man's fall in reverse; and a figure dressed in dark woolen tunic and trousers standing behind him. Focusing on the murderer, she tried to scan him, but felt nothing. She tried harder, and detected the cloaking spells that hid his thoughts. The murderer, then, had Talent. But the solving of that spell was another story. Try as she might, she couldn't unweave enough to get any hint of who the person was, and why he had murdered this perfect stranger in the village. She couldn't even tell if the murderer was a villager, or someone who had followed the victim here from someplace else. Gytha made what observation she could, and backed off.

Back to the body. Time to seek out the man's spirit. Clinging to Moth with one part of her mind, she sped Out along the path to the Land of the Dead, hoping to catch the spirit before it had utterly fled or was dissipated. Deeper and deeper in trance she sank, scarcely breathing as she followed the victim's life-force. As she flew in pursuit, she began to detect a roiling in the trace, as if the dead man's spirit was fighting every step of the way to the Land of the Dead. Closer and closer she came to it, and then she spotted it in the distance, a silvery shape struggling to return but being dragged inexorably to the Dark Mountain by the Death Winds. Gytha made an extra effort, coming as close as she dared lest her own spirit be caught in the flow and be snatched into the Mountain along with that of the victim. Clinging fast to the golden thread which connected her to Moth, she reached out, sending a whisper-thin rainbow thread of energy toward the silvery man-shape as it thrashed and twisted.

"Tell me! Who are you, who killed you, and what is your mission?" The thought was punched down the thin thread as it touched the other's spirit. There was a flashing burst of thought which came back to Gytha, and then the thread snapped and the man's spirit was sucked into the maw of the Mountain. Gytha had to struggle against the sudden inflow, much as a sailor tries to outswim the suction of a sinking ship. Moth was steady and firm, and her golden thread was a lifeline to Gytha, who painfully pulled herself back, fluttering in the Death Winds, hand over hand back toward the land of the living.

Well it was that Gytha was richly Talented and held more than a little Power. Never before had she gotten so close to the Dark Mountain, and it took all of her Power to keep her moving away from it, hauling her spirit back to Moth and the here-and-now. Her spirit arms trembled with the strain, but she doggedly kept moving, feeling the terrible winds ebb as she clawed herself away from the Last Gate. As she neared the Real World, the golden lifeline thickened and gave her strength, and she moved more and more quickly and easily toward her anchor.

Moth was almost unconscious, but held as long as she could. Her claws dug into the dirt beneath her, and her body was as stiff as a rock. She saw her mistress coming closer and closer . . . could she hold out just a bit longer? And then just a bit longer?

Gytha transited out of the Path just as the kitten fainted. The Wise Woman's spirit shape hovered briefly over Moth's still form, returning some of the energy that the kitten had expended in holding the lifeline. When she was satisfied that Moth wouldn't die on the spot, Gytha re-entered her own body, totally wrung out, and fell into a faint herself. The golden dome shimmered around and above them as the two utterly exhausted Workers lay unconscious on the ground.

# CHAPTER 14

The beast or troll, or whatever it was, was gone. Sven was disappointed that it didn't have any companions; he'd been looking forward to nailing them, too. The fog was lifting, and the path ahead of them was clear. Svarting jumped up onto the wagon, and from there into Diccon's open rucksack, which was wedged between two of Sven's barrels of ale. He was too excited to go to sleep right away, but he settled himself comfortably on the soft clean clothing in the pack, swivelling his head around so that he might catch sight of any other dangers which might threaten them.

They had another week or so's journey ahead of them before they would come to the flat lands to the south. Once there, they'd have an excellent chance of finding a boatman to take them across the wide, shallow inlet to Asugisalas' territory. Diccon, still wearing his chain shirt under his outer tunic, exercised with his heaviest hammer, swinging it around and mock-fighting imaginary opponents. He knew that he would all too soon be going into battle for real, and he didn't want his muscles to soften and betray him.

Moth awoke first, groggy from her exertions. She tried to rise to her feet, but her legs were like bits of yarn, and all she could do was lie there, panting and aching all over her body. Slowly she gathered strength from the good earth below her, and after a while, she could raise her head a little. She mewed softly, then louder, trying to wake her mistress. Gytha lay slumped on the ground where she'd fallen from the step, breathing heavily. Moth sensed that the Wise Woman was merely sleeping now, and soon her head dropped back onto her front paws and she slept, too.

The sun was much higher in the sky when Moth woke again. Gytha was stirring uncomfortably, so the kitten sent her an inquiring thought. Gytha's eyes slowly opened, and then she groaned aloud. This brought Moth to her unsteady feet; creeping toward her mistress, trying to mew her awake. Gytha smiled at the kitten's face, now almost touching hers. *We did it*, she mind-sent to the kitten, *you and I did it! I saw the man die, and thanks to you, I was able to follow him and get his last message. Well done, little one!* Moth chirruped back at her, agreeing. *I almost couldn't hold on, but I did! I'm glad you're safe!*

Gytha was startled to mind-hear the words coming from Moth. Cats aren't supposed to talk. But something had happened here; Moth's thoughts were clear and cogent. Usually when one spoke with animals, it was in pictures, smells, and sounds. Moth was using human speech. Gytha extended her special senses to the kitten, looking her over to make sure that she was all right, and maybe to see what had opened up her Talent so. *We were together*, Moth sent, *I was you and you were me. I'm glad that I can* really *talk to you now.*

Gytha pushed herself up into a sitting position and gathered Moth onto her lap, crooning and rubbing her head. The kitten's feet made starfish, and she purred blissfully as the two of them gathered more energy from the generous earth.

After a while, they noticed that there were people standing outside the misty dome of the protective circle. They were sort of blurry, like looking at things through water. Gytha set Moth back on the ground, and slowly got to her feet. She then retrieved her alder wand and went to the northern part of the circle. Holding the wand waist-high, she muttered a few words, and then she poked the wand's tip forward and up with a slashing motion. The circle was broken, so the shimmering dome winked out like a soap bubble. Suddenly the chill of the morning reached the two exhausted Workers, who shivered as they faced their now clearly-visible audience. The chieftain and the villagers were standing silently, waiting for the Wise Woman to speak.

"What have you learned?" he asked quietly, leaning forward. "You were away for a long time!" Soti Jarl's brow was furrowed with concern as he spoke. "Could you tell what happened?"

"The dead man's name was Arinbjorn Egil's son, and he came from seven valleys to the south. His chieftain had heard that there were people of Talent to the north, and sent him up this way to warn folks that raiders from south-oversea were seeking out and killing all Talented people they could find. The warning had passed northwards from coast watch to coast watch. Arinbjorn carried a message, set down in the ancient code. I must see if he still has it on his person, or whether the murderer was able to destroy or make off with it!"

The chieftain summoned his thralls to bring Gytha a chair and some ale. When the Wise Woman had settled herself and eased her parched throat, she spoke again.

"The one who killed this man also came from the south, but much farther so. He'd arrived at their village two days before Arinbjorn was to go north. Arinbjorn, who held some of the Talent, was suspicious of the fellow, and together with their Wise Ones was able to send him packing. It was then decided that the warning should immediately be sent to those of us in the north, valley after valley, so that we wouldn't think the man was a simple, innocent traveler as he'd claimed. Our friend, carrying the message, headed up the coast, but apparently the man who would slay him followed him, and caught up with him here. The murderer had plenty of time to make off with any message carved on a stick. Arinbjorn's spirit told me that the real message was hidden in his clothes. Any message sticks that he had were decoys, written in gibberish. I tried to see who the murderer was, but all I could find out was that he wasn't from around here, and that he has Talent . . . or at least has cloaking amulets made by one who has real Power. Look for a man half a hand shorter than you, clad in a dark blue tunic, dark brown trousers, and a wolfskin cloak fastened with a Roman-style bronze fibula. I wasn't able to see his face, but I think he had a long brown mustache and no beard. Arinbjorn had very little time to tell me his death-message; I am sorry that it's not more complete."

"That's a pretty good description! I'm amazed that you got as much as you did!" the chieftain said approvingly, "Has anyone seen this man? No? Well, if you do, for Thor's sake, come right back here as fast as you can and tell me or Gytha! If he's killed once, he'll do it again. If he finds out that our Wise Woman has gotten his true message, I think we'll be facing a real danger. We'd also better send our own messengers north as soon as possible to warn the folks up there. But first, we've got to find that secret message!"

Gytha stirred in her chair and continued, "We have to look carefully at Arinbjorn's clothes. He'd said that the message was there. First, we should pour some mead for his spirit. He must also be buried carefully; I don't want his spirit to return to his corpse and walk the land. I've heard of such, and misfortune follows where the again-walker treads. Murder victims, like stillborn babies, have been known to come back, looking for the life they lost. Arinbjorn had been trying to tell me more when the Death Winds sucked him through the gates of the Dark Mountain.

"Try to take his clothes off without touching them with your skin! Any tools or cloth that you use for this must be buried with him; they will be tainted and can never be trusted again. I will prepare the spell to bind him to his howe. Tosti, you're a carpenter, do you have the wood to make a coffin? And you, Arni and Thorstein, get some picks and shovels and follow me! I must choose a place for his burial which won't disturb the good *vettir* of the village!

"You children, go out about the village as if you were playing. But be careful! Look for any traces of the man that I described to you . . . and if you see him, send one of you back to us while the others keep watch. Remember to think only of your game, say, something like hide-and-seek. If you see the man, begin reciting your runes in your head; that'll be good practice for you, and your mind will be occupied with that. If the murderer has Talent and can hear thoughts, that should be a good screen against his probing!"

The children, pleased to have a part in the goings-on, departed in a swarm. Simple Grinulf, one of the thralls, went along with them; he liked to play hide-and-seek, too. He often played with the children, and didn't mind that they usually outsmarted him. The game let the children run all over the place and go looking in various hidey-holes. Gytha assured the chieftain that the children shouldn't come to any harm; they were making enough noise to scare off any intruder. Moth was recovering nicely, and wanted to help, too. Gytha silently asked Moth to keep her eyes on the children; kittens were good at games, and nobody would suspect a kitten as being a spy. Moth's keen senses of smell and hearing might just pick up something that the children missed.

The game went roistering off toward the beach. Moth began to follow, but then her head turned toward the opposite side of the village, toward the valley and the path leading into the mountains. Her little ears pricked up as far as they could. *Something isn't right there*, she mind-sent to Gytha, *I think the killer ran that way.* Gytha looked and listened with all her senses in the direction of Moth's focus, but she was still weary and couldn't pick up anything definite. The chieftain noticed her sudden, intent look toward the valley path. Quietly, he beckoned to Arni and Thorstein, discreetly signaling them that they should follow him into the longhouse. The picks and shovels could wait. Once inside, he asked them to get their bows. He handed each man two of the arrows on which Muha had inscribed good-luck runes. Both men were champion hunters, but it wasn't deer that they would hunt now.

Arni took some charcoal out of the firepit, and streaked his face and hands with it. He handed the stump over to Thorstein, who followed suit. They made large black smears on their clothing; this would break up their outlines and make them harder to spot in the woods. A little lard blended with flour made white streaks, which they applied to their necks in patches, as well as on the "low-light" areas of their faces and bodies. Each man took his bow from the wall, where they had been hanging near the high seat. The hunters owned several bows, and kept them in different places so that they were always near their favorite weapon just in case. You never knew when you needed a bow, but bows were clumsy to carry with you everywhere.

The two men went out the back door, stopping at a handy cow pat to add brown to their disguise. Cow pats are also good at masking human scent. The hunters headed out toward the path, their keen eyes searching for traces of the murderer's passage. They moved without noise, and with surprising speed. A skilled woodsman can cover amazing distances, knowing by instinct where to put his feet and how to avoid twigs and dry leaves. Their ready-strung bows were held close to their bodies, so that they wouldn't snag on brush and branches. Thorstein and Arni intended to get within sure arrow-shot range of their quarry without making any undue noise. They were used to sneaking up on deer and, since humans' hearing wasn't as keen as that of deer, the hunters felt safe in picking up their pace, half-running as they followed the faint clues left by their prey.

Marit's birds told her the news, and where both hunters and hunted were relative to herself. The young dairy witch and her little sister were up on the high grassy plateau above the valley tending to their cows and goats, leading them from one grassy pasture to another, and in the evenings, making cheeses and churning butter. She sensed a darkish blotch where the murderer moved, so she gathered her herd with a low whistle and a gentle mental nudge, urging them away from the blotch, hoping that that blotch wouldn't come any closer to them. The hunters were gaining on it slowly, but they wouldn't catch their quarry before nightfall if the latter kept up his present pace. Marit got the herd into a shallow dell, which effectively concealed them, and then asked her birds to keep their eyes on the Dark man who was being chased by the village's best hunters. She then wove a simple, passive coverlet of a spell, a "this is only a grassy meadow with nothing on it" cantrip. It was like making a mirage, and didn't require a heavy use of the Power. If the fellow being chased by the hunters had Talent, any active spell or mind-query would give the girls away. Her little sister kept the animals quiet and together while Marit maintained the concealment spell.

Wodurid was still feeling pleased with himself as he loped tirelessly along. He'd managed to catch that fellow who'd been raising the alarm, so no further warning could now possibly go to the settlements to the north. He knew that he might be pursued, but he was used to running long distances at the same steady, ground-eating pace. His wolfskin cloak was bundled up on his back so that it wouldn't flap and hinder his motions. Bending his course around to the south, the assassin ran on. Alone, he couldn't face a number of Talented defenders, but with his war-band . . . aaah, with his war-band and the wizard, he could clear the coast, village by village, until no Talented people remained. And if he were very, very lucky, he might even find that dratted child that Agnold the Black was looking high and low for! Agnold had offered a huge sum in gold to anyone who brought the child to him. Wodurid intended to be that person.

Arni and Thorstein reached the high plateau about two hours behind Wodurid. They could see faint traces of his passage, and they hastened their pace, sipping from water-skins now and again as they ran. The chieftain had asked them to hunt the murderer down, and there had been no mention of them stopping when they got to the borders of their land and that of the neighboring village. The hunters would have to rely on their own judgement.

Marit's birds saw the hunted man turn towards the south, away from them. When he was truly out of range and possible line-of-sight, Marit gradually and cautiously released her spell and let the herd wander again. The grass was lush and sweet, and the animals hadn't even noticed Marit's spell. Relieved that the black blotch hadn't detected them, Marit decided that it was time for her to teach her little sister how to talk to birds and other beings. Inga was quite comfortable with her goats, but goats don't fly. They also aren't good at carrying messages. Inga was interested, but any birds that passed by were not. Oh, they chatted with Marit, but Inga couldn't hear them. Or them, her. It was only when the sun set and the day birds had gone that Marit came to the conclusion that Inga's thoughts were where birds couldn't hear them. Goats could . . . . now what else listens where goats listen?

# CHAPTER 15

Arinbjorn's clothes lay in a heap at Gytha's feet. The dead man, now covered with an old linen sheet donated by the chieftain's wife, lay on a wide plank. Soti Jarl had found three other men to dig Arinbjorn's grave, since his first two choices were now hunting the murderer. The chieftain, as *goði* or high priest, then went into the temple of the gods to prepare himself for the funerary rites.

It would be up to Gytha to find the message Arinbjorn had died trying to deliver. Not touching the clothes with her flesh, she spread the dead man's cloak, tunic, clout, trousers, belt with its attached pouch and sheath-knife, stockings, and boots out on the ground, manipulating them with two sticks. Moth watched for a while with her intent kitten stare, but the young thing was soon bored and found an interesting ant to follow.

At first look, the clothes seemed to be just that. The man's pouch contained a smallish lump of flint, an iron strike-a-light, and three flax seeds; his belt was plain leather, and his tunic was old and patched. But wait . . . . the patch . . . the stitches attaching the patch to the cloth . . . . some were short and others were long. The code! Hidden in what looked like hasty stitchery! Gytha fetched a wax tablet and stylus, and then leaned close to the patch. The first question was where the coded sequence began. She started at the upper left corner of the patch and drew slashes, short and long, corresponding to the stitches. One short stitch, then four long ones; one short stitch and seven long ones . . . . yes, this was it! Gytha knew her runes, and knew that the rune-row was divided into three families. She called them *ættir*. The first family would have one short stroke to mark it, the second two, and the third three. Then, each letter in a given family would be numbered in long strokes. One short stitch . . . that would be Frey/Freyja's family, the first of the *ættir*. Then four long stitches, that made it the fourth rune in that family, Á. Gytha worked swiftly, and before long, had the encoded message solved.

"Ágnold seeks Biornulf child. Wigilaz Froðuwarða his. Also Freada, Grimfrið, and Wodgrim."

Only one of the names made sense to the Wise Woman. She had heard of Agnold, but the others were unknowns. Must be his henchmen, she thought. Then she thought of Diccon, who was headed south towards Agnold's lands. She wondered how she could get this information to him. Gytha knew that Diccon's ostensible reason to travel south was to study with Muha, as well as that the covert reason was to help the latter defeat Agnold for good. Agnold's reach had grown . . . stretching even as far as to this small northern village. If he weren't stopped, he would surely eradicate all of the Talented in the northlands, and then rule them all with a cruel iron fist. The Wise Woman wished the young man success every time she thought of him, which was often. Marit, of course, did likewise.

The southernmost adept-members of the secretive Bear-Star Clan, whose members were only known to their fellows, had finally realized that the man had to be stopped. Muha, as a Clan member, had taken the opportunity of his journey north to covertly seek out any of the Talented who might have a good chance of success. And if those other names in the coded message belonged to wizards, this could make things definitely challenging. Gytha, also a Clan member, was therefore obliged to do all she could to make that success possible.

This information was important. Arinbjorn had died attempting to deliver it. Gytha knew of its urgency from her contact with Arinbjorn's spirit, so she hiked up her skirts and trudged all the way up to Marit and Inga's summer cottage on the high plateau. There, she asked Marit to bespeak one of her birds to carry the news south to Diccon and Muha. Marit knew Diccon so well now that she could imprint his image and identity in the bird's mind. It would seek out this one human being and none other, as if it were an iron filing drawn by a piece of lodestone. The Wise Woman cut a long narrow strip from one of Marit's cheese-making linen towels while Marit sent out her call, and hemmed it all around with the short and long stitches of the coded message. The narrow interior portion of the strip got a simple decorative pattern and the runes "Gytha sends."

A young bachelor falcon came to Marit's summoning. The young dairy witch quickly wrapped her apron around her left wrist, and the falcon settled, curious about this human who could talk to him. As Gytha took her last few stitches, Marit asked Kraii . . . for so the falcon named himself . . . if he would be willing to carry a message south to a land where there was a distinct possibility of meeting a number of young unattached female falcons of his kind. Kraii thought that this was a dandy idea, and held out his rough, scaly leg to Gytha, who carefully knotted the message-rag on his ankle. Marit linked to Kraii, telling him what he needed to know to find Diccon. She also warned him to keep well away from any humans who were not Diccon. She then kissed the message-cloth, imprinting the kiss on it so that when Diccon touched it, Marit's kiss would caress his hand. Then Inga and Gytha watched as Marit launched Kraii into the air, following him with their eyes as he arrowed up into the sky, headed due south.

Diccon and Sven were at that moment rattling into a small settlement. Sven's barrels had been hard hit during the trip, and there were many miles yet to go. They'd been avoiding civilization as much as possible, but things (and supplies) had gotten to desperate straits. For one thing, the front left wheel of the wagon urgently needed a wheelwright's attention. For another, they were low on food. For a third, Sven was low on booze. For a fourth, Diccon was sick and tired of having to listen to Sven hour after hour. Sven did love to tell stories, jokes, and long disjointed meanderings which made little sense to his listeners. Seems the man couldn't stand a few minutes of silence! Diccon, who had wanted the luxury of thinking about Marit, and especially of that incredible last night when they were together, was hoping that his chattering wagon-mate would inflict himself on someone else for a while.

The village consisted of nine dwellings, a number of out-buildings and a few ancient barns. A small weatherbeaten temple to the gods stood next to the largest dwelling. A smallish creek ran through the village, with a clearly marked fording place. Here and there a chicken picked at something in the tough grass, and a dog yapped from one of the back buildings. Other than that, there seemed to be no life about. Diccon hopped off the wagon and went to the door of the large longhouse next to the temple. The door was slightly ajar, and it creaked as Diccon pushed it open.

"Hallloooo . . ." he called, "Anybody home?"

Silence greeted him. Diccon began looking around; maybe they were all asleep. He went through the whole house, but no luck. The firepit was dead; no warmth remained to the ashes. Looking up, Diccon noticed that the usual forest of hams, bacon, hardtack bread, and dried fish had been cut down, and that only an array of smoke-blackened twine and rope ends hung from the roof-beams. He leaped onto the heavy oaken table and inspected the rope-ends. Slashed in haste, they were. Either the villagers had left very quickly, or they had been robbed.

Diccon hopped down to the floor as Sven entered the building. The old man, no longer chattering, started thumping on casks and looking into boxes and chests. Diccon was sure that Sven was hunting for a refill source for his kegs, but the intensity of the search and the items examined soon dispelled that notion.

"What're you looking for?" the young man finally asked, "Beer doesn't usually live in blanket chests like the one you're poking around in!"

"Shomething'sh wrong here. Hic. No people. No food. And no drink, unlesh you go to the urrrp! creek!" Sven's nose twitched, and he continued, "I don't shmell anything dead. But . . . . I *do* shmell shomething rotten!" His nose twitched again, and his head swung around to face the cluttered back area of the house. "Shtronger here . . . . hic! . . . . closher I come, shhtronger it ish . . . ." His voice trailed off as he walked toward a low clothes chest at the back of the room. He stopped just out of reach of the box, sniffing cautiously. He sidled to one side and then to the other of the box, studying it and the floor around it with some care.

"Diccon, get the fire going! Right now! Hic!"

The urgency in the old man's voice spurred Diccon into blurring action. He tossed some dried pine cones and grass twists from the nearby firewood box into the firepit, and then added what few twigs remained in the box. Looking quickly around, he spotted a spindly child-sized stool which he smashed over his knee, adding its wood to the pile. He noticed some other bits of wood nearby, which he stacked up, cone-fashion, around the tinder. Next, a small shred of char-cloth was threaded in with care, and then he struck a spark with flint and iron onto its protruding end. The char-cloth ignited instantly, and it wasn't long before a merry little blaze was crackling in the firepit. Diccon went outside to find more wood, while Sven felt around in one of the many pouches hanging from his disreputable belt, never taking his eyes off the small clothes chest that had attracted his attention. Eventually he pulled out a stubby wand made of mistletoe wood with a short splinter of rowan wood jutting from its end.

Diccon, followed by Svarting, came back with an armload of split logs, which he carefully arranged around the young fire. The "magic feeling" now simmering in the room roughed up the hair on his forearms and nape of the neck. Svarting looked like a puffball; his fur was standing on end all over his body. Sven had hunched over, and was busy scribing something on the floor near the box. Diccon and Svarting started over to see what he was doing as the old man straightened up.

"Tricky kinda curshe here," he mumbled, "Diccon, go find me a plank and some shturdy polesh. Hic. I got it neutralizhed for now, but we gotta burn it, chest and all."

"Why can't we just pick up the box and toss it in the fire? It doesn't look very heavy to me!"

"No, don't touch it, don't open it, an' fer Frey'sh sake, don't even *think* at it! Hic! Wanna have your life-shpirit shucked outta your body and shent to the Dark Landsh in agony? Hic?"

A plank. Right. Where to get a plank. Hmmm . . . the main table has planks . . . It didn't take Diccon's smith-trained muscles long to come up with a plank. The poles were wrenched from the fence outside. Diccon brought them to Sven, who told the youth to sharpen the ends of each pole into a chisel point. When that was done, Sven had Diccon hold the poles by their unsharpened ends while he drew a pattern halfway down the length of each one with his wand. Faint greenish-golden lines and sigils hovered over the wood before sinking into it. Sven then drew more sigils on one end of the plank. Next, he told Diccon to wedge the sharpened ends of the poles under the clothes chest and lever it up, so that the plank's unscribed end could be shoved under it. Sven then stood on the sigil-inscribed end while Diccon levered the chest farther onto the plank and away from the wall.

When the chest was sitting in the middle of the plank, Sven drew a protective corridor on the ground from it to and around the firepit with his wand. The fire was by now burning with vigor, as if it eagerly awaited the feast to come. Sven had Diccon lift the scribed end of the plank slightly so that he could drag it to the firepit. As he did so, Sven darted behind it with his wand at the ready, drawing sigils in the air and then on the wall behind where the box had stood, and finally drew a line where the wall met the floor. He didn't move his hand over the spot where the box had lain, though. Diccon got the laden plank up to the firepit, and stepped aside. He then took up the poles and began shoving the plank over the edge toward the fire. Sven stopped him just before the plank and box would tumble into the fire.

"Itsh not gonnnna go easily. Hic. Thish is more than your ordinary ill-wishing cursshe. Go to the other shide of the firepit, an' lay the polesh over the fire sho that we can wedge the sharp endsh under the plank again. We gotta get that thing hanging over the fire sho that we can be far away when the plank burnsh through. Hic. Mother of a cursh in that boxsh, there is! When that goesh, the whole house will go. Maybe the whole village. Hic. I'd rather have plenty of real eshtate between me and it, I would!"

"Won't the curse sense that it's in danger and try to escape and nail us?"

"Naww, the shtuff I drew with my little marker here will keep it bottled up. I hope. Hic."

Between the two of them, they got the plank resting on the two poles, with the fire directly underneath the part where the box lay. Sven dashed out the door to the wagon, still holding his mistletoe wand tightly in one fist, followed by Svarting and Diccon. The old gelding was more than ready to depart at speed, even though he had been on the move for hours. Sven and Diccon held on for dear life as the horse bolted. Svarting's claws tacked him to Diccon's back, but fortunately for the kitten, Diccon's mail shirt prevented them from penetrating skin.

The wagon careered down the rutted road, with humans and kegs bouncing about inside. They veered around one bend, another, and a third. As they swerved behind a large rock outcropping, there was a large explosion and an even louder shrieking behind them. A purple-black pillar of smoke shot towards the heavens, furiously coiling and twisting like a huge enraged serpent, but it was caged in by a fence of greenish-gold lines and sigils which extended upwards around it like a tube. The gelding screamed in terror, put his ears back, and ran for his life. Sven screamed with joy that he'd successfully disarmed the curse with no harm to them, and then he screamed again with anger as the mostly-empty kegs bounced out of the speeding wagon and smashed on the stony ground behind them.

Eventually the horse slowed down. It wasn't used to running long distances, but it had managed almost a mile this time. Sven was rather bruised and banged up, but he was still in the wagon, still clutching his wand. Diccon had held fast with his smith's muscles and he'd had the weight of his mail shirt to help him. Svarting's needle-sharp claws, snagged in Diccon's over-tunic, had kept the kitten from being tossed out along with the kegs. Behind them, the cloud-serpent still raged, but it was beginning to get torn apart by the winds in the upper air, which could penetrate the magical cage imprisoning the serpent-demon. Sven and Diccon watched as the cloud-beast made a final, furious attempt to escape, gnawing on the greenish-gold bars of light, but they held fast and before long, the purple-black cloud beast sank back into itself and vanished.

"Took it long enough to die! Never shaw a cursh like that one before! I was shorta guesshing on what would deshtroy it. Glad I guesshed right! Hic!"

"You—you *guessed*??"

"Yep! When you meet shomething like that, itsh much better to guessh than to do nothing at all. You might jusht get lucky! Which remindsh me, I could sure use a drink!" Sven looked around the wagon, and then realized that there were no drinkables left on board. His face went white and he began to tremble. "Diccon, we got to get me shomething! I can feel me sobering up, and when I'm shober, I lose my Talent!"

Diccon tried to urge the gelding onward, but it shivered and hunched its back, panting from its recent exertions. Clearly, the horse wasn't going anywhere at all for the foreseeable future. They would have to make camp right there where they were. The sun was sloping toward the west, but they still had some hours of daylight left. In the high summer, the sun didn't spend much time below the horizon, and even the darkest part of night wasn't really all that dark. Diccon unhitched the gelding and led it to the side of the road, where there was some grass. The horse was tethered to a nearby tree with a long rope so that it wouldn't wander, and then Diccon set out to do some exploring. If he was lucky, he might find someplace that had some ale or mead for Sven.

Marit was wistfully thinking of Diccon at that moment. She'd found that her thoughts often strayed to that subject of late. A small, secret smile curved her lips upward as she watched the sun sink toward the horizon, its rays painting her cows and goats golden. And then, as one, the cows raised their heads and ambled toward her. It was evening milking time. Time to get back to business.

# CHAPTER 16

Wodurid was still trotting easily as the sun set. He had a feeling that he was pursued, so he decided to keep up his ground-eating pace as long as he could. Fortunately for him, the moon was rising, and his sharp eyes could easily pick out his path. He smiled slowly to himself as he thought of the message sticks he'd taken from the body of that fellow. Surely there could be no clue back there at that dinky little settlement as to the victim's mission. Wodurid was content; he would be with his war band in two days' time. Then they could head back to the Northlands and continue their own mission. The assassin loped on, mile after mile, as the moon sailed on its path through the heavens. He would only stop to rest when the sun rose once again.

Arni and Thorstein, skilled hunters and woodsmen that they were, realized that they were falling behind, and that their prey would not wait for them. They were far better at sneaking up on a slow-moving or stationary target than running down one which never seemed to need any rest. The sun was rising, and they'd run through the night. Even so, their quarry had apparently been able to keep up his blazing speed without resting, and there was no way that the two stumbling, weary hunters could catch him now. They came to a halt on a stony bluff many miles to the south of their village, and looked at the seemingly unending land in front of them. Arni looked at Thorstein, and Thorstein looked at Arni. As one, they sighed, nodded, and turned back.

It was finally time to lay Arinbjorn in his newly dug grave. The children and women of the village had gathered a mound of stones. Tosti the carpenter had lined the deep, rectangular hole in the ground with freshly hewn fir planks. The children gathered soft pine and fir branches to lay on the grave's floor so that Arinbjorn's body would be comfortable. They also strewed the bed with sweet-smelling herbs and bright meadow flowers.

A funeral was a big thing in those parts. There weren't all that many people around, and maybe you got one or two deaths per year. Some were fishermen who drowned at sea, and that meant that there wouldn't be a body to bury. The occasional dog or cat burial was a matter for the children, who played at the serious ceremonies accorded to a human. Now they had a real body, even though he was a stranger. That minor drawback was more than countered by the fact that Arinbjorn had been foully murdered in cold blood, which would mean a funeral with all the bells and ribbons, a multi-day affair involving funerary games, ritual processions, and the gloriously drunken wake after the last stone had been laid. People would come from miles around for this one.

Sigrun, the chieftain's wife, opined that Arinbjorn should not go to his grave as a poor man. He could take what he'd brought with him, save the code-bearing tunic, but he'd travelled light and had no family there to present him with pottery urns of mead, weaponry, bread and cheese, or animal companions to see him to the Land of the Dead. A poorly-equipped body sometimes came back to the land of the living to take what had been begrudged him at his funeral. The "again-walker" was something to be feared, and even more so if that again-walker had been murdered. Sigrun had an old bead necklace that she could give him, and she had her sons bring a sword and spear from the smithy so that Arinbjorn would not be unarmed in his new home. Gytha sewed the Hel-shoes for Arinbjorn, with stout leather soles inscribed with a triple-Týr bind-rune so that his spirit would be able to tread the paths of the dead with courage and in safety. Each and every one in the village did or gave something, lest ill luck befall them. Berit, who could do little in the way of physical activity, sat next to the body, singing all the songs she knew in her fragile, sweet soprano voice, so that Arinbjorn's spirit would not get bored and restless. Skogi, Moth, and Mist also did their part, keeping flies and other vermin away from the body.

The morning of the funeral dawned bright and clear, a good omen. Soti Jarl, dressed in his best tunic, raised a long birch bark horn to his lips and sounded a loud clear note which rang through the valley. Sunlight gleamed on his ruddy amber necklace, on the silver inlay in his ceremonial spear's head, and on the thick gold arm-ring dedicated to Thor that he wore when carrying out his official duties as *goði*. In front of him lay Arinbjorn on his plank, covered from head to toe with a linen sheet. The smith, carrying his symbol-engraved Great Hammer, arrived with his two apprentices in tow. Odd carried a small vessel containing thunder-water, and Ulfgeir held a small box containing ashes from the forge. Jan Sverre's son, the brewer, arrived at the same time as Sven's wife. Magni Wrongfoot, who was so skilled at climbing for birds' eggs, brought a battered willow bark basket with three gull's eggs and an owl feather as a grave-offering. Eirik and Egill Tune's sons, who were twins and who did everything together, brought an enormous dried codfish fillet and three of those large flat dark brown seeds which had floated to their beach from far away. These seeds, called "Beads of Brisingamen," were sacred to Freyja, and would ensure that Arinbjorn would not be lonely, as it were, in the afterlife.

Before long, everyone that could attend was there. It was time for the ceremony to begin. The chieftain blew three long notes, one for Frey and Freyja, one for Thor, and one for Týr. This would bring the attention of the gods to the ceremony. Then his sons, who had laid their offerings at the head and foot of Arinbjorn's plank, went into the temple to get the hastily carved animal head post which was attached to one end of a longish board. The board, narrow side up, was inserted at a right angle into a vertical slot in the base of the ornate animal head post, and pegged in place. The animal head, studded with iron nails, had wide eyes, flaring nostrils, and a gaping mouth. Similar heads were put up on the bow-posts of ships going into battle or on raids; the signs of fear carved on their wooden faces would induce that same emotion in any unseen supernatural beings which were in range. Raiders raised the fear-animal to scare off the protective land spirits so that their target would lie open and supernaturally undefended.

For funerary use, a long linen rope was strung through the gaping mouth and held in place by the wooden canine teeth, which met to form a hole through which the line ran. On one end of the rope was the *krók*, a large iron hook with a knob on its end. The knotted rope end was fastened within the ferrule by means of two iron nails piercing it at right angles through holes in the ferrule. The *rangle*, or "rattle," was an elongated loop of iron mounted on a ferrule, with three elongated oval rings holding smaller round rings threaded on it. This item was attached to the other end of the linen line. The *krók* and *rangle* arrangement was normally used to herd sheep . . . those sure-footed Northern sheep could dash up the straight side of a boulder face, where a pony or human could not go with any ease. The herdsman, who had hooked the *krók* to his belt, could throw the *rangle* to the length of the long line so that it would smash on the rocks ahead of the sheep, turning them back downhill. From herding sheep to herding malign supernatural spirits was an easy leap . . . as on the physical plane, so on the supernatural one. Odd and Ulfgeir, as the sons of a chieftain-*goði* and as chieftain-*goðis*-in-training, would walk on either side of the animal head, which was to be carried by four men, leading the funeral procession to the howe. Odd was supposed to throw the *rangle* about in front of them, clearing the way so that no evil spirits would be anywhere near the deceased on his last journey to his grave. Ulfgeir was tasked to be anchor man, with the *krók* hooked securely on his belt.

The chieftain led the way, followed by Odd, Ulfgeir, and the eight-legged "Death-Horse," which in turn was followed by two men bearing Arinbjorn on his plank. The smith led the men and Gytha the women in the procession that followed the deceased, chanting under their breaths as they walked.

When they got to the open grave, the "Death Horse" walked around it three times sunwise, and then stood at its northernmost edge, facing south across the hole. The smith raised his Great Hammer and hallowed the grave in Thor's name. Gytha called upon Frey and Freyja to watch over this man who had died so suddenly from a hateful deed. Soti Jarl raised his spear high, calling upon the warrior's god Týr to see that Arinbjorn would have a place of honor in the next life. Arinbjorn's plank was then lowered into the grave by means of a linen rope looped around the head end and a similar rope looped around the foot. The ropes, having touched the funerary board, were let fall into the grave. Likewise, anything that had come in contact with the corpse was placed in the grave, alongside the weapons and provisions laid in for Arinbjorn's protection and sustenance in the afterlife. Finally, the animal head post, with board, *krók,* and *rangle* still attached, was laid over the prostrate, stiff figure which lay under its linen sheet. A few final flowers and one half-gnawed pork rib were tossed in as Tosti lowered the rectangular wooden top onto Arinbjorn's box. The smith then nailed it shut, using iron spikes that had been quenched in thunder-water, pounding them in with his symbol-carved Hammer. Finally, Gytha laid a small piece of slate inscribed with certain runes on the top of the box. That "thistil-mistil-kistil" rune spell would ensure that Arinbjorn would stay put in his grave as long as the runes remained legible.

A wall of thick fir poles were then laid cross-ways over the grave, and fir branches laid on top of them. A layer of blue clay came next, followed by a layer of sand. Then, everyone helped pile rocks on top of the grave, heaping them in a smooth mound. Finally, a tall fir pole was raised on the very top of the mound, wedged firmly in place by more stones. The runes on the flattest side of the pole read "Soti Jarl and Odd and Ulfgeir had this howe raised to Arinbjorn, who was murdered. Ketill carved the runes." The inscription, set down in the traditional format, would be repeated word-for-word on the elaborate permanent stone marker, which would take Ketill Thorarin's son, the stonecarver, several weeks to complete.

It was now time for the funeral games to begin. Arinbjorn was safely ensconced within his tomb, and wouldn't interfere with the goings-on. A large firepit, which had been dug and filled with charcoal the day before and lit when the sun rose, was emitting glorious smells from the roasting horsemeat which was rotating slowly on several spits, thanks to the efforts of the chieftain's thralls. It was time for foot races, spear throwing, archery contests, wrestling matches, and other acrobatic endeavors. Anybody who could play an instrument was pressed into service, and ale and mead flowed like water. The level of exuberance raised during the games would give energy to Arinbjorn's spirit as it fared along the dangerous path to the Land of the Dead. The brewer was heard by more than a few attendees to bemoan Old Sven's absence from the festivities and, more to the point, from the chugging contests.

All too soon, the sun was setting and it was getting dark. The large bonfire in the middle of the field took care of most of that problem; torches were erected in a wide circle beyond it, and the party roistered on. Thord the Clumsy, Orn's son, managed to break his left leg when he fell from a perfectly steady keg of ale. He'd been standing on top of it, serenading the company with one of his rowdier ballads, and had gotten a bit too enthusiastic.

Six or seven other fellows decided to carve Arinbjorn's permanent runestone memorial on the spot, so they hunted up a sturdy cold-chisel, a hammer, a boulder, and a full keg. The runes came out rather higgledy-piggledy, since the fellas were laughing and falling off the stone and swigging copious amounts of ale. They'd neglected to bring a torch for illumination, but they were pretty well lit as it was, and the dark didn't really bother them all that much.

A few couples took the opportunity to sneak off into the underbrush for some intensive worship, as it were, of the fertility deities Frey and Freyja. Children ran amok, snatching forbidden swigs of mead when nobody was looking, eventually dropping from fatigue here and there, scattered all about the field. Before long, adults were following their example, and when the sun finally rose again, its first rays shone down on a field littered with sleeping people.

During the next few days, the funeral was the first and main topic of conversation. They'd done this one up brown, they had, and Arinbjorn's ghost would surely not walk again. True, more than a few of the village men weren't ambulatory for a day or so and had to be solicitously tended by wives, mothers, and sweethearts. Thorstein and Arni were quite annoyed that they'd only gotten home in time for the hangover part.

Wodurid was far to the south, being welcomed back by his war-band. They were grim, hard men, led by a hard, dour man who answered to the name Grimfrið Irontooth. To a man, they were utterly dedicated to their overlord, Agnold the Black. Agnold was an ambitious man. That ambition had already won him vast tracts of lands, and his loyal adherents were awarded lordship over the peasants who dwelt therein. He commanded wizards of power. Those who were in the know feared Agnold's own command of the Power. But great power begets a thirst for more, and Agnold was far from sated.

He sat there, on a heavy oaken throne covered with black bear skins. Agnold's fingers were adorned with massive gold rings, and several gold chains hung around his thick neck. Long greasy black hair tied back in a ponytail cascaded down his back, and his heavy features bespoke cruelty and wilfulness. He'd grown up in a harsh world where brother fought brother, and treachery was rewarded . . . or not. The conquerors from the Empire were gone, and Pax Romana no longer kept things in check. It was every man for himself, and Agnold intended to grab as much as he could. All he needed now was to get his hands on one certain child, one who the soothsayers had told him would be a great danger to him. Agnold's first step was to cleanse his lands of the Talented. He didn't want any competition from them. He craved the position of absolute ruler, and absolute rulers didn't flourish where uncontrolled Talents dwelt. Already, his war-bands had exterminated hundreds of them. Soon, he would extend his overlordship into the rich lands of the north. Furs, unicorn horns, dried fish, honey, and wool would be tithed to him. His kingdom and tame sorcerers would effectively bar any loose Talents of the wild barbarians of the north from coming south and making trouble. Agnold smiled to himself as he dreamed, snapping his fingers for a slave to fill his wine goblet again.

Within a woodsman's cabin in a distant forest, an orphaned boy-child awoke from a bad dream, whimpering, and then fell asleep again.

# CHAPTER 17

It turned out that Inga could talk, after a fashion, with certain bugs. Marit was surprised at this; bugs weren't supposed to be aware of much outside of their own small lives. But some bugs were surprisingly intelligent, especially bees, ants, and flies. The first two were hive insects, members of a greater mind. Flies were survivalists, and could be found wherever there was food and warmth. Inga's goats were survivalists, too, and maybe that had something to do with it.

Marit realized that Inga's Talent could serve the village as well as her own did. Inga's bugs were able to go anywhere, and no attacker would think to waste an arrow on a bee or a fly. Marit still mourned Greyman's death. A bee could carry a warning and dance that news to Inga; especially what direction danger was coming from, how far away it was, and how fast it was approaching. Ants used smell as their primary sense. If there was poison in something, an ant could detect it. Flies, well, flies could enter a building without being especially noticed, and hear all that was said. If one was attuned with such a fly, that person might as well have been present, even if she were a mile away in the flesh. Flies made excellent spies.

Odd and Ulfgeir awoke slowly and painfully. Both were murderously hung over, but the geas which ruled them forced them to their feet and toward the smithy. The smith was already at work, his hammer clanging away on a half-forged sword. The noise was almost more than the boys could bear, but their feet carried them through the door and into the heart of the din. Thorgrim, seeing their extreme discomfort, laid his hammer aside and sat his apprentices down on a bench. A faceful of cold water followed by a short lecture on overindulgence was directed at each, and then the smith chuckled deep in his chest, mindful of his own youthful introduction to all the ale he could hold. How well he remembered the face of his own master, blearily swooping through a headache-y drink-befuddled field of vision. No, it wasn't lecture time; it was Hair of the Dog time. The smith kept a small flask of a thick, viscous brownish-greenish-purplish herbal extract which was sovereign for hangovers. It tasted horrible, but the results were well worth it.

Before the sun rose much higher, both Odd and Ulfgeir were feeling much better, Their mouths still tasted like a February henhouse floor with overtones of pig manure and ashes, but their headaches were miraculously gone. The tuxedo cat sighed with relief that the apprentices no longer broadcast thoughts of pain, wretchedness, and stomach-turning queasy sickness. She loved comfort, and the smith's magic elixir had blessedly banished the apprentices' poundingly miserable thought-intrusions which had inhibited that comfort.

"You have to learn how to drink and not get falling-down drunk if you want to lead men," Thorgrim said sternly. "I think it's time to introduce you to some of the elements of the Warrior's Way lore. Some parts are purely physical, practical precautions; others involve Men's Magic. Yes, there are differences between some of the magics used by women and by men; each is powerful in its own right. It's a rare person who can call on the Way of the opposite sex. You both know Hilda, don't you?"

Both heads nodded; Hilda was one of Aun's "sisters." They knew her *very* well.

"Well, Hilda's older sister, Ragny, is one of the rare ones, a *seiðkona*, one who can call on both sides of the magic. *Seið* is a kind of magic that carries the practitioner between the Worlds, to speak to and learn from the dead and from the supernatural Powers. Pure gender-based magic can't go there very easily. Only those people who are between the sexes, who can call on both the Men's Way and Women's Way, dare go on a *seið* Voyage. It's a powerful Way, and one to be feared by those of closed minds. A chieftain must be open to *all* his people, equally and fairly. Every single person has a Purpose, something that only he or she can do well. Even Simple Grinulf, Dagfinn's thrall. The children all love him, and he can keep them amused for hours. His Way is one of innocence and discovery. True, he forgets easily, but that makes everything new to him all over again. Sometimes one must see things with new eyes. If one gets used to the world about him, he often misses things. Think about it!"

This was a heavy lesson for the boys, especially in their present condition. The smith knew that in their misery, the lads wouldn't automatically push away this lesson and its import, or reject the concept that "otherness" was actually a good thing. Thorgrim was more than a simple metal-pounder; he was a Master in the Smithcrafter's Way. He was also, though none in the village save his fellow members Gytha and Marit knew it, a member of the secretive Bear-Star Clan, a loose association of Master Talents throughout the Northlands. His lessons held more meat than those of most teachers, and not infrequently wandered from the specialized lore of the forge.

Agnold the Black had no knowledge of the Clan. None of his tame wizards were members, although many of them were certainly known to the Clan. The nearest Clan member, geographically speaking, to Agnold's headquarters was a balding, wiry old seaman whose small double-ended lapstrake fishing boat was at that moment careened on a shale beach for a fresh coat of pitch on its bottom.

Hroðulf Hroðgar's son was his name, though everybody simply called him Hrof. Hrof was a Master Seaman, skilled in the lore of the waters and its denizens, and a far-traveler who had lived in many lands. His wife was his boat, and his mistress the sea. And he was utterly faithful to them both.

Sven, who was not a Clan member, awoke stone sober. He stretched carefully, automatically trying to extend his senses to see if aught was amiss. It felt as if he was wrapped in layers of deadening woolen blankets; he couldn't sense out of his body. The old man lurched to his feet, managing to kick Diccon awake in the process, which in turn awoke Svarting, who'd been asleep on Diccon's stomach. The gelding, somewhat rested, had finished off all the grass within reach, and was now working on the tender leaves of the willow tree to which he was tied. Sven stumbled over to the wagon, hopeful that he would find even a small cask that might have wedged itself fast and not been lost during their flight the day before. Diccon sat up, displacing Svarting, who scampered off into the woods in search of breakfast, an adventure, or something.

The young man's eyes fastened on the front left wheel of the wagon. It had been badly battered, and it was a miracle that it had held together this long. It wouldn't survive even a short, gentle trip now . . . it was almost falling off the axle! . . . and repairs would have to be done on the spot. Diccon was not a wheelwright, but he'd had enough experience around the forge to know how to fix a wide variety of things. While Sven started backtracking their yesterday's journey in hopes of finding an intact cask or jug, Diccon fetched some bits of metal and an axe from his heavy bundle of tools. It didn't take him long to chop down a smallish beech tree, and then to hew a log from its trunk to use as a prop for the front of the wagon. Once the log was wedged solidly under the wagon, Diccon pulled out the linchpin and hauled the offending wheel off the end of the axle.

The wheel was in terrible shape. It was a solid disc of wood planks, bolted to cross-beams and shod with iron. The wood had cracked on one side and begun splintering away, with fissures reaching almost to the axle-hole in one section, which meant that the iron rim had bent inwards, giving the wheel a distinctly lopsided profile. Each time the wheel rotated and the flat section contacted the road, some more wood would shower off it, and the metal bend even more. No wonder the headlong flight yesterday had been so bumpy, and why they lost all of Sven's booze, as well as clothes, bedding, food supplies, and anything else that wasn't tied down, too heavy to budge, or a part of the wagon. The Spear in its case was safe; it had been lashed to the inside frame of the cart.

Good it was that the smith had made Diccon fell trees and prepare wood for the charcoal burner. The young man had skill enough to fashion rough planks of the beech trunk to replace the damaged wood of the wheel. He had to make a small hot fire in order to work the iron rim back into shape and then onto the repaired wheel. Sven had returned as this process was in its early stages in order to fetch the gelding, its harness, and some rope. He made several trips back and forth, with rescued items roped to the horse's back or loaded on several fanned-out pine branches dragged with the rope tied to the harness.

Sven returned with the last of their lost gear as the sun dipped toward the northwest horizon. He was as hungry as a wolf, but had held off devouring the last of their small store of food. Wild animals had made off with most of their edibles, even taking the plank-hard dried codfish fillets and bits of dried fruit. Sven had a partial cask of butter, obviously licked over by a variety of rodents, foxes, and other small animals who could put their snouts in the narrow opening of the small cask. He had also rescued a string of smoked sausages which had gotten tossed high and landed on the outstretched limb of a linden tree, and a cloth-wrapped bundle containing one of his wife's journey cakes. Not even a winter-starved bear would dream of touching one of Helga's cakes! They were as hard as the smith's anvil, would never go rotten, and they tasted like fir bark. Sven had, early on, learned the trick of soaking one in mead for a day. Then it was edible, especially if accompanied by lots and lots of mead.

By the time the wheel was fixed, it was too late to travel much further. They had a simple supper of sausage cooked over the erstwhile forge fire, cold water from a nearby spring, and crumbled bits of the journey cake mixed with butter. Diccon had had to use his medium smith's hammer on the cake to smash it into bite-sized pieces, and the cloth it was wrapped in kept shards from flying all over the place. As they were finishing up, Svarting returned from his hunt with a very large rabbit dragging from his jaws, which he dropped at Diccon's feet. The latter immediately took the hint and thanked Svarting for his lovely gift. The rabbit was quickly skinned, dressed, threaded on a hastily-cut wooden spit, and set to roast over the coals of the fire. Sven hunted up some more wood, while Svarting cheerfully snacked on the offal. The rabbit smelled delicious as it cooked, and before long, the three of them had a lovely second supper. They slept that night under the wagon, which was still standing in the middle of the road.

Hrof spent that day applying pitch to the bottom of his boat. The next day, he would apply a second coat, and then maybe the day after, he could re-launch her and get his nets ready for some more fishing. The herring were running, and he didn't want to miss out.

Gytha carried her healer's basket to Berit's home. Mist had run all the way from there to Gytha's place to ask for the healer's help; her mistress was in pain and could hardly breathe. There was room in the basket for the kitten to ride home, and Mist took advantage of that opportunity. Berit had spent much of her failing energy during the funerary rites, and had taken to her bed. The herb-woman took Berit's thin hands in her own, trying to warm them and also to send energy into her limp body. Mist's eyes were huge in her kitten face as she also tried to bolster her mistress' reserves.

Then Gytha cocked her head to one side and listened hard, scarcely breathing herself. She dropped Berit's hands and placed her hands over the young woman's belly. Yes! Berit was with child! No wonder she'd gotten so exhausted! Gytha sighed unhappily. It would be a race between the growth of the tumor and that of the child. It was a girl child, and Gytha could sense even at this early stage in its development that the infant would become aware in a matter of a few months. She would have rare Talent, would be a Healer like Gytha. The problem would be to keep Berit alive and as strong as possible until the birth, and for as long afterwards as the gods would permit.

Gytha would have to fight for the lives of both of them. Leaning back, she scanned Berit from head to toe. There was only one tumor, but it was deep within her, attacking the bones of her spine. It hadn't yet touched the tender nerve cord within, but its tendrils reached for it. Gytha lowered her head, took a deep breath, and focused on the tumor and the bones it was eating. First, she would have to tell the body to wall it off, stop any fingers of the tumor from extending any further. Cell by cell, the body would have to erect a sturdy wall which the malignant growth could not pierce. The cancer was a beast, a hungry beast, and would not be sated until it had conquered all. It was greedy; it sucked blood into itself and built many veins so that even more rich blood could penetrate to its depths. Gytha's eyes flickered as she saw that last. Blood was the secret, the weak spot . . . . and a part of the Healer's Way was the skill of blood-stopping. If somebody slashed themselves with an axe while hewing wood, the blood-stopper's skill could save his life. Maybe this would save the child's life . . . and perhaps, if she were very, very lucky, also save Berit's life!

The chieftain examined his largest ale-casks with sorrow. As *jarl* and *goði*, it was up to him to provide the wherewithal for community ceremonials. Arinbjorn's funeral had been simple in that everybody had brought food for the wake, and the smith had donated the *krók* and *rangle*. Tosti the carpenter had supplied the plank, coffin, and the animal head post. But the ale, that was what the chieftain had had to kick in. Thirty-two gallons. Pfffft! All gone! He himself was an indifferent brewer, and his wife was too busy rescuing the kitten, spinning, making bread, soap, and clothes, rescuing the kitten, dying yarn, repairing torn tunics, overseeing the thralls, rescuing the kitten, gossiping with neighbors, rescuing the kitten, tending the firepit, making butter, rescuing the kitten, and rescuing the kitten. It was up to him to oversee the ale department. This meant that he called in three of the thralls to roll the empty barrels over to the brewer's for a refill. The latter would bring them back in his wagon in a week or three, but in the meantime, there were going to be thirsty times in the *hof*, the chieftain's hall.

Inga was getting better and better at talking to her bugs. It had been kind of a shock at first . . . bugs??? Not dignified like birds or horses or even rabbits. Nobody she'd ever heard of talked to bugs! Turned out that she could also talk to wasps and hornets. Like bees and ants, they also had a hive mentality. When she found some termites, she would have to see if those answered to her, too. If so, she could tell them to avoid the wooden buildings, barns, and boats of the village. There was plenty of dead wood in the forest for them.

# CHAPTER 18

Halfdan was overjoyed and deeply saddened by the news that Berit was with child. Any man who loved his wife as much as Halfdan loved Berit would have been overwhelmed by that welter of emotions. He'd finally become resigned to losing Berit . . . and now, with their child in her belly . . . their beautiful, Talented daughter at risk . . . he desperately wanted *both* to live. A white-hot hope flared in him as Gytha described what she would like to try, the blood-stopping technique which might, just possibly might save the lives of Berit and little Solfinna . . . they'd already named the child. Halfdan dreamed at night of cradling her in his arms. He was a *father!* He'd do *anything* to save and protect his own child and her mother. Gytha warned them both that she'd never tried this technique in this way before, but both Halfdan and Berit pleaded with her to try her best. Berit knew that she was dying as it was, and if things didn't work out, at least she'd lose nothing that wasn't already forfeit to the Death Winds.

The Wise Woman wanted Berit to gain some strength before she underwent the procedure. Berit had to rest in the sun, eat as much meat, fish, bread and honey, cream and *kvann* as she could hold, and focus on what it was to be alive. That "awakeness," the awareness that was her. Other people tasted what they ate, but Berit was to focus on her *own* sense of taste. What it was that she, *Berit*, and nobody else, tasted. She was to look at colors . . . and know that it was *her* Life Force, the "ego," if you will, the unique consciousness that was Berit which studied the green grass, blue sky, white clouds, and her own pink hands stroking (and feeling) the soft fur of her grey kitten. Taste, smell, sight, hearing, and touch. Gytha told Berit that she must become aware of her own life-force; aware that she was a unique being who lived in this world, in the Here and Now. She could have been born a frog or a slave in ancient Rome, or not born at all. But, her particular spirit had been called by her parents, and she, Berit, had been born into this world. There must have been a *reason* why she had been come into this body and unique awareness. The young woman stroked Mist's ears gently, feeling the soft fur and the tremble of a silent purr as Mist smiled up at her mistress and goddess.

Thorgrim, Odd, and Ulfgeir were working on spearheads today. The boys' education had progressed, thanks in great part to the geas, and the two lads were actually beginning to take pride in each day's work. The smith grinned in his beard as he supervised the work. First, Odd would man the bellows and Ulfgeir the forge. Then they'd switch positions. Ulfgeir, now a muscular fellow and not a puffy, servile spoiled kid, really enjoyed wielding the hammers and feeling the metal move under his hands. The first time he made a decent spearhead, he had held it for a long time in his hands, marveling that he, Ulfgeir, made this. Not the smith. Not his brother Odd. Himself. Ulfgeir. *I* made this! *This* could be the very spearhead that slays an enemy! He could hardly wait to show it to his parents.

Marit was worried. Something was not right. Her birds and Inga's bugs didn't report anything out of the ordinary, but Marit's hunches had been accurate in the past. Something coming up . . . time to do some soothsaying. Consult the auguries. Check out the omens. She asked Inga . . . you always *ask* Inga, you don't *tell* her . . . if she would be so kind as to watch over the cows for a while. Inga, whose developing Talent also knew that there was something Not Right, agreed in a flash. Marit thanked her, and then went out alone on the high plateau where they lived during the summer, taking nothing with her except a cloak, a loaf of bread, one of Inga's goat cheeses, a smallish flask of ale, and her scrying crystal. This would require an all night session, when the world was asleep and not making thought-static.

Diccon, Sven, Svarting, and the gelding were finally underway again. Sven bitched and moaned under his breath about his current sobriety, but nothing could be done to correct that situation. Diccon almost prayed for a keg to drop from the heavens, so that he wouldn't have to listen to Sven droning on and on and on and on.

They eventually came to a small village that had real live people walking about in it. This affair with deserted villages was all well and good, but there was generally no hooch to be had there. Real people walking around in a living village drank ale and mead. Sven was quiveringly alert to the possibilities. The wagon rattled into the center of what passed for activity, and Sven quickly hopped off the wagon to hunt up what he needed. Diccon, meanwhile, was confronted by the local chieftain.

"What'cher want?" that worthy asked suspiciously, "We *don't* like strangers here! Yew passin' by, or yew plannin' to stay?"

"Actually, me an' my ol' man're gonna visit his folks down south," Diccon replied in what he hoped was the local dialect, "But we gotta get us some stuff, like ale and food, before we move on. We ain't lowlife, and mean no harm to you an' yer folks!"

"Yew sure? We been havin' some right queer folks comin' about an' askin' questions, we have! Ah'd run 'em outta town if we had enough fellas to do the job! Ptui! Ah *hate* strangers!"

"Hey, we're just passin' through, OK? All we need is some staples, an' we're gone!"

"Awright, yew gotta deal! Yew got gold or silver? We could shore use some gold an' silver!"

"No, but I'm a smith, and can shoe horses, fix ploughshares, and repair metal fittings!"

"Awwwwriiiight! We don't have our own smith, an' we need a buncha stuff fixed! OK, I'll give ya two kegs of ale an' a half cow carcass if yew can fix some stuff fer me!"

"Four kegs," said Diccon, who knew the value of a smith's work, "Four kegs, the half cow carcass, two hams . . . and I mean *good* hams and not last year's wormy hams, one good large cheese, some honeycomb, and bread. I don't care if it's hardtack or soft loaf."

The chieftain thought a bit, but the possibility of him getting his horse shod overweighed his innate greed, and he nodded his assent. Diccon insisted on being paid the aforesaid kegs, hams, etc. before he laid hammer to any repair work. While the locals were assembling the comestibles, Diccon and a flock of hastily-recruited teenaged boys scavenged a pile of rocks, which he built into a crude firebox. A large flat-topped boulder would serve as an anvil. His medium-sized bellows poked its snout through a hole in the side of the firebox, and was to be manned by a local. A board balanced on two rocks would have to act as his work bench.

The young smith loaded the firebox with charcoal supplied by the chieftain, and then kindled a nice, hot fire. Those villagers who had stayed for the show saw Diccon pull out his smith's tools and get ready to work, waking the makeshift anvil (the stone sort of thudded; it didn't ring) with his Great Hammer. They were awed by the young man's demeanor, the professionalism that he showed. A real *smith*! Wow! Diccon, realizing that he was the Big Show, laid it on for the locals. If his master back home had seen the shenanigans he performed, he might have approved, or he might have ripped Diccon's head off. But Thorgrim was far away, and this was the here and now. It was Showtime!

Old Sven had disappeared during this first part of the goings-on. He had his own search, that of getting his Talent back. Before long, he scored a smallish hornful of mead. Then he bet a prosperous-looking fellow a half silver neck ring . . . he had various bits of hack-silver, and this was the biggest piece . . . that he could empty a pitcher of ale . . . the local could choose the pitcher . . . in ten swallows or less. That worthy, seeing that this was a nice, heavy piece of silver, promptly hunted down the largest jug he could find, and filled it to the brim with ale.

Sven had owned that piece of silver for over twenty years, and it had won him many a pitcher. The prosperous fellow was sure that this scrawny, scruffy old derelict wouldn't be able to drink all *that* ale, and in ten swallows???? Needless to say, Sven won the bet. It only took him seven swallows. He had this trick of opening up his gullet and pouring the suds down. Occasionally he'd swallow, come up for air, and then go back to pouring. The man was awed and amazed, and Sven's Talent came roaring back. The old lush zig-zagged off down the street, looking for another likely sucker . . . er, sporting fellow.

Wodurid knew that he had lost any pursuit. His Talent ran that way. He could tell if someone was taking an interest in him or following him. Grimfrið Irontooth had been pleased with his report, and determined to take his band north in order to wipe out any Talents there. Agnold the Black was getting itchy, which meant that he wanted, nay, *demanded*, action. He was balked by Asugisalas in the peninsula directly to his north, but in the far lands where his tame wizards said the great Talents lived, *there* was the place where that child he sought called home. The wizards had determined that this child, now known to be named Biornulf, did not live in any lands he controlled. Yet.

Grimfrið Irontooth was a realist. At least, he thought that he was a realist. And any realist worth his salt would know that Black Agnold was an up-and-coming Power, which meant that it would behoove Grimfrið to anticipate his overlord's wants, which meant that he and his men started packing up for an extended campaign. They had two missions: first, to wipe out any and all Talents in their path, and second, to get their hands on Biornulf. Agnold hadn't said *why* this particular child was of importance, and Irontooth wasn't about to ask. If he managed to snag the kid and bring him to Agnold, so much the better for Grimfrið Irontooth. And having Wodgrim *wigilaz* along with the band would *surely* ensure victory!

Wodgrim *wigilaz* wasn't at all thrilled about having to go north again. He was a trained wizard, not a petty hack-and-slash type, and he was *not* pleased to have to associate with a crude bunch of hack-and-slash barbarians. Agnold had insisted, and one obeyed Agnold. Wodgrim sourly packed a few clothes and checked over his Tool bag. The last time he'd gone north, it was in a smallish twelve-oar boat which had rocked villainously. He'd spent a lot of time with his head hanging over the lee rail, cursing his queasy stomach. When they finally headed into shore, he'd had to quash his vomiting, get out his inscribed human thighbone wand, and focus on his magic. His primary mission had been to cast his Terror spell, which would render the locals unable to work magic and unable to face a sudden attack. Then the boys would simply splash ashore and go to work, hacking and slashing, looting and so forth. Wodgrim was to wait until the messy part was over, and then point out any of the Talented among the prisoners and ferret out any that were in hiding. They'd be still befuddled by Wodgrim's spell, which would make them easy meat.

This sequence had gone fine for the first twenty or so villages, but then he'd run up against one which had a real Power-user, some freak who'd apparently been immune to his Terror spell and who'd countered with an even more powerful spell which made the earth move and swallow some of the raiding party. Those that had avoided being swallowed got nailed by a giant demonic blue serpent. He himself, along with the skipper and another two men, had managed to escape thanks to a hastily cast Dark Contagion spell; they'd still been ankle deep in the water when the villagers' spells struck. That had been a singularly nasty surprise! Wodgrim's Terror spell had always worked before. Like many short men, he had a big chip on his shoulder, and he bitterly resented anyone whose spells were stronger than his own.

Upon his return home, Wodgrim had gone into conference with his fellow wizards, and a Great Working was done. Wodgrim's thighbone wand was augmented during this working; its spell would now kill, not simply terrify. He would only have to deal with a short sea voyage. Then, Grimfrið's band would head inland and approach their targets from the rear. Their targets would all be out fishing and looking seaward. Their backs would be to him, which was just fine. Any time you could nail someone from behind, that meant that they wouldn't be alert or actively fighting him. This time, Wodgrim's wand would kill everything in its path, including grass, trees, and the insects in the air. The war-band would leave on the morrow, and this time, he'd level that wretched village which had thumbed its nose at him.

That same night, high on a grassy hillock, a dairy witch looked deep into her moon-struck crystal and saw a long black bony wand which spat death.

# Chapter 19

It took almost two days for Diccon to finish all the jobs that the chieftain had lined up for him. That individual, a canny middle-aged balding fellow with ruddy cheeks and a full white-blond beard which nearly reached his belt, had gotten the word out to all of his people that they should bring their holed-through pots, unshod horses, and broken hasps to Diccon's impromptu smithy. No charge to the customer; the chieftain would take care of the tab. It was worth it to the chieftain to fork over some ale and food in exchange for getting a real smith's work, and it seemed as if every citizen of the village had something that needed to be made or repaired, especially if he or she didn't have to pay for it. The villagers praised the generosity of their wonderful chieftain, and praised the skills and efficiency of the smith. Sven encouraged the latter, letting it be known that smithcraft was a thirsty trade, and that poor Diccon was slaving his heart out over a hot fire without a drop to wet his parched mouth. The housewives, pleased with their repaired pots, were generous with their ale, mead, and pails of water. Needless to say, poor Diccon only got the water.

When all the smith's work was done, the chieftain decreed that since he'd have half a cow carcass left after he'd paid Diccon, and since the meat would spoil if it weren't eaten, that they would spit-roast that carcass over the bed of glowing coals in the erstwhile forge box. Diccon suggested that they could roast the entire beast at one time, and that he'd take that part of his pay in cooked meat. Everybody that was in the neighborhood came to the feast, and everybody, yet again, praised the generosity of their wonderful chieftain.

Sven wound up on the beach, giggling and hiccuping at the broad track of moonlight on the water. After a little while, he began to get drowsy, so he crept into a handy beached boat. The little weather gods guided his steps, so he didn't even wake Hrof, who was already asleep in that same boat. Diccon, who'd taken delivery of the rest of his pay, slept in his wagon along with his smith's tools. Svarting, whose little tummy was full of roast beef, had night guard duty. If he napped, nobody caught him at it.

The next morning, Sven and Hrof were awakened by a clam dropped into the vessel from an altitude. Gulls picked up clams from a low-tide beach, flew up into the air, and then dropped them on the rocks. Then they'd flap down and feast on the smashed clam. This particular clam missed the rocks and landed right next to Sven's head, which made a terrible bang on the wooden decking. Sven's hoarse scream woke Hrof. Then there was silence as the two men looked at each other, at the still intact clam, and at one frustrated gull. They had a good laugh, introduced themselves, and had a wee drink. Sven had brought a small cask with him to the beach, and it still had some hooch in it. Hrof expertly opened the clam and ate it for breakfast, still laughing at the gull.

Before long, Diccon showed up. He'd been hunting for Sven all over the place, and had finally heard the old lush's voice from the direction of the beach. Diccon had brought some of the bread and a biggish hunk of cold roast beef with him. He knew that Sven wouldn't be thinking of food when there was mead to be had. As the three men ate, they discussed various and sundry things. Diccon mentioned that he was interested in getting to the flat lands across the bay, and that this would require help from someone who had a boat. Hrof said that he wanted to launch today and go fishing, but that he'd be willing to ferry them across for the shoulder of Diccon's roasted half cow. After a bit more dickering and an agreement, Diccon trotted back to his wagon, to be met by a worried Svarting.

The kitten's eyes were huge, and his tail was all bottle-brushed out. He tried to send his message to Diccon, who bent close and touched Svarting's head between his ears with one callused finger. Then Svarting's message got through: a blurry image of a group of men who had muddy auras; they exuded Darkness, and they skulked and hid while the village slept. They only came out after Diccon had gone down to the beach, watching the young smith with some interest, and ducking into a handy hiding place whenever the youth looked in their direction. They'd taken no notice, fortunately, of a certain tuxedo kitten. The men hadn't approached the wagon yet . . . it had been rolled into a shed. It was obvious to Svarting that the men were looking for something. They had bright swords, too.

Diccon silently thanked Svarting and asked him to keep a watch out in front of the shed while he quickly and as quietly as possible harnessed the gelding and hitched him to the wagon. He then tossed some loose hay on top of all the supplies in the wagon. Remembering how Muha had disguised himself for his journey, he appropriated a large floppy hat which was hanging on a peg in the barn, and dotted red ochre spots all over his face, arms, and hands. From a distance, it would look as if he had the pox, which should keep any marauders at bay. He also made sure that his amulet was handy, and that the Spear was safe in its case near-to-hand. Lastly, he recited a charm which would cause people's eyes to veer away from him and the wagon, sort of an avoidance spell. It had to be a very quiet bit of magic, because if these men were looking for the Talented, he didn't want any tingle of active spellcraft to give him away.

Svarting gave the "all-clear," and Diccon led the gelding out of the shed. The wheels of the wagon were newly greased with the fat of the cow they'd roasted the day before, and everything in it had been lashed down so that in case of another mad dash, they'd not lose everything all over the road again. Diccon turned the horse's head toward the beach, and slowly led him across the grassiest and sandiest places he could find, lest the clip-clop of the horse's hooves attract unwanted attention. They had gotten down to the beach, explained the fake pox marks to a startled Hrof, and gotten the horse unhitched when Svarting suddenly hissed, spat, and leaped off the wagon. He ran as fast as he could, with the cat's up-and-down teeter-totter gait, heading back toward the village.

"Let's get the boat launched and our stuff aboard, fast!" Diccon half-whispered as he pushed against the bow of the boat, "I think that we've been spotted by a bunch of those Dark raiders! Svarting, Freyja bless him, must have picked up on them and gone back to cause a diversion, while we save what we can!"

Sven and Hrof helped push, and got the boat launched and floating in thigh-deep water. Diccon leaped into the wagon and slashed the ropes securing various casks and bundles, his smith's tools in their sack, food, chests of clothing, the Spear in its case, Gytha's carefully packed medical kit, and Sven's kegs. They handed things from man to man, hastily stowing them in the boat. Diccon had to lift Sven's kegs; he was the only one with the strength to do so. As they started loading the cow carcass, they heard a horrible drawn-out scream from somewhere in the village. It was shrill, unnerving, ear-shattering, and blood-curdling. Diccon laughed, for he realized that Svarting had tacked himself to the back of a pig and was swiping a clawed paw across something tender. Pigs scream like banshees, and Svarting was making sure that this one really opened up. Made for a great diversion!

The men hopped into the boat . . . they'd have to abandon the horse and wagon . . . as Svarting's dark body pelted across the beach toward them. Diccon held out an oar, blade flat-side to the water, and Svarting unhesitatingly hopped onto it, scrabbling with his claws at the wet wood. As the young man carefully and quickly pulled in the oar, Hrof set the small craft's sail while Sven tried to row.

A hung-over drunk isn't very good at rowing. As soon as the kitten was safely aboard, Diccon evicted Sven from his seat and then put his smith's muscles behind the oars. He'd taken just six strokes when he heard shouts coming from the land, and saw seven or eight figures running toward the beach, swords drawn. Hrof immediately dived for a small sea chest, and pulled out a short length of rope with three knots in it. Swiftly, he untied the first knot . . . and a spanking breeze sprang up, filling the sail, carrying them away from the land. The men with swords skidded to a halt at water's edge. One of them started fumbling in a pouch at his side.

"Hold your ears!" shouted Hrof as he leaped to the very stern of the boat, "This is gonna be loud!" He then cupped his hands around his mouth, took a deep breath, and then started chanting in almost a whisper. Diccon had to take one hand away from his ears to grab the tiller, so that the boat wouldn't veer and come into the wind . . . with that wind, it might broach as it came around, and capsize. Hrof's voice got louder and louder and louder until it was a giant shriek, a vast wind-scream aimed at the men on the beach. Diccon tried to stop up his bare ear by laying his head over on his shoulder, but the sound kept coming through. Svarting screamed and laid his ears back, but the sound kept getting even louder and louder. Sven's teeth rattled as the sound crested, pushing against the very air around Hrof's head. The men on the beach, who had been in direct line of Hrof's shout, were running back toward the village, hands clapped against their ears. Hrof laughed, and then set out to do one last bit of magic.

This next spell was familiar to Diccon. Hrof was calling the fog. He summoned wisps of it to arise behind them and spread out and up, hiding them from the land. Thicker and thicker the fog got, and Diccon lent his strength to Hrof's working. Before long, a real pea-souper masked the shoreline behind them, and Hrof was able to relax and take over the helm again.

"I don't think I can go back there again," said Hrof slowly, "The way those men were acting, I'd be dead meat if I came back. They must be some of those strangers we've been hearing about, the ones who've been nosing about and causing trouble. I think that I'll just see if the folks up ahead will buy my herring as eagerly as that village did!"

"But what about your home, your family?" asked Diccon, "What about them?"

"Wave-Cleaver *is* my home and my family," replied Hrof, patting the tiller. "All I have is aboard her. I can come and go where I please. Right now, it pleases me to bring us all to safety across the bay."

"*I'll* drink to that!" exclaimed Sven, fumbling for his half-emptied small cask of mead, and that's exactly what he did. Before all of the mead was gone, he politely handed the cask around. Then he finished off what was left.

The fog bank swelled behind them, and Hrof knew that they'd not be pursued by the raiders. He'd heard about Black Agnold's men, and didn't want to meet them at close range. On the sea, however, he was in his element. Wave-Cleaver scudded toward the far shore, her sail bellied out with Hrof's magical wind, riding the waves toward her new homeland.

Wodgrim *wigilaz* was content. Following his recommendation, Irontooth was taking their band north to continue their work of eradicating anyone with Talent who might object to Agnold's overlordship. They'd start where they'd left off, at that one-horse village which had chased him off so ignominiously. Before they left, they'd sacrifice to their grim god, Wod, so that his battle-frenzy would carry them to victory.

# Chapter 20

It was good to be home again. Muha liked people, but in his role as a leper during his journey south, he'd been avoided like the plague. Made for a mighty lonely trip, bereft of any social interactions save the frequent shouts of "Move on, ya filthy beggar!" "Get outta here before I sic my dogs on ya!" or worse. He didn't mind the curses and shouting; it was the thrown rocks that bothered him the most. Those hurt.

Asugisalas, Muha's patron, was a forty-ish broad, hearty man with red-blond hair and beard. His mustache was wheat-blond, which was rather startling to those who didn't know him. Called "Sugi Jarl" by all and sundry . . . his full name was a mouthful and not easily spat out if you were in a hurry . . . the big chieftain was mightily relieved to see his *erilaz* return safely. He'd heard tales of the wild lands of the North, where dragons prowled and freak blizzards waylaid the June traveler; also, Agnold's forces had been getting over-bold of late. A bunch of swordsmen could only do so much, defense-wise; there was nothing like a top-bracket wizard to even the scales . . . or tilt them in Sugi Jarl's favor. Muha had some really interesting and creative spells. It was a very good thing to have a truly innovative wizard with a wicked sense of humor in one's employ! Needless to say, Sugi Jarl had a wicked sense of humor, too. Wizard and lord got along very well together.

Sugi's advisors brought Muha up to date. The situation was worrisome. Bands of marauders, presumably Agnold's thugs, had been testing the jarl's defenses. They'd started out with pinprick raids and terror-inducing quickie atrocities, but now they were thrusting deeper into the jarl's lands and staying longer before being beaten off. If nothing were done, the raids would only get worse and worse until Agnold launched a full-blown attack, with the aim of overwhelming the defenders and flooding into Sugi Jarl's rich lands. Sometimes the only thing those ambitious, greedy sons-of-Hel understood was superior strength, delivered unhesitatingly and thoroughly. Sugi Jarl was totally fed up with the situation, and had only awaited the return of his *erilaz* to take the battle south to Agnold's front door.

Sven, who'd discovered that ale didn't appreciate being tossed around in a bouncy craft, was doing his best to keep ahead of the flow of suds exuding from the bungs of his four kegs. The yeast had been roused, which meant that the ale was fermenting almost explosively. The old man hopped from keg to keg like a demented bird, shlurrrping up the tongues of foam as they snaked down the sides of the kegs. This left the far less important task of handling the boat to Hrof and Diccon. The latter, who had grown up in small boats on the river, was able to be a real help to Hrof, who had to focus not only on his seacrafter's magic, but also on navigation and making sure that his rope-magic wind carried them in the proper direction.

The voyage across the bay took the better part of a day, but Hrof wanted more distance between himself and the Dark Raiders, for so he named them. They scudded along the shore, passing village after village, until the slowly sinking sun finally touched the horizon. They made landfall on an uninhabited beach and pulled Wave-Cleaver close into shore. Hrof tossed his four-pronged anchor off the stern as they neared the beach, and paid out the anchor's line to twice the depth of the water above the anchor before setting the hook. As the bow's keel-board touched bottom, Hrof leaped off the bow with another line in hand, and fastened it to a sturdy tree. This arrangement would keep the boat's bow in and secure while they slept that night. While Sven continued at his self-appointed task with the kegs, Hrof went off to gather mussels and clams, and Diccon dug a firepit, chopped some driftwood for a fire, and got the campfire going. Hrof came back with his large basket brimming with bivalves, and then he went inland to look for wild *hvitlauk*, which we call garlic. Diccon hunted up a large kettle and a smallish pot, into which he tossed a chunk of butter. Hrof was successful, and soon chopped garlic was added to the butter, and the small pot placed at the edge of the fire to heat. The mussels and clams were steamed in the large kettle. As dusk proceeded into night, Sven, Hrof, Diccon, and Svarting feasted on a perfectly wonderful dinner of clams and mussels dipped in garlic butter, ale, bread, cold roast beef, cheese, and more ale. Svarting passed on the ale, bread, and garlic butter, though.

Agnold the Black was not sitting on his thumbs. One of his bands of armed men had set off to the north, bent on continuing the mission of exterminating any of the Talented who might threaten his ambitions. Now, it was time to assemble the forces which would take out Asugisalas. That particular fellow was standing in his way, and Agnold did not tolerate folks who stood in his way. He took a last swig of wine, and abruptly gestured at the slave girl who crouched at his feet. He would ease his anger with her tonight, and then on the morrow, start preparing for the next stage in his plans.

Gytha went to bed early that night. Tomorrow, she would start working on Berit. She tossed and turned, worrying about the procedure, worrying that she'd do something wrong, and prematurely snuff out Berit's life . . . and that of little Solfinna. Moth did her best to purr her mistress to sleep, and when that didn't work, tried something else. Cats have a spell of their own. If a cat sits or lies on her human and sends sleepy thoughts at him or her, like as not, that person will get drowsy. Moth snuggled close and did the sleep magic bit. It took almost a half hour, but eventually Gytha's breathing became long and regular as she sank into sleep. Moth purred faintly, and then fell asleep herself, a captive of her own spell.

Ulfgeir was also restless. He didn't know why he couldn't get to sleep, but anything he did to attain that state wouldn't work. Something was niggling at him, and it wasn't letting go. He couldn't fasten on it, couldn't identify it. He rolled over and tried counting sheep. But they turned into black wolves, and the wolves kept coming closer and closer, threatening him with slavering, widely-gaping jaws. Their yellow eyes fastened on him . . . Ulfgeir sat up suddenly on his cot, thrashing his arms to chase them away.

He was wide awake. No way could he fall asleep now. He pulled on his tunic and trousers, stuck his feet into his boots, and headed out the door to the smithy. He'd found that sometimes being right next to the anvil and forge fire that he'd somehow attain a higher awareness. Whatever had been niggling at him was still there, and maybe if he could focus in on it and identify it, he could finally grab some Z's. He could see stars above in the not-quite-dark summer night sky as he made his way to the smithy.

The tuxedo cat was also awake, and greeted him at the door. She, too, was uneasy, and hadn't been able to get to sleep either. The threshold wards were quiet, ditto those of the chimney. But the anvil was awake, and the forge fire stirred restlessly in its bed of ashes. Ulfgeir put his hands on the anvil, hoping for some kind of insight. Wolves, black wolves were coming; he saw them coming from the south, leaping and panting, their noses pointed directly at him and their yellow eyes never leaving his. The tuxedo cat, catching Ulfgeir's vision, spat and bristled. The wolves were still distant, but they were coming fast, and they would be at his throat very, very soon. Ulfgeir looked over at the banked forge fire, and saw the glow of paired eyes like those of wolves peering at him through chinks in the ash. The youth trembled with fear; cold sweat breaking out on his body. He debated waking the smith, but a mere apprentice didn't just go in and wake the smith unless the smithy were burning down or a similarly urgent emergency was an immediate threat. But the vision was so strong . . . and he'd seen it more than once. And the tuxedo cat had seen it though his eyes. Her ears were back, and she was crowded into one corner of the room, eyes wide and glowing in the moonlight streaming through the open smithy door.

Ulfgeir didn't know what to do. He put his hands on the anvil and felt it hum under his palms. Usually, after the day's work was done and the anvil thanked for its work, it slept until the next day when the smith's hammer woke it. There was a kind of urgency in the anvil's note. That was what decided Ulfgeir to head over to the smith's cottage, open the door, and call to him quietly from the doorway. One never shook the smith awake or shouted in his ear. The smith could move very quickly, and he kept an axe hung on the wall next to his bed. Ulfgeir had to time his summons to fall in the quiet moments between his master's snores, as he called again.

The smith awoke, growling. "Ulfgeir, there had better be a damned *good* reason for waking me up like this!"

"I-I think I've had a vision," the youth stammered, "I couldn't get to sleep, so I went to the smithy. The anvil's awake, and so's the forge fire! They see it, too! Evil black wolves running north, coming to kill us!"

"The anvil's awake?" the smith asked in a low tone, "And the fire, too? What about the cat? The wards?"

"The wards seem to be quiet, but the cat saw what I saw, I'm sure of it! She's terrified!"

The smith grunted deep in his chest and reached for his tunic. "OK, Ulfgeir, let's see what's up. If you're right, I think we're going to be very busy from here on out!"

Ulfgeir led the way to the smithy. The smith stopped short of the threshold, sensing its hum. Everything seemed normal there. When he stepped inside, his head went up suddenly and the last wisps of sleep fled. Ulfgeir had definitely picked up on something. The smith went to the anvil, apologizing to it for asking it to work during a rest period. Then he laid his callused hands flat on its surface, closed his eyes, and waited for its message.

Black wolves. But these had spears and ran on two legs. There was Darkness about them, and they were coming from the south. The smith could tell that they were aiming for his village, and that they would arrive in three or four days if they kept up their present pace. The smith glanced over at the forge fire, listening to it crackle softly as if it wanted to be fed right then. The anvil hummed, seeming to thrust up at the smith's hands. It was still night, but it was time to get to work.

"You really *do* have the true Smithcrafter's Talent!" he said approvingly to Ulfgeir. "Your sensitivity may have bought us a day or more! It's not everybody who can hear the forge like that!"

Ulfgeir swelled with pride. He'd found that working in the smithy filled some need in him, and he really enjoyed his work. Unlike Odd, he'd quickly outgrown his geas. As a matter of fact, he'd been thinking of becoming a smith for real, instead of playing second fiddle to his brother as a kind of sub-chieftain. The smith had *praised* him! Ulfgeir's smile split his face as he breathed in the familiar acrid forge-smells. Yes, this is where he truly belonged. Suddenly a kind of peace descended on him. He had a Purpose. It was *right* that he follow the smith's Path.

The smith's voice broke the youth's reverie. "You'd better go wake up your brother! And bring some ale, bread, and cheese back with you; I'll get the forge fire going. It's going to be a long day."

Grimfrið Irontooth finally called a halt. His war-band would need to get some rest; the men had been on the move for almost three days after they'd left the boats. They were all mounted on rangy, hardy little horses which were used to long days on the trail. The pack animals kept pace with them easily, thanks in good part to one of Wodgrim *wigilaz*' spells. Irontooth led his men into a grove of fir trees, which would hide them while they slept. The horses were given grain bags and hobbled so that they wouldn't wander. Wodgrim then placed a silence spell on them so that they wouldn't whinny or make any noise that would attract unwanted attention while the men slept. Finally, Wodgrim brought forth two owls from a shrouded cage that had been fastened to one of the pack horses. These birds were tasked to watch while the humans and horses ate and rested. The men would need their sleep. Soon they would descend on that miserable village, and after they had wiped it from the face of the earth, they would continue their northward thrust.

# Chapter 21

Wiegand *wigilaz* rose early that morning. His magical tools, clothes, and other gear were already packed for the coming battle. Agnold himself would be in on this one; the opportunity of killing Asugisalas and wiping out his forces was more than he could resist. Agnold had made it absolutely clear that he himself would be the one to personally slit Asugisalas' throat. Wiegand could have Muha, though. The lean wizard smiled slowly in his dark beard; he'd recently picked up some seriously lethal spells from the warm lands on the southern inland sea. Muha wouldn't have a clue . . . or a chance. It was going to be soooo good. Wiegand was really looking forward to this encounter. It would be like spearing fish in a bucket. Chuckling quietly, he went outside to join the troops.

Agnold, for his part, was busy overseeing the assembling of his army. He'd put together what he thought would be an irresistible force, one that would crush Asugisalas like a bug. He'd pulled over a thousand men from his territory, and hired another three hundred or so mercenaries from the mountain lands to the south. There were even several wild men from the east, whose people worshiped an eternal flame in an oak grove and whose gods were alien to those of Agnold and his kinsmen. That wouldn't bother Wod, the grim tempest and death-god whose halls would soon be enriched with hundreds of battle-slain dead, and whose ravens would feast until they could hardly flap themselves into the air. Agnold would make sure that Wod got a very rich offering in battle-slain warriors. In return, the god would surely favor Agnold's forces, even those of his troops who worshiped other gods.

The first to leave were the scouts. Agnold wanted reliable reports of the land and people he would be meeting. The scouts, riding swift, nondescript horses, would travel in pairs. That way, one could ride back with a report while the other waited in place for his return. They would range a half-day's march from the main force of the army, which was composed not only of hundreds of foot soldiers, but also mounted shock troops, his wizards, and a train of supply wagons. There was also a small advance party which would quietly ride into Asugisalas' lands in order to alert and activate Agnold's "moles" who had settled there a while ago and who had lived quietly, awaiting Wiegand's summons. One of these, a jolly merchant named Freada Gormur's son, was to poison Asugisalas' drinking water sources. The other man, Froðuwarða *wigilaz* Dugrim's son, would activate a talisman whose Terror spell would chase off the local *vettir*, the protective land-spirits, so that Asugisalas' realm would be vulnerable to the invaders' attack. This talisman was hidden in a sealed lead box so that it could not be detected by Sugi Jarl's Wise Ones. Once the box was opened, though, the spell would instantly flood the area out to the distance of a day's ride. The *vettir* would suddenly be uprooted and pushed out in front of the onrushing shock wave of the spell. This meant that they wouldn't have a chance to warn Asugisalas' Talents. Wiegand *wigilaz* was especially pleased with that talisman; it had taken him a full month to craft it. Nine men had been hung in Wod's grove in the making, thrice three, to make the spell even stronger.

It was time to depart. Agnold mounted his massive black stallion and gave the signal to march. Jingling and tramping, the huge army began its advance, led by Black Agnold and his troop of picked warriors. He estimated that they'd reach Asugisalas' lands in three or four days. Then, ah, then there would be an epic battle to gladden the heart of his divine patron!

Grimfrið Irontooth's band spent the night (and several thereafter) in ruined villages. True, some of the villages had been occupied and prosperous when Irontooth's band arrived, but Wodgrim's now-lethal wand spell followed by a sudden armed assault quickly rectified that situation. The dead bodies of those villagers who hadn't escaped were hung in trees as offerings to Wod. And those villagers who ran away . . . well, arrows took care of that. The men feasted, drank, slept, and set out again the next morning, always headed north.

Berit was excited about what would happen, but she also feared it. Gytha assured her gently that there would be no pain, and that she'd work as carefully and precisely as possible. Halfdan held his wife's hand as the poppy juice took effect. When Berit fell into a doze, Gytha asked Moth and Mist to snuggle close to the sleeping woman's belly, one on each side. The kittens were to hold Berit and Solfinna while Gytha's mind entered Berit's body and dealt with the tumor. Moth had to show Mist what to do, but as has been said before, Mist was a very smart kitten, and she caught on quickly. Halfdan could stay, but he'd have to sit absolutely still and not make a noise, no matter what happened. The Wise Woman relaxed in her comfortable chair, clearing her mind and preparing herself for the delicate procedure.

As Mist linked with Berit and Moth with Solfinna, they began to purr faintly, cradling the Linkages in cat-song. Gytha raised her hands, palms hovering over Berit's chest, just where the ribs in front met under her breasts. Her healer's senses felt around the tumor, identifying its borders and its thin fingers reaching out into healthy tissue and bone. First, she would have to stop the wispy tips of those fingers from stretching further. This was easier done for the parts of the tumor embedded in flesh than for those parts which had invaded bone. The Wise Woman knew that this task alone would take many hours, while the kittens held fast and Halfdan silently prayed to all the gods and goddesses that Berit . . . and Solfinna! would live.

Gytha first asked the healthy bone and flesh bordering the tumor to form a thick wall of shiny white cartilage and impenetrable bone around the tumor, so as to fence it in. This took quite a long time, since she had to tell each cell what to do. In a way, it was like commanding a huge army without having any sub-commanders to help out. Gytha had to activate and teach every single soldier, as it were. Mist and Moth purred on, as Halfdan's eyes followed the graceful movements of the healing-woman's hands as she worked.

The tumor itself was a large irregular lump clinging to the spine behind Berit's heart and stomach. It had eaten into four of the vertebrae, weakening them. The new bone that Gytha commanded to form in each vertebra as a barrier to the tumor, would also give support to the damaged bones. When Berit's healthy tissue had finished building the shell around the tumor, Gytha was finally able to begin the next task, that of choking off the growth's blood supply. The Wise Woman would have to be awfully careful with her blood-stopping skills here. She didn't want to miss her target and block a perfectly healthy blood vessel. It was the ones entering the tumor that she wanted to close off. She started with the tiny vessels, sealing them off one by one. The sun rose high in the sky and began to sink into the west as she worked, heedless of fatigue and hunger, steadily pruning the tumor from its supply of rich blood.

Finally, there were only three large vessels left. Gytha's hands hovered over Berit's sleeping body as she tackled the first one. She saw the vessel clearly, and commanded a belt of cells to grow around it where it entered the shell surrounding the tumor, and then when that was done, to contract until no more blood flowed past the stricture. The tumor fought her, craving its nourishment, but the belt held as Gytha's Power told it to stay tight. Next, the belt had to be locked in place, never to open again. Gytha's hands moved in a sudden, intricate gesture as she sealed it. After checking her work, Gytha moved on to the next large vessel. Again, a constricting band was formed, tightened, and locked. Gytha was now also fighting her weariness, weaving slightly in her seat as she faced the final vessel. Slowly and patiently she called the last belt into place, pulled it tight, and locked it. The tumor was now totally encapsulated and shut off from its blood supply, and it would slowly begin to die. Before she withdrew from her patient, Gytha made absolutely sure that the shell surrounding the tumor was solid, and that not even a single cell of the malignant growth could sneak out of its prison.

The Wise Woman leaned back, groaning with exhaustion. Halfdan looked up at her, hope in his eyes, silently questioning. Gytha nodded once, and let her hands fall to her lap.

"I've done what I could for now," she mumbled, "I'll need to rest before I can proceed with the next step. The tumor is dying, true, but the mass of dead tissue will eventually have to be removed from her body. But for now, Berit should remain in bed, resting and gathering her strength until I can see to that."

"How are you going to do that? Are you going to cut into her?"

"No. I will tell Berit's body how to slowly squeeze the tumor into a hard ball and then to force it away from the bones of her spine. When we get the last of it out of the vertebrae, I will tell the damaged bones how to make healthy new parts, and how to regrow into strong bone. Until I can do this, Berit must stay in bed and not try to rise. Her back is so weak now that it might shatter, and then all my work would come to naught. Finally, the hard ball will have to be slowly moved through Berit's body until it comes to the skin surface. It'll be an easy matter then to pop it out."

"But you've killed the tumor?"

"It's dying as we speak. It may take a day or two for the last of it to perish. I shall stay here . . . you do have a spare bed, don't you? I don't think I can manage the walk back to my home right now." Gytha arched her back and stretched, realizing that she was ravenously hungry. "Halfdan, do you have some ale and food handy? I could eat a horse!"

Halfdan didn't quite giggle at the vision of Gytha chowing down on a whole horse, but he did give a great, gusty sigh of relief as he nodded. He was exhausted and starving, too. Mist and Moth raised their heads; their task done. Berit and Solfinna were safe, and healing sleep was what they needed now. Moth, sensing the hunger of her mistress, squeaked her empty-tummy plaint, and Mist followed suit. Halfdan rose, a gentle smile playing on his face as he nodded his thanks to the kittens, and went to fetch dinner. He knew that a great Working had been done, and that for the rest of his, Berit's and his daughter's lives, that they would be beholden to the Wise Woman. Gytha hadn't even asked for payment . . . she knew that Halfdan was struggling, financially speaking, but the young fisherman vowed to himself that somehow, someday, he would return the favor.

Hrof awoke early; he wanted to get underway as soon as possible. Though he didn't say so to Diccon and Sven, he also wanted to get in some morning fishing so that he'd have a nice catch to sell when he got to civilization. Diccon was anxious to get to Muha's homeland; out here he was vulnerable to whatever was feeling its oats that day. Sven, who was already (or still?) half in the bag, was amenable to whatever the others decided.

They made good speed, considering that Hrof set his net several times. This net was a wide circle with weights around its edges. It also had a running line along its edge, so that it could be pulled closed like a purse. When Hrof saw a ruffled patch on the surface of the water indicating a school of herring, he would deftly throw his net over the patch and start hauling on the drawstring lines. The weights pulled the edges of the net down around the fish, and as the purse closed, the fish were hauled in. Hrof had it down to a science. All he had to do was to come into the wind, toss his net, and within a very short time Diccon would help him pull in a bulging load of silvery herring. As he emptied the fish into empty barrels, Diccon got the boat underway again. Sven did his share by monitoring his kegs.

The low, flat land slipped past them, and then they faced another wide stretch of water. The straight violet smudge of land ahead beckoned them, and before the sun set again, Wave-Cleaver was partially drawn up on the beach of a small settlement, where Hrof sold almost all his fish. There was enough left for supper, though. Hrof gutted them with his fingers, and grilled the flattened fillets like pancakes on a flat piece of buttered shale. He found some wild thyme, which he scattered over the cooking fish. There was also roast beef, honeycomb, cheese, bread and, of course, a mug or three of Sven's ale. The locals told Diccon that Asugisalas' lands were only a short sail to the south. The young man was looking forward to seeing his mentor again.

Marit and Inga spent the day smoking some of their cheeses. They had a small smoke-house near their cottage, and they fired it with dampened chips and twigs of alder wood. The cheeses were laid on racks in the smoke-house so that the fragrant smoke would get at as much of their surface as possible. While Marit minded the fire, Inga went out with a small goat-drawn wagon, looking for tawny cloudberries, ruby lingonberries, wild mushrooms, and blueberries. She had a basket for each, and had grown up knowing the good mushrooms from the bad ones. She sang as she picked berries, warbling like her sister's birds, and laughing to see the occasional butterfly bouncing in the warm summer air.

Odd was dispatched to his father's longhouse to alert the village that the raiders were coming again. Soti Jarl was worried, because he had so few of the Talented to call upon. Gytha was tending to Berit, and Marit was up in the high grassy mountain meadows with her cows and goats. Ragny, the *seið* witch, had traveled north two weeks before, to visit some friends. Sven Bluemouth and Diccon were far away, which left only the smith and Ulfgeir to provide any immediate magical protection. Some of the smithcrafter's Way fit into battle magic, but much did not. And from what Ulfgeir said, this attack was going to make the others look like child's play.

The chieftain dispatched his best hunters, Thorstein and Arni, to set up watch stations on the southern pass through the mountains above the village. They were accompanied by the swiftest runners in the village: Magni Wrongfoot, young Assur Tosti's son, Gufi Gylfi's son, and Dagfinn Thord the Clumsy's son.

Thorstein, Gufi, and Dagfinn set up camp on one side of the pass, where they could survey the lands to the east and north. The others settled in on a rise to the south, where they could cover the south and the west, including the river and their village. Each watch station was within line of sight with the other, so that if one picked up on an invading force, this news would go to the other by means of a hastily lit torch waved in the air. Then one runner would tear down to the village, leaving the rest still on duty.

The smith and Ulfgeir spent the day sharpening swords, spearheads, axes, arrowheads, daggers, and so forth, making sure that hilts were solid, spearheads and arrowheads were securely socketed on their wooden shafts, and that everybody . . . including the women . . . had at least one weapon to hand. The two also checked the bear and wolf traps, re-setting some that had snapped shut on fallen branches or unlucky small game. Odd wound up helping his father organize the physical defense of the village.

The smith knew that this raid would be "make or break" for the village. He wished that Diccon and Sven were there, but wishes couldn't swing swords or chant curses. If he had time, tomorrow he would forge another magical Spearhead with the help of Ulfgeir. Maybe it wouldn't be as fancy as the one sent south with Diccon, but it should have a similar effect on an invading force. If the raiders split up and attacked from two directions, that would be a bad thing. The smith could only be in one place at one time.

# CHAPTER 22

The winds were fair, driving Wave-Cleaver south towards Asugisalas' lands. Sven was pleased (and not pleased) that there was a following sea, which meant that the boat wasn't pitching much, which meant that the yeast in his kegs was relatively quiet, which meant that he didn't have to tend to his kegs all the time. Gulls wheeled over their heads in the deep blue sky, and danger seemed far away.

This was, however, not necessarily the case. Agnold's advance men, two nondescript fellows on nondescript horses, entered Asugisalas' lands one at a time. One advance man was tasked to give the secret signal to Freada Gormur's son. Poison took a while to work, so the merchant was to immediately carry out his mission. Once the advance man had left, Freada sat down and thought. He'd been sent north to Asugisalas' lands about three years before, and set up in business with Agnold's money. Freada had also brought his family with him. The peace of his new home, and the freedom to pursue his trade without various officials from Agnold demanding this or that from his wares . . . no mention of payment . . . had made an impression on him. He was not eager to place his family and future under Black Agnold's thumb again. True, he'd been promised a mountain of gold coins. But Agnold's promises were a sometimes thing. Freada had had several years of peace, but now it was crunch time, and Agnold would expect his investment to pay off. Agnold had supplied the poison, a noxious compound sealed in a waxed mini-keg, to Freada when he'd left his homeland. That mini-keg had spent the following years buried in a mound of dirt behind Freada's outhouse.

What to do? Agnold's men would certainly be watching, and they would kill him and his family if he didn't fulfill his original mission. Agnold's men didn't know what his poison supply looked like, surely they didn't. What if Freada took sea salt, poured it into a smallish keg, and then dumped that into the various springs and wells? The original keg was well-hidden, with a rather healthy bush growing on its mound. Agnold's men would report that yes, Freada had carried out his mission. Since poison took a while to act, that would give Freada time enough to get his family and his money to safety. The merchant nodded, nodded again, and began his preparations.

The advance man sent to alert Froðuwarða *wigilaz* had to hunt him down. Froðuwarða didn't spend much time in his home. Fortunately for Agnold's plans, the *wigilaz*' spell was to be released only when Agnold's men were closing in on Asugisalas' borders. The man was finally located at the local brewery, testing the new ale. The advance man waited outside, hidden in some bushes, until much, much later when Froðuwarða finally staggered out. He tried to give his message, but his target was in no condition to comprehend it. The advance man sourly followed Froðuwarða home, occasionally having to lend the wight his arm. Once there, he got Froðuwarða to bed, and then he bunked out on the floor next to the firepit. The wizard would be sober in the morning, and could then be given his marching orders.

Marit was worried. Her birds brought her some unsettling news. A band of men on horses were heading north toward the village, and several of them were frightening to the birds. The dairy witch was supposed to remain up there with her herd on the high, grassy plateau during the summer and early fall, but this news had to be gotten to the village right away. Inga volunteered to run the news to the chieftain, and Marit asked her birds to keep close watch on the riders. Just in case, she started moving her cows and Inga's goats farther inland to a shallow grassy valley in the plateau. She then ringed that valley around with a magical "Do Not Pass" fence. There was plenty of water and forage there, enough to last the animals for many weeks. The cows were still in milk, but Marit could distance-milk them if necessary. Each animal had a collar with a unique pendant. Mama Cow bore Diccon's sweet sounding cow bell; Flossi, her daughter, had a quartz crystal caged in copper. Marit would be able to tell each one in turn to stand still while her telekinetic "fingers" stripped the milk from the udder, bringing it forth from a knife driven into a wooden pillar, and filling her buckets below.

The smith worked his apprentices hard. Ulfgeir rose to the challenge as if he were a smith born, and found to his astonishment (and delight) that he was able to tell his brother what to do, for once. Piles of spearheads and arrowheads were made, and by late afternoon, Ulfgeir was knocking them out almost as fast as the smith. Ulfgeir used a small anvil set to the side of the forge box, which meant that two anvils were in use at the same time. By default, Odd got to man the bellows. He bitched and moaned about it, but the smith was adamant. If Odd slacked off, the village would suffer. The smith would report truly to Odd's father about his behavior, which meant that Odd would stand a scant chance of inheriting the chieftainship after his father.

When the day was done and the anvils thanked for their work, Ulfgeir and the smith sat on a bench next to the forge fire's warm stone box, horns of ale in hand. Odd had taken the opportunity to beat it to Aun's place, where he would find sympathetic ears, among other things.

"Odd will never learn," Ulfgeir said meditatively, "The only thing *he* thinks with stands below his belt. I don't see how he can follow in Pop's footsteps!"

"I agree," replied the smith. "You have the Talent, Ulfgeir. I think it's time to teach you some more of the smithcrafter's lore. Go over to that pile of iron bars there, and try to sense which one wants to be your Great Hammer!"

"Y-you think I'm ready for a *Great Hammer*???"

"Yes, lad, I do. You were *born* to be a smith! And the time to forge one's Great Hammer is now, when the moon is at its fullest and none shall disturb us. You'll need this Hammer in the days to come, if the visions we've had are correct. I'm sure in my mind that you saw truly, and that we're in imminent danger!"

The smith stoked the forge fire, apologizing to it for awaking it so very soon after bedding it. He then had Ulfgeir spread his hands over the few bits of star-metal he'd emptied onto the work table from a small oaken box. Ulfgeir, eyes closed, waved his hands uncertainly over the table . . . and suddenly it was if they were grabbed by something. He barely got his eyes open in time to see his fingers close on a twisted nugget lying off to the side of the main pile. Not touching the other bits, the wide-eyed Ulfgeir brought the piece which had chosen him over to the smith. The smith grinned, stretched, and waved the youth toward the common iron.

"You'll have to make your own Hammer," he said. "The most that I'm allowed to do is to work the bellows. You must select the metal, blend the star-metal with the cold iron, forge the hammer's head, and set the symbol or symbols on it. Tomorrow, you'll go into the woods to find the proper handle for it. Remember that you'll have to ask the tree's permission before harvesting the wood, and that you must shape the handle there, giving back to the tree all you do not take with you. I can offer advice from the side, but only until the forging begins. A smith's Great Hammer must be his work alone!"

Ulfgeir gulped. Up to now, he'd been simply pounding metal, but this was a major step for him. Only a true smith had a Great Hammer. Joyously, he turned to the forge fire, greeting it and asking it to help him with tonight's work. The fire crackled and grew, swelling in its bed, reaching out for the pieces of iron thrust into its maw by the young man. While the metal heated, Ulfgeir took up the smith's four-pound sledge and saluted the anvil. He apologized to it formally for waking it so soon, but its help was needed to forge the Hammer. Ulfgeir brought the sledge down on the flat surface of the anvil, whose bell tone woke up the sleeping tuxedo cat with a start. Twice more the young man struck, and with each stroke, the anvil shivered and rang, and the tuxedo cat's fur stood out more. Great magic was going to happen in the smithy that night, and the now wide-eyed cat wasn't going to miss a bit of it.

The smith pumped the bellows slowly. He knew that he couldn't nod to his apprentice to cue him when the metal was ready; a smith had to know when to do what. This was indeed a test for the young man who watched the metal heat in the forge fire. At precisely the right time, Ulfgeir reached in with his tongs and fished out the "cold" iron which had come from the earth, and immediately thereafter, the star-metal. Placing the latter on top of the former on the anvil, he held both in place with carefully placed tongs, and began beating the metals together.

The star-metal welded itself to the earth-iron, and the whole mass flattened under Ulfgeir's hammer. Then it was returned to the forge fire to heat some more. The next time it lay on the anvil, it was bent over and flattened again. Nine times it had to be so folded, and then and only then could the Hammer's head be shaped. The metal was formed into a longish thick bar and then doubled over, with a central hole where the shaft would go. Then Ulfgeir worked each peen into shape, hammering the metal into solid square-faced ends.

When the final shape was attained, the smith paused briefly from his work at the bellows. Ulfgeir took up a metal punch and, with a small hammer in one hand, tacked a dotted pattern on the side of the still-soft metal of his Hammer. This symbol was one which had come to him; it was not of the smith's supplying. Each smith had to learn his own Power symbols. Ulfgeir then placed the Hammer's head into the forge fire for the last time, heating it to white-hot. When it was almost there, he poured a small sip of rowan mead on the fire and asked Thor to bless his work. Then he pulled the incandescent metal out of the fire, laid it on the anvil and, with various straight and curved smith's chisels, filled in the lines of his symbols between the dots.

When that was done, it was over to the barrel of thunder-water, dipping the Hammer's head into it again and again until the metal cooled enough to not explode or shatter if submerged. Great clouds of hissing steam fumed forth from the barrel during the dipping process, subsiding only after Ulfgeir let the semi-cooled metal fall into the water. The young man then thanked the anvil for its work, thanked the forge fire, and thirdly, thanked Thor. When he withdrew the dripping Hammer's head from the barrel of thunder-water, the smith was at his shoulder.

"It is good. You are now a true smith!" Ulfgeir swelled with pride at the smith's words. He'd *earned* his position, and being named a smith now filled him with almost giddy elation. He remembered back to the day when his Mom had hauled him and Odd to the smithy, and his attitude back then. He'd thought that a smith was down there with being a thrall, or worse. The young man blushed in anguish at the memory, remembering how callow and young he'd been, how thoughtless and insipid! And now he was a real *smith*! Ulfgeir felt very manly as he shook his master's hand as one smith to another.

Berit slept the night through, and well into the morning. She awoke to the rumble of two kittens purring in their sleep, one wedged on each side of her body, and a sleeping Halfdan leaning forward from his stool, his upper torso lying across the bed by Berit's feet, and her hand still lying in his. A distant snore told Berit that someone else was in the house, too. She drew in a breath of air, remarking to herself how *good* it felt to breathe. There was no pain, but she hesitated to move lest it bite in. She half-floated on her comfortable featherbed, surrounded by her friends. Her eyes closed, and she slept again.

When she woke, there were good smells coming from the cooking area, and Halfdan and the kittens were gone. She mentally reached within herself, fearing what she'd find . . . but Solfinna was still there, slumbering as she developed. Gytha came in at that moment, carrying a hot pan of broth. She helped Berit sort of sit up, her back firmly propped with pillows, and watched the young woman sip the hot, nutritious liquid. There was no pain as Berit moved . . . a miracle! Berit questioned the Healer with her eyes, and Gytha smiled back at her.

"The tumor is dying," the Wise Woman said, still smiling, "I still have work to do with you, but the worst of the danger is now past."

"I'll live to see my daughter?"

"I don't see why not! But first, we'll have to work on your back bones, and then get the dead tumor out of you." Gytha's hand brushed the air. "That shouldn't be too difficult. The scary part was yesterday. Thanks be to the gods and goddesses that I didn't make any mistakes! To my knowledge, nobody has done this kind of Healing before. I was just guessing at what might work. I was scared stiff during the whole process, you'd better believe!"

Halfdan came in at that point, dark circles under his eyes, but with a wonderful grin on his face. He'd picked a bunch of wild flowers, and laid them on his beloved's breast. Half sobbing with joy, he bent over to carefully kiss her, and the fervent response prompted Gytha to insist that Berit not strain her back so. Berit laughed, lay back, and held her husband's head close as he kissed her again and again through the salty tears running down his face.

Wave-Cleaver entered a narrow river, passing into Ausgisalas' lands. A short sail brought it to the dock near the center of the city . . . for this huge settlement was surely a city! Diccon hopped off, intent on finding Muha. Sven opted to stay with his kegs, and Hrof set in to selling his fish to the dinner-rush crowd.

# CHAPTER 23

It took Diccon several hours to locate Muha. The latter had been closeted with Sugi Jarl for much of the day and evening. The *erilaz* had needed to brief Sugi Jarl; he'd had warnings that Black Agnold was on his way north, finally making his big move. When Diccon showed up at the chieftain's house, he'd had to wait, and wait, and wait. Eventually Muha came out of that inner room, recognized his pupil, and greeted him with real pleasure. He then introduced Diccon to Asugisalas, who was happy that he'd have another smith to help forge spear and arrowheads against the oncoming threat. Muha then took Diccon aside and quietly asked him if he had the Spear with him.

"Yes, as a matter of fact, take a close look at this walking staff I'm holding!"

Muha looked, looked again, and then Looked hard at the staff. He grinned and began to chuckle. "You did a good job on those concealment spells!" he said, "Took me a bit to solve them! You've learned a lot since we parted!"

Sugi Jarl then suggested that the three of them sit down with a keg of ale and discuss the upcoming battle. Miraculously, as soon as Asugisalas popped the keg open, Old Sven materialized in the room, drinking horn at the ready. Muha chuckled again, his eyes crinkling up at the corners. He knew that Wiegand *erilaz* would be with the attackers, and he also knew that Wiegand knew what he, Muha, could do. But . . . and this was the big "But" . . . Wiegand *erilaz* was ignorant of what Diccon and Sven could do. Diccon had the Spear and his amulet, as well as Tiw-knew-what smithcrafter's spells . . . the warrior-god whom Diccon and Sven knew as Týr was called Tiw in Sugi's southern lands. Sven Bluemouth was unparalleled at curses. The more mead and ale was in him, the more erratic and creative he got. Muha poured the old lush a generous tankard, and the four men began to talk.

They had hardly started . . . Sven was still on his third hornful . . . when there was a rapping at the window. That orifice, covered with thin oiled goat hide, was closed during the night. Whatever was striking it made the hide rattle in its frame. Muha took a short rune-inscribed amber wand out of his pouch and warily approached the window, wand at the ready. The window rattled again, and a distinct "Keeeeeeeee!" sounded outside. Muha sensed no evil, so he lowered his wand and opened the window. A weary young falcon popped into the room and arrowed through the air straight to Diccon. The latter caught the bird and felt

Marit's kiss. He knew it was her kiss, and his head swam with joy. He cradled the bird close, and was about to kiss it back when he realized that this was a falcon, not his sweetie.

Muha noticed the rag tied on the falcon's foot. While Diccon cradled the bird, the old *erilaz* untied the cloth and spread it on the table. He studied it for a while . . . the message "Gytha sends" was clear enough . . . but there had to be more. Hmmmm . . . . the only other thing was the stitches hemming the strip of cloth . . . Muha looked closer . . . yes! It was the ancient code! "Ágnold seeks Biornulf child. Wigilaz Froðuwarða his. Also Freada, Grimfrið and Wodgrim." Muha, having lived in Sugi Jarl's holdings for much of his life, thought he recognized three of the names. Froðuwarða wasn't a common name, but there was a fellow with that moniker living out near the edge of town. He was named *wigilaz* in Gytha's message . . . and the word *wigilaz* was the same as *erilaz* in his dialect. Hoo-boy! A worker of Power that he didn't know about, and one that he'd missed for years! Freada, now . . . yes, there was a successful merchant by that name, but the Freada he knew was a jolly fellow who loved children and who laughed a lot. Wodgrim, of course, was a well known name to those of the Bear-Star Clan. Muha didn't have a clue about Biornulf child or Grimfrið.

Grimfrið Irontooth was far to the north, organizing his band's campsite. They'd marched for days, and on the morrow, they would descend upon that wretched village which had put Wodgrim *wigilaz*' nose so out of joint. His men were ready. Last-minute knife and arrowhead sharpening was carried out around the small campfires. Grimfrið was unaware of a barn owl who just happened to glide over his camp on silent wings.

The owl continued on her invisible way until she came to Marit's cottage. She rapped at the door, and Marit welcomed her in. She showed Marit fuzzy mind-pictures of Grimfrið's campsite, and gave her an idea of the short flight between those men and the village. They would come in from the east, avoiding the southern pass which would surely be watched. Marit quickly scratched a short message on a slim slat of wood and asked the owl to carry it to the lookouts to the south. Marit's birds had told her all about them, and where they were located. The owl agreed, especially after Marit told her where the mousing was especially good. Owls will work honestly for their pay, unlike some other birds we might mention. Arni was startled when the slip of wood tumbled out of the silent, dark sky to land on his lap, but when he read the runes, he sent one of his runners to the other watch site. The two groups got together, and then repositioned themselves so as to more closely monitor the eastern approaches.

Gytha had Berit drink a lot of buttermilk; she also fed her a gruel which had finely ground bone meal in it. Like to like . . . if there was extra bone inside

Berit, Gytha could coax it to where it was needed. Berit gagged down the nasty tasting potion, after which Gytha gave her a bite of honeycomb to get rid of the icky taste in her mouth. Berit was to rest. On the morrow, Gytha would proceed with the next step, that of rebuilding Berit's spine.

Odd wound up back at his father's place. He was to lead a small group of men into battle; it was obvious that the lad wasn't taking to the forge. Maybe Odd would shape up as a warrior. So far, the only skills Odd had shown were of the kinds appreciated by Aun and her "sisters."

Ulfgeir found the shaft for his Hammer in a relatively short time. It seemed to him as if many of the trees around wanted to give of their wood for such a sacred purpose. He looked at them all, but selected a nice, straight branch offered to him by a middle-aged ash tree. After gravely thanking the tree, he carefully harvested the offered bough so that the cut surface left on the tree would heal over well. Following instructions, he whittled the bough to shape and inserted it in the Hammer's head, giving back the bark, twigs, and shavings to the tree and the good earth.

When he got back to the smithy, both the smith and the tuxedo cat were anxiously waiting for him. The smith knew . . . he'd read it in the forge fire and heard it from the anvil . . . that on the morrow, the village would be under attack. Ulfgeir was promising, thought the smith, but what we need right now is some serious battle-Talent. Gytha was involved with Berit, but she could surely be pried loose to help save everybody's lives. Marit was up in the boonies, and Ragny, Sven Bluemouth, and Diccon were out of the picture. The worried smith sent Ulfgeir to warn Gytha. Then, Ulfgeir was to stretch his young legs and find Marit. Two smiths, one Wise Woman, and a dairy witch . . . this was the extent of magical protection available to face the oncomers. The smith hoped that the men of the village were up to snuff. The anvil and forge fire had indicated that this was a large group of raiders . . . and that it included the wizard who had cast that hateful Contagion spell on Diccon.

Soti Jarl wasn't napping that afternoon. He'd had his men set many trip-lines with clay jugs full of pebbles tied to their ends so that they would crash to the ground when the soot-blackened string was disturbed. Thralls were put to work digging deep pits and wedging sharpened sticks upright in their bottoms. These pits were covered over with thin branches, hay, and forest litter, so as to look like innocent pieces of ground. There were a variety of other traps prepared; the villagers were nothing if not creative.

Gytha left Berit and Halfdan . . . they understood that she had to work for the good of the village now. She told Halfdan to carry his wife carefully down to his boat, and row to one of the islands just off the coast. That way, at least they'd be safe. Halfdan was all for joining the fighting men, but the Wise Woman insisted. She told him that he could keep watch outward toward the sea, while Mist watched Berit. If there was one force attacking from the land, maybe there would be another coordinated attack from the sea. Then, Gytha went to her workshop to prepare the spear and arrow poison that the warriors would need the next day.

One who followed the Path of the Light didn't, as a rule, prepare poison. Gytha walked on the narrow edge of that prohibition as she mixed up a big batch of a paste which was mostly made from crushed mistletoe berries, foxglove juice, and soft old cheese. The mistletoe berries would stun the muscles, foxglove would make the heart race, and the cheese would ensure that the wound would suppurate. Nasty, but not lethal in itself. She put the paste in large empty mussel shells; that way, each man could have his own supply with him for use as needed. All he'd have to do before going into battle would be to scrape off the beeswax sealing the top and bottom shells together, and then stroke his arrow or spearhead across the paste. He could prepare several arrowheads ahead of time, so as to be ready when an enemy appeared.

Ulfgeir found Marit and Inga after running what seemed to him miles over the high, grassy plateau. The girls had prepared for their departure, and their herd was safe in its refuge. The three of them got back to the smithy as the sun set. Marit's birds would warn her when the raiders started marching again. Inga found a nice fat white-faced hornet nest in Thord the Clumsy's outhouse . . . it was situated high under the peaked roof, and hadn't been noticed yet. She found another nest in the large tree outside the chieftain's longhouse, and several more in the woods near the village. Honeybees, of course, were all over the place.

Sugi Jarl sent some of his retainers to find Froðuwarða and Freada. The former was not in his house, so the men spread out, looking for him. Freada was located at a spring near the jarl's longhouse. He was promptly apprehended and brought before the jarl, Muha, Sven, and Diccon. Muha looked the man over, sensing that the man was hiding something. He pressured Freada to yield his secret, saying that he had information that Freada was one of Black Agnold's spies. Freada's shoulders drooped, and he reluctantly told the men that yes, he'd been tasked to poison the water supply. But he'd been happy in Sugi Jarl's realm, and had substituted sea salt for the poison in case he was watched. He loved his family very much, and didn't want Agnold to find out that he'd reneged on his deal. Muha checked the small keg that Freada had with him, and determined that the man was, indeed, telling the truth.

"You and your family will be safe with us," Sugi Jarl promised, "I appreciate your change of heart! Now, do you know of any other spies that Agnold has sent here?"

Freada did not. But that was not to say that there weren't any such. This Froðuwarða was unknown to him, and he said as much. Muha sat back and began to scan for any Talents in the area. He picked up Diccon, Sven, and Svarting, of course. He also identified three of his apprentices, who were hard at work preparing for the onslaught to come, plus the other loyal Talents. Froðuwarða was either out of range, or so well shielded that he couldn't be detected.

Froðuwarða lay hidden in the cavity of an old lightning-blasted oak tree to the south of the main city. His wards were up, and Muha's scan passed over him without noting him. The *wigilaz* curled up and slept, knowing that he'd need all his skills and strength in the glorious day to come.

# CHAPTER 24

Grimfrið Irontooth got his men up early that morning. The sun had barely risen when the war-band gathered around a sturdy oak tree for the sacrifice to Wod on this, a battle day. Wodurid had selected three of the band by lot, unbeknownst to them, to have the honor to greet their grim patron god in person. Nine of Irontooth's strongest warriors casually surrounded the chosen, three to a man. Others of the band threw ropes bearing hangman's nooses over three high, sturdy, horizontal branches, and then pulled the nooses down to neck height, widening the loops to receive their burdens.

Upon Irontooth's signal, all of the warriors began to beat their swords on their shields, making a fearful din. A second signal cued the nine warriors to grab the swords and shields from the selected sacrificial victims, and then to drag the struggling, screaming men to the nooses. Wodurid and Wodgrim, both named for the god, raised their battle-horns, blowing a mighty, prolonged blast as the nooses were thrust over the victims' heads, tightened, and then ten men on the other end of each rope ran back with them, hauling the thrashing byrnie-clad bodies high in the air.

The horn-blowers had to hold their note for that entire sequence in order to call Wod's active attention to his newest recruits as they departed from the land of the living, and to grant victory to this particular war-band. The rope-runners were merciful; they had jerked the rope at the beginning to break the necks of the victims, so that they would not suffer a slow death. Only when the bodies hung slack could the horn-blowers cease their note. By having two of them, one could snatch a breath while the other held the note, alternating for as long as it took the victims to reach Val Halla.

The hoarse horns were noticed by every bird, bug, and small animal all around Grimfrið Irontooth's campsite. Many of those birds took off to alert Marit, and the bees and hornets told Inga the same thing. Various birds and bugs were tasked to keep a watch over the war-band, while Marit and Inga hot-footed it to the chieftain's longhouse, screaming the news. Soti Jarl was over at the smithy, so his wife dispatched a thrall to alert him. Inga headed down to the beach to rouse the boatmen, while Marit raced to Gytha's low-slung abode. Gytha was at home, finishing up the last of the mussel-shell packets of arrow paste for the troops. The Wise Woman drafted Marit to help seal the mussel shells with beeswax, and put them in baskets from which the warriors could help themselves.

Moth had stayed with Mist, monitoring Berit and Solfinna. They were safely hidden in a scruffy topknot of weatherbeaten brush and water-worn boulders atop one of the anonymous little islands just off the coast. Halfdan had pulled his rowboat ashore and hauled it into the topknot, balancing it upside down on two rocks, and then camouflaged it with branches and seaweed. Berit lay underneath it on a soft featherbed, which had been laid on a flattened pile of brush.

While the kittens explored the island, Halfdan baited a three-hook handline, attached a soapstone sinker just above the topmost hook, and then tied a wooden float to the line thrice a man's height above the sinker. He cast the baited line well out into the sea to leeward of the island, right where he knew there would be fish. The float bobbed in the gentle waves, keeping the weighted "business end" of the line just off the bottom. The other end of the line was tied to a whippy tall bush, along with a wisp of red yarn. If a fish took the bait, the line would jerk the bush, waving the yarn flag. Halfdan set two more such lines, after which he built a small campfire with driftwood and twigs. He'd just gotten the fire going when Berit, who could see the wisps of red yarn, called to him that one of the lines had a fish on it. Halfdan hauled in a fat red-speckled flounder, and re-set the line. By the time the fire had burned down to a bed of glowing coals, there was enough fish to feed everyone quite well.

Berit insisted that she could help her husband stand watch, since she could see a good part of the seaward horizon from where she lay, simply by turning her head. Her back wouldn't be involved at all. Halfdan started to protest, but Berit was adamant. It wouldn't do any good if the person on watch fell asleep. Two people, keeping watch in turn, could maintain continual vigilance. If there was an attack coming in from the sea, Halfdan would signal the shore with lit torches. The latter, longish poles with pine tar-soaked rag heads, lay close at hand, ready to be thrust into the campfire.

Inga scampered as fast as she could to the smithy, passing the chieftain's slowly-moving messenger enroute. She stumbled into the building, nearly falling to her knees from weariness. Ulfgeir rushed to catch her; he was the closest to the door when Inga burst in. The young man had noticed Inga about the village, but hadn't dared let her know that he'd noticed her. But now he had his arms full of panting, exhausted novice witch. What the youth didn't know was that Inga had noticed him, too.

The smith and the chieftain snapped to as Inga gasped out her warning. Ulfgeir sensed the urgency, and reluctantly released the girl. He sat her down on a bench and brought her a horn of ale. As the chieftain and the smith had a hurried conference, Ulfgeir packed up the most recently-made weaponry for the chieftain's thrall, who had finally arrived, to carry back to the village. Since he was already clad in his mail shirt, all Ulfgeir had to do was to don his helmet, belt on his sword, tuck his Great Hammer into his belt, grab an axe and a shield, and he was ready to go to war. The smith took up his Great Hammer, amber-hilted scramasax, a heavy broadsword in its sheath, shield, and various and sundry other tools and incidentalia. He, too, headed down to the village where Soti Jarl would be mustering the defenses.

The first of the lookouts came streaking down to the village. The raiders were on the march, and would reach the lookout posts before the sun stood at its highest point in the sky. Arni and Thorstein knew to bail out before Agnold's men got to them. They'd already laid false trails across some of the more interesting arrangements of bear and wolf traps interspersed with staked pits. Thorstein had had the bright idea of stringing an ankle-high trip-line across one trail, anchored on one side by a tree and with the other end tied to a brick-sized rock precariously balanced on a low branch above a cluster of small holes in the ground below. When the line was yanked, that brick-sized rock would fall with a thud, and a furious cloud of mean black dirt-bees would fume out of those little holes and take sweet revenge on whoever dared disturb their slumber.

Arni, meanwhile, bent over some sturdy, whippy young trees, anchored the tops with ropes, and then tied loops in the other ends of the ropes with slip-knots. Those loops were laid on the trail, disguised with forest litter and leaves. Whoever stepped within one of those loops would suddenly find himself hanging upside down, dangling by one foot from a now-straightened tree. If a horse got caught, that animal would be flipped over, one leg high in the air, spooked out of its mind and thrashing around, which should spook all the other nearby horses. Or so Arni hoped. Odd's little band contented itself with stringing throat-high fishline here and there, liberally rubbed down with soot and stinging nettles, and digging small stumble-pits loosely covered with twigs and forest litter.

A number of these traps suckered some of Irontooth's advance men, but soon the more obvious remaining traps were disarmed or marked so that the main body of the invading force wouldn't fall victim to them before the actual battle. Every now and again, though, there would be a scream or several screams as an undetected Learning Experience found a customer or three.

Soti Jarl knew that he would be facing a trained force of professional fighting men. His people were fishermen, farmers, craftsmen, woodworkers, shipwrights, traders, and so forth. This meant that the idea of a solid, disciplined phalanx of armed men facing the invaders would be out of the question. The chieftain dispatched various groups of men in different directions. They would strike fast and retreat, hopefully pulling the opposing force apart, which would make them more vulnerable to be picked off bit by bit by the archers. Nibbled to death by ducks, as it were.

Helga, Sven Bluemouth's wife, took the village children to the beach. They would watch for Halfdan's signal if the raiders also came from the sea. Sigrun, the chieftain's wife, grabbed her heaviest iron skillet and a freshly sharpened carving knife, and joined the village defenders. No way was *she* going to be left out of the fray!

The smith and Ulfgeir headed east, to stand between any magical assault and the non-Talented folk of the village. Odd, Arni, and Thorstein took their guerilla bands off to the sides of the line of attack . . . they now knew the direction from which the invaders would approach. They wanted to nail as many men as they could, and doing so from the sides would be the most profitable. Marit and Inga bespoke their birds and bugs, asking them to help in the defense. Gytha, meanwhile, linked with the *vettir*, the good gnomes of the earth, protecting them from any magical attack that might frighten them into flight.

The villagers were as ready as they could get. Before long, Marit's birds reported that the enemy force was forming up, ready to charge into the middle of the village in a shock attack. They also reported that there was one who had a long black wand, which he was beginning to wave in the air in intricate patterns.

The smith felt the spell-summoning, and raised his Great Hammer high in the air, calling upon Thor. Then he brought forth his rune-inscribed scramasax, ready to part the lethal spell that he knew was in the making, splitting it asunder so that its main force would not fall upon the *vettir* and humans in its path. Gytha strengthened her sending, enfolding the *vettir* and the defenders in a safe dome of Power. Skogi, the chieftain's tiger tom kitten, backed her up. He had the fighting spirit, and wasn't about to let some rabble overwhelm *his* people.

Wodgrim shouted the last words of his deadly spell, which launched itself in a black wave fanning out in front of Irontooth's host. There was a droning, tearing sound in the air as it moved forward, sucking the life out of all within its path. The wall of Darkness rushed upon the smith and Ulfgeir, who stood nearest to the oncoming enemy forces. Thorgrim stood steady, scramasax and Hammer raised in the air, and Ulfgeir held his Hammer aloft as well, calling upon Thor to *please* hurry. Marit's birds and Inga's bees and hornets flew high to avoid the Dark wave, and then they ducked down after it had passed them to do their part in the battle.

Back in the well-warded smithy, the tuxedo cat noted the passage of the Dark wave, which seemed to leap over her home without touching it.

Grimfrið was sure that Wodgrim's spell would flatten the village's defenses, and that all he and his men would have to do was a little bit of mopping up. Thorgrim, Ulfgeir, Gytha, and Skogi held firm, and Wodgrim's lethal spell was cleaved in two, each part rushing toward the sea, missing the village and the small offshore island where Halfdan, Berit, and two kittens stood sea-watch. The guerilla bands led by Odd, Arni, and Thorstein began picking off men with arrows, loosing one flight and then moving swiftly to another position in order to avoid any return fire. Irontooth's men kept coming, kicking their horses into a gallop. Marit, who knew what spooked horses, waved a linen towel in the air, chanting as she flipped it in sudden jerks, aiming her spell at the oncoming raiders. The local *vettir*, protected from Wodgrim's spell by Gytha and Skogi, marshalled the land's defenses, guiding the feet of the onrushing horses into gopher holes and soft patches of ground which gave way under their weight, and adding their own images to Marit's spook-horse spell.

Grimfrið Irontooth got a nasty surprise when Thord the Clumsy's outhouse hornets all targeted his face and hands. Hornets can sting again and again and again. A hundred or so hornets could ruin one's whole day. He screamed, clawing at his face, blinded by the many stings which penetrated his eyeballs. There were plenty of other hornets and bees to go around. Before long, Grimfrið's men were all screaming, swatting, and cursing. Their spooked horses ran hither and yon, many of them chased by clouds of angry insects. Marit's birds flew at the horses' heads, flapping their wings to spook the horses even more. Needless to say, the disorganized attackers were easy meat for the archers, and each bowman took care to aim at faces, not mailed torsos.

A few of the attackers managed to make it to the village, to be met by everybody who could bear a weapon. The smith and Ulfgeir wrought gory havoc with axe and sword. Sigrun beaned one fellow from behind with her skillet, right on top of his helm, driving it down hard on his head. Her carving knife took out the wight's throat. Then Sigrun went looking for another customer.

Marit now brought her dairy magic into play. Her hands swept the air as she did her distance-milking spell, pulling blood from the invaders' bodies through each and every sting-hole and wound. She'd driven a knife into a pillar of the chieftain's house, and stroked it as if she were stripping milk from a cow's teat. Streams of blood flowed freely, puddling at her feet and running into the street. Heedless of her sodden shoes, Marit milked on, sucking the blood out of a hundred or more men.

Wodgrim got special attention from Thor, who finally arrived in a towering purple-black cloud. The god's fiery hammer came sizzling down from the skies, frying the fellow in his own grease. Wodurid came next. He tried to duck, but ducking under a tree was a bad mistake. His tunic burned merrily under his white-hot byrnie as he fell, great chunks of the tree smashing him into the ground. When Thor came through, he did it in a big way.

When the shouting died down, it was the villagers who did the mopping-up. Not a single man of Grimfrið's war-band survived. The villagers stripped the weapons, mail shirts, helms, and anything else of value from the blood-spattered bodies, and then hauled the corpses to the beach. Helga had herded the children away so that they wouldn't see the gory bodies, and anyone who had a boat roped up strings of cadavers,like fish on a line. Then they rowed out beyond the mouth of the fjord, dragging their grisly burdens behind them. When they were at the edge of the strong offshore current, they cut their lines loose, letting the sea take the bodies to the place where blind sea-worms, sharks, and monsters of the deep dwelled. Wod had not favored his men that day. Ægir and Ran would collect them; they would never join the fabled warriors of Val Halla.

Not a man of the village had been killed. There were various nicks, slashes and stab wounds, which Gytha and Marit tended. Inga rounded up the loose horses, most of which could be sold to neighboring villages. The guerilla forces returned, every arrow spent, with big grins on their faces. Their targets would be food for the vultures, wolves, weasels, and worms where they lay. Wod's ravens could feast on them, too. Gytha's arrow poison had worked as advertised, although none of the raiders had lived long enough for the cheese to kick in. Inga's hornets returned home to replenish their venom; but many of her bees had died since they can sting only once, leaving their stingers and much of their guts in their victims. The village was safe, and Jan Sverre's son, the brewer, opened his doors to all for the victory celebration. There was plenty of ale and mead to go around, especially since Old Sven wasn't at the party.

# CHAPTER 25

Asugisalas wasn't a successful chieftain thanks just to his good looks, capacity for holding ale, and abundance of gold. He was an intelligent, astute man, and he knew full well how dire was the threat facing him. In the false dawn of morning, a flock of his scouts clad in mottled mossy-colored tunics scattered in all directions. Sugi Jarl wasn't sure from which direction or directions Agnold's attack would come, so he deployed his outermost screen a half hour's run ahead of the next layer of defense. Sugi had planned the positioning of his forces like the layers of an onion.

As soon as the vector or vectors of attack was/were identified, the scout(s) detecting such would dash back to the next-to-outermost layer. A continuous watch and tracking of the enemy would be maintained, lest Agnold pull a fast one and come at Sugi's lands from an unexpected direction. There would be frequent news bulletins and intelligence relayed back in stages through the various layers, so that Sugi Jarl could then strengthen up the areas in and around Agnold's path or paths. Muha, Diccon, and Sven would be one of several units of the Talented to face Agnold. Svarting was firmly told by Diccon to remain at Sugi Jarl's home but, as has been said before, sometimes kittens can be over-bold. Svarting waited until Diccon was just out of sight before surreptitiously following him. His Mama had charged him with the duty of aiding and protecting his human to the very best of his abilities. When Mama said something like that, it had better be done.

Agnold, astride his prancing black stallion, was pleased with the discipline of his troops. They pushed on straight ahead towards Asugisalas' lands and did not stop, as was their usual wont, to sack, pillage, rape, and burn along the way. He had thought deeply on his strategy the night before, weighing whether to mount a two or three-pronged attack, or to send his entire force against one spot. There were advantages and disadvantages to each tactic. A pronged attack would spread out Asugisalas' forces, but each of the attacking groups would be more vulnerable than in a massed attack. The one-thrust concept would put immense weight to bear on one part of Asugisalas' lines, but it would be vulnerable to a flank attack. Eggs in one basket, as it were.

He finally settled on the single weighted thrust, with scouts sent well out to each side. If his men could punch through Asugisalas' lines, they could then fan out and overwhelm the defenders from behind, and wreak bloody havoc on those who stood in his way. Once Asugisalas was defeated, the whole of his lands would lie open to Agnold, who could extend his rule over those rich fields and good harbors. He smiled as he rode, dreaming of his victory to come.

Two of Agnold's scouts were spotted by a small group of well-concealed men. One of them slipped away noiselessly, and ran back to warn the next line of defense. The rest fell back slightly, trying to map out the enemy's strength and path of advance. It soon became clear to the defending forces that Agnold would be making a focused attack from one line of advance. A number of Sugi Jarl's Wise Ones joined the fourth line of defense, as the fresh relay headed back towards the next layer of defense along the projected path of attack.

By the time the final runner reached Asugisalas in person, the jarl's men were swinging into their predetermined positions. Muha, Sven, and Diccon headed out, along with a small keg of the jarl's strongest mead. A tuxedo kitten trailed behind the three, unnoticed by them as he darted and hid. Before the small group reached the fourth line of defense, Sven's small keg was empty and its owner was quiveringly eager to trot out some of his more interesting curses. Diccon, who carried the Spear, was concerned about his role in the upcoming fray. He would be the one who would stand in the open and, with his smith's powerful muscles, throw the Spear as hard as he could so that it would fly over the heads of as many of the enemy as possible. Muha and Sven would have to mount his magical defense, since Diccon's concentration would be focused on the Spear and its flight. He would be totally open and vulnerable during that action. Sven mumbled under his breath, getting ready for the fun to start.

Wiegand *wigilaz* was one of nine wizards in Agnold's train. Each wizard was accompanied by a small group of bodyguards, who would see to his safety. It's impossible to get off a spell if you're fighting for your life. When Agnold's scouts made contact with Asugisalas' forces, the bodyguards would form a loose ring around their principal, keeping close, but not so close as to impede the wizard's work.

As Agnold's scouts ranged forward, Sugi Jarl's men directly in their path silently faded back and to the sides. This was to lull the enemy scouts, and also to let the van of Agnold's forces be surrounded on three sides. Oh, there were enemy scouts who fanned out to the sides just in case the defenders would be doing just that. Sugi's advance men, who knew the land like the backs of their hands, were able to take out those enemy scouts, one by one, quietly and permanently. Nothing crude like bopping them on the head with a club; this was silent, deadly woodscraft that let a hidden man suddenly snag a passing enemy by clapping one hand over that wight's nose and mouth, cutting off his wind and bending him backwards off his feet, and then dropping him in his tracks with a quick bit of knifework. If there were two enemy scouts, two of Sugi's men acted simultaneously so that there could be no warning given. It was critical that there be no screams, no thrashing about, and no escapes. The dead men were then hidden in the underbrush. Sugi's men worked quickly and in absolute silence.

The first hint that something was not right came in the form of a hoarse scream off to the left of the marching invaders. A vassal chieftain who was passing nearest that spot dispatched five men to see what was up. The men angled off into the beech and linden forest, heading slightly to the left of the spot from whence the scream had come so that they could sneak up on whatever caused it from a different direction. The forest was pretty much young growth, and occasional blackened stumps of an old forest fire showed through the mossy ground cover.

The men, archers all, had their bows strung and arrows nocked, ready to aim and fire in less than a second. Suddenly, a leaping, thrashing noise was heard, as of a heavy man running as fast as he could, going away from them in huge leaps and bounds. The archers quickened their pace. Surely this had to be a mail-clad warrior . . . had he left his place in the lines to go water a tree? Had that man stumbled across one of Agnold's side-scouts and surprised him?

It wasn't easy running through the woods with a nocked arrow sitting on one's bowstring, but it was an easy matter for the archers to swivel the fletched end of the arrow down parallel to the lower limb of the bow, and then to hold the weapon in one hand close to the body while the other hand fended off brush and low hanging branches.

The lead archer had taken less than twenty half-running steps when he saw the first signs of flight. The woods were opening up into a smallish clearing, and deep gouges could be seen, obviously left by the heavy feet of a running man, headed straight across that smallish clearing. The fleeing man was not in sight; he had obviously just gotten into the forest on the far side. The crunching footsteps suddenly slowed and stopped, as if the man were exhausted. The archers, as one, ran across the meadow, eager to pot their quarry.

Well, that's what the archers *meant* to do. But that verdant clearing was actually a bog, with a nice wide patch of algae-covered quicksand right in the middle. Three of Sugi's scouts had found a man's height-length log, and had tied long ropes to each end of it. The log had then been carefully balanced on a low-slung beech bough off to one side of the bog, and the lines paid out by two of the men, who skirted the bog on either side and hunkered down in some bushes on its far side, directly across from the log. The third member of the group had shinnied up a lone fir tree, hiding in the thick branches, and waiting until a good part of Agnold's men had passed him. Then he gave out the hoarse scream to attract attention, and also to signal his cohorts to be ready to spring their trap.

Five crow calls announced the number of men homing in on that scream, and one more told the men in the bushes to alternately haul in their lines as fast as they could, causing the log to bound over the ground end-over-end, smack across the bog and quicksand patch. The log fetched up under the bushes concealing the two, leaving alternating gashes in the ground. The two men then dropped the ropes and took off, running lightly in their soft leather shoes, hopping from rock to rock along their pre-selected exit path.

They didn't have to run far. Wings of Sugi Jarl's forces were already folding in on the intruders, much as folds the Venus flytrap's eating-leaf around a bluebottle. The plan was to draw men out of the line of march and into the bog trap, thus thinning the attack force in one spot. Sugi's flankers would then race in from either side in a coordinated pincers attack, smash through the thinned part of Agnold's troop train, and nip off the front part of Agnold's army containing the shock troops and berserkers. They would then englobe this cut-off group, attacking it from all sides, while the rest of Sugi's forces and Wise Ones flowed in behind them to deal with the main body of Agnold's warriors.

Agnold's five archers had spread out, but not quite far enough. As one man, they hit the quicksand running. Their screams and thrashing diverted more of Agnold's troops, which was just fine by Sugi's men. Some of the latter were archers, too, and each of their arrowheads was smeared with mistletoe berry paste. The active agent, which we call *viscotoxin*, had been used since the dawn of time in that geographical region for hunting large dangerous game such as the now rare wild giant bulls. Pincushion the haunches of such with enough mistletoe-smeared projectile points, and the back end of the animal would go to sleep, pinning the animal to one location, making it much safer for the hunters to dart in and kill it.

Mistletoe was a sacred plant, especially linked to the destructive bolts of Thunor the Thunderer. Since it had no roots, lived high in trees, and was evergreen, it was firmly believed to have been planted there as a result of the passage of the god's thunderbolt; and as such, it lived off the cosmic energy of the sky-fire rather than from any terrestrial nourishment. Any projectile point smeared with mistletoe would thus act as a proxy thunderbolt, and it would be just as effective on the physical plane of existence as on the divine plane.

There was a local myth about a tricksy fellow named Loke, who had convinced the blind Od to throw such a projectile at one of the gods, the dew and freshwater deity Balder. Loke, of course, was terrestrial wildfire; and it was well known that dew, mist and rain tended to damp out loose wildfire. Loke *had* to remove Balder in order to remain alive himself. Od, by reason of his blindness, was unknowing and innocent, and could thus handle the weapon of the Thunderer where Loke could not.

Loke had only one projectile; Sugi's archers had many. They could also see their targets, which meant that their arrows flew to the faces and unarmored parts of Agnold's men across that so-innocent looking clearing. Oh, there were a few odd bubbles here and there, but the five advance archers had vanished as if they had never existed. One of Agnold's men, a berserker by trade, got an arrow in his cheek and promptly went amok. Since he was to the rear of the group that had burst through the woods, this immediately caused his compatriots to dash as far and fast away from him as possible. A maniac with an axe is not a good neighbor!

A few of Agnold's men actually missed the quicksand. The berserker followed most of the men into it, and mighty indeed was the thrashing and yelling that ensued. Sugi's swordsmen swarmed over the others, who were trying to simultaneously pull arrows out of themselves and fight.

Meanwhile, in the pinched-off forward part of Agnold's army, things were getting interesting. It was, as one berserker happily remarked to another, a target-rich environment. Asugisalas' forces were all around them, and the hunting would be good. Or so they thought.

News finally trickled back to Agnold that his van had met the enemy. He ordered his army to charge ahead as fast as it could and to broaden out. Surprise was now lost, so it was critical to strike as heavy a blow as possible at Asugisalas' lines. It was time for the piledriver. Time for the wizards to earn their pay. By now, Froðuwarða should have opened the Terror spell-box, and Asugisalas' forces should be seriously vulnerable, since the local *vettir* would have fled.

Wiegand *wigilaz*, along with his fellow wizards, was to make a concerted attack. Nine spells at one time. Each spell was different, and each was designed so as to not set up a frequency beat or interfere with any of the others. Ulfrid *wigilaz* was to cast a forgetfulness spell so that Asugisalas' men wouldn't remember what they were supposed to be doing. Modri and Wilifrid collaborated on a clumsiness spell; one was to cast the "fumbles" and the other cast the "confusion" element. Ulrich Hairynose would trot out his famous diarrhea spell, and Halidogorid prepared his Doomsday spell, the one his sweet little grey-haired Momma had taught him. Mikal, who sort of followed the path of the Christians, was to loose a curse, one which should surely bring Beelzebub in person to torment the opposing force. Little Theodoric . . . actually, he was well over six feet tall . . . would send a tempest screaming onto Asugisalas' host. Finally, there was Piotr; he came from the eastern lands beyond Agnold's realm. Dulling weapons was his specialty. Wiegand would seek out Asugisalas' Talents, negating their special senses, and causing their spells to fizzle.

Agnold blew a mighty blast on his silver hunting horn, giving the "get ready!" signal. The nine began their final preparations. On Agnold's next horn blast, the wizards would simultaneously loose their various spells. Then Agnold's army would charge, smashing any residual resistance. Asugisalas and his men would not see another dawn!

# CHAPTER 26

Svarting had somehow gotten separated from his human. Maybe he'd been distracted by a rustling leaf or a cricket. In any case, the young tom was now on his own; a stranger in a strange, dangerous land. He kept heading out in the direction that he thought his human had gone, but in actuality, he was running on a path much farther to the north than he should have followed.

Suddenly, his fur stood on end. Magic was in the air! It sure wasn't his human's type of magic; this stuff stank like rotten fish, staining the air. The kitten's ears flattened back, and his nose wrinkled with disgust bordering on nausea. Something really evil lurked right nearby, and Svarting now realized, to his dismay, that he was the only one who knew about it.

Svarting came of a long line of Helpers-of-the-Human-Wise-Ones. For a cat, he held an uncommon amount of Talent; surpassing many humans in that regard. He also knew that it would be up to him, and him alone, to deal with this effluvium, this terrifying, malignant menace. He gritted his kitten teeth and headed in the direction from whence the evil was flowing most strongly.

Froðuwarða waited patiently in his oak-tree refuge for the signal. Surely it would come today! It was Wod's day, auspicious for the god's attention. Agnold knew where to find him; this was a pre-arranged rendezvous site. One of several. If Sugi Jarl had stumbled on this particular tree, Froðuwarða would fall back on the next rendezvous site. A symbol-engraved lead box lay on his lap. His hands rested on its lid, ready to break the wax seal and release the dreadful spell pent within.

Svarting homed in on Froðuwarða's hidey-hole like a bee to honey. But this wasn't honey, not at all. The kitten sensed that this was unspeakable evil, waiting for Freyja-knew-what . . . and that this evil had better be dealt with right now.

Not in the future.

No chance to run and find his human to help.

Now.

All by himself.

One kitten against one human.

Now.

One kitten, all by himself, isn't strong enough to overpower a human by sheer muscular effort. But there were other ways. Svarting, his senses incredibly alert, heard the rustle of a rat nosing around in the forest litter beneath the oak. He leaped on the rat, seizing it by the nape of the neck. That alone was a foolish thing for a kitten to do; mature cats would think twice before tackling a full-grown rat. But kittens have to learn somehow.

The rat was surprised, too. Its forepaws scrabbled briefly in the air, and then found a good grip on the tree's bark. It zipped up the tree, and that meant that Svarting, whose teeth were clenched on the loose neck-skin below the rat's ears, had perforce to zip up that same tree. His clawed feet straddled the rat as the two of them climbed.

They got up about twice a person's height when the rat spied a rat-sized hole in the tree. Naturally, the rat ducked down the hole, slamming the kitten's nose against the lip of the hole. Svarting let go, falling backwards off the tree, his nose bloodied and torn by the rough bark. The rat, also losing its grip, fell down through the hole smack onto Froðuwarða's head, and thence onto his hands.

Ever hear of a cornered rat? Froðuwarða immediately found out first hand about this phenomenon when the scared rodent went on the attack, repeatedly biting the man's hands with its long yellow teeth. In the flurry and muffled screaming that ensued, the lead box slipped from the wizard's lap and landed somewhere in the inky darkness near his feet. Flailing around didn't help the man at all; it brought the rat's teeth close to his face, which was Not Good for the man. The violent action inside the hollow bole of the tree went on for a while, as neither rat nor man could escape or kill the other in such close confines. Meanwhile, Svarting managed to land on all fours next to the tree trunk.

Screwing up his courage, he snaked in the hole the man had used to enter the tree's hollow space. One forepaw stubbed itself on the heavy brick-shaped box, which had fallen to one side of the man's wildly kicking feet. The lead spell-box was far too heavy for the kitten to pick up, but he could (and did) sink needle-sharp teeth into the man's ankle. Froðuwarða screamed, his attention turning to his new attacker. The rat took advantage of this opportunity, lunging forward and clamping on the man's nose, biting down hard until its yellow teeth met. The man shrieked again, grasping with both hands for the rat, trying to pull it off his face. His feet thrashed violently, kicking the box to one side, and Svarting was able to guide it with deft white paws down a fox hole in the very base of the tree's cavity. He then darted quick paw-strokes in order to cover the hole. The human was kicking up great chunks of rotten wood and soft earth, which made that part easy for the kitten. The hard part was avoiding the man's flailing legs.

After a short while the rat saw its opportunity, dropped free, and shot out the main entrance hole.

It wasn't much the worse for wear, but Froðuwarða sure was. Now the wizard frantically groped around for his box, blood streaming from his face and hands. His scrabbling fingers met only churned-up fluffy rotted wood and earth. No box. It was as if it had vanished from the face of the earth. He tried to sense where it was, but the cloaking spell incised on the outside of the box was still effective, even at that close range. He couldn't feel its presence at all.

The box was gone. Obviously, some evil magic had somehow found it, picked it up, and carried it far away. Due to no fault of his own, Froðuwarða couldn't carry out his mission, which meant that Froðuwarða had better leg it out of there, heading away from Agnold and all he stood for, as quickly as possible. Agnold didn't take kindly at all to being disappointed. His messenger hadn't arrived yet to give the final cue to the wizard, but Froðuwarða wasn't about to wait around for him. He valued his own head, and he wanted to keep it firmly attached to the rest of his body for many years to come. Hoping that he'd not run across either Asugisalas' forces or Agnold's merry men, he ran due north for two straight hours, and then angled west to the sea. He found a small river-fishing boat drawn up on the shore, which he promptly commandeered. It had a sail and mast, and the winds were fair for him to scud south along the coast until he got to a land inhabited by folks who didn't speak any tongue he knew. Only then would he be beyond Agnold's ken and eventual revenge.

What Froðuwarða hadn't calculated on was that there was a freak rapid sea-current which swept his little vessel to the southwest and then to the west. Two weeks later, his boat would wash up on a shale beach jutting out from a thickly-forested land on the far side of the great salty sea. At last the half-dead wizard would be safe, since the kind copper-skinned natives who rescued him spoke no tongue he knew.

Hrof wasn't idle that day. He'd sold all his fish and gotten orders for more. But Sugi Jarl wanted to hire Hrof and his boat for a special mission that should take only a few days. The price they settled on was certainly fair, especially since danger pay was included in the sum. Hrof's mission was to ferry twelve men and ten huge dogs to a certain small creek which led to a marshy area to one side of Agnold's line of march. He was then to conceal his boat and wait. If the men and/or the dogs didn't return by the second sunset after they landed, Hrof was to return. Hopefully, Sugi Jarl would have beaten Agnold's forces by then. If not, Hrof would have to head north to the safety of lands beyond Agnold's reach. Hrof insisted on getting paid up front, and Sugi Jarl anted up half the total; the remaining half to be paid to Hrof when he returned.

At that point in the discussion, the men and dogs arrived. Big dogs, with huge mouths full of gleaming white teeth, and suspicious white-rimmed dark eyes which watched Hrof's every move. The Master Seaman cut off the negotiations at that point; those teeth were altogether too close for comfort. Negotiations, done properly, usually involve a bit of dramatic gesticulation and snarling argument. Big dogs don't like things like that.

Muha was uneasy. There was a sort of indrawing magic feel to the air. Sven hiccuped, hiccuped again, and rubbed the side of his nose. He was picking up the same thing. So did Diccon, whose Great Hammer vibrated slightly against his stomach where it was thrust through his wide belt. Sugi Jarl's other Talents felt it, too. All realized that this wasn't going to be some simple spellcasting; this was going to be an all-out blitz. Diccon still grasped the Spear, but he wasn't within visual range of Agnold's army. He couldn't throw the Spear until he was facing them and could see to throw it over the entire host.

The indrawing got stronger. Muha screamed at the other Talents to loose what they had handy. A magical cacophony would be better than waiting like sitting ducks. He who strikes first frequently gets a second chance. They had to act before the enemy released their spells if they were going to survive. Agnold didn't hire second-rate Talent.

Sven got his curse off first. He'd been assembling it as he'd moved into position. Muha was still in mid-shout when the old lush acted. With a smallish keg of strong mead helping him power his curse, Sven screamed a long string of words, followed by a world-class burrrp. A brilliant blueish fireball accompanied by a whistling, tearing sound shot from his mouth toward the as-yet-unseen enemy Talents. The fireball jigged and flared erratically in its path as it disappeared into the forest. Sven then dramatically raised one hand straight up in the air, forefinger pointing toward the heavens, and stretched his other hand pointing out in front of him, mouthing another curse. Diccon could feel other spells being launched all around him as he hurriedly stripped the case off the Spear to ready it for action. With the Spear in his right hand and his left hand at the small amulet pouch hanging from a thong around his neck, the young smith dashed forward, knowing that he had to get in his Big Hit in as soon as possible. Hopefully, he'd make it before Agnold's *erilaz* corps let loose.

Wodurid felt the Power shudder into him, filling him beyond full. All he needed was Agnold's signal to loose his spell. He was so focused on his magic that he didn't see Agnold raise his horn to his lips to sound that signal.

The cut-off van of Agnold's army was now engaged in hand-to-hand combat. There wasn't room for spear work; their attackers pressed in with their shields and darting swords, pushing them backwards into a tightly packed grouping. The men in the middle of that group could hardly move, much less fight. Only those on the periphery of the group could bring weapons to bear. Even then, they were hampered by their close neighbors, who were also trying to swing swords and axes.

Sugi Jarl's men pushed forward, shield against enemy shield, buttressed from behind by the second tier of fighters. The first line's mission was simply to push. Every other men of the second tier of attackers stabbed out with sword and spear at the enemy's faces. Then, eight or nine of Sugi's shortest warriors went down on hands and knees, crept through the forest of legs, and began hamstringing enemy warriors from ankle level. The latter couldn't reach them; they were too tightly packed to get their axes and swords down far enough to do any good. They hopped and kicked, but since their legs and feet weren't armored, that didn't hinder the hamstringing crew much at all. Once a hamstrung warrior fell to the earth, Sugi's men would finish him off and then move on to the next customer.

Sugi Jarl's pincer maneuver had worked. The remaining wings of his forces had now folded in far enough to bring the battle to the flanks of Agnold's men. The shrieking, clanging, crunching, bleeding, and dying had begun.

Agnold drew in his breath. His silver horn's clarion sound echoed over the clangor of battle. As one, the nine wizards began to launch their spells.

Sven's curse-fireball arrived at that moment, homing in on Wiegand first. It smashed against his head, flowed over it; then shot off at an angle toward Halidogorid, whose arms were windmilling in the air. Halidogorid's bodyguard raised their shields to fend it off, but it moved too quickly and shot into the wizard's mouth, oozed out his ears, re-formed, and shot off at angle. It wasn't as bright or quick as before, but it was still going.

Three other spells came roaring in at that point. One struck Agnold's horse, causing it to panic. Agnold had to hurriedly drop his horn, which had split his lip and knocked out a tooth in the first lunge. He had to exert all his strength and horsemanship to remain atop his crazed stallion, cursing in great jerks as he hauled on the reins to bring his mount's head up and back so that the stallion couldn't buck him off. A second spell caused a sudden spate of vomiting among Agnold's front-line troops. Those of Sugi's men who were battling those afflicted could only grin and bear it. Their swords and axes splashed through the enemy barrage, snaking in to chop necks. The third spell, too-hastily gabbled out and blurred in the casting, merely turned an over-eager raven who'd been hanging in the air over the rear part of Agnold's army into a large blue walrus. Since a walrus doesn't fly very well, about twenty or so of Agnold's rear-echelon troops got a big fat surprise.

It was fortunate indeed for Sugi Jarl and his men that Svarting had managed to neutralize Froðuwarða. The *vettir* protecting the land weren't forced to flee, which meant that they joined in the battle to protect their homes. Right now, six out of nine enemy spells had been launched. The *vettir* summoned up all their Powers to fend off what they could.

# CHAPTER 27

Diccon raced through the woods, heading toward the sounds of battle. Sven, who was focusing on his curses, stayed put, backed up by a few of Sugi Jarl's older warriors. As Diccon headed out, first one, then several, then a whole bunch of men followed him, swords and axes thirsty for battle. As they ran, ducking the tough knots of brush and low hanging branches in their way, the screaming, yelling, and clash of weapons got louder and louder.

Sven's first curse had knocked out Wiegand, Halidogorid, and Ulfrid. Literally. It was an "Instant Inebriation" spell. The three wizards lay smashed to the gills, cheerfully burbling and hiccuping on the ground. Needless to say, their spells never got activated. The bodyguards for each of the three picked up their charges and trotted to the rear, hoping that they might come across a cold brook or spring so that they might be able to quickly sober up their principals and get them back into action. Sven's second hastily-mouthed curse got Modri and Wilifrid . . . they'd been working almost arm-in-arm . . . instantly inflicting them with blinding headaches, an overpowering ringing in their ears, and visions of flashing, gyrating multicolored lights. Sven had loosely modeled that curse on some of his more spectacular hangovers. Modri and Wilifrid, unused to such excursions and alarums, staggered and fell to their knees, moaning and shaking their heads in a vain attempt to clear them. Their initial spells, however, had already been launched. Sven, as yet untouched by spell or sword, started in on his Blue Serpent of Death curse, focused toward the main body of Agnold's fighting men.

Muha was busy, too. He told Sugi Jarl's other Talents to scatter so that an aimed spell or curse couldn't take out a whole clump of Wise Ones all at once. It was clear that the first phase of this battle would belong to the magicians and sorcerers; the armed men would finish things up.

The first and only Working that the old *erilaz* did was to strengthen and support the *vettir*, the protective land-spirits, who were arousing the land to reject the invaders. Muha had to continually maintain this support; it wasn't like a "shout and point" one-shot spell. As senior Wise One to Sugi Jarl, it fell to him to stand motionless, with arms outspread toward the earth and head raised, to maintain this linkage as long as it was needed. Sugi's younger wizards were more eager to jump in and perform the spectacular spells and flashy curses which they'd learned as teenagers.

Spells and curses crossed paths as the armed men hurried into position, charging into the thunder and shouting of hand-to-hand combat. Staying behind the lines and waving their hands wasn't for the fighting men; they wanted to feel their swords and axes cleave the wind and slice into enemy bodies. Their teeth bared in feral grimaces, they fought shield-to-shield and steel-to-steel.

One of Agnold's warriors, locked in combat with one of Sugi's men, spat at his opponent's eyes to divert him. He quickly swung his axe around, aiming for the neck. Sugi's man, experienced in the ways of war, barely blinked as he parried the heavy weapon so that it swung wide. He then shoved his shield forward in a strong, sudden punch as Agnold's man recovered from the parry, knocking the man back on his heels. A quick thrust with his sword over the opponent's shield-rim finished things, and Sugi Jarl's man stepped forward to meet his next opponent.

A huge black hairy demonic shape, bat-winged and bull-horned, red-eyed and cruelly tailed, suddenly appeared in the midst of one wing of the men attacking the main body of Agnold's forces. This was Mikal *wigilaz'* demon . . . perhaps not Beelzebub himself, but certainly more than impressive in its own right. It roared and reached filthy long-taloned hands downwards toward the now terrified men of Sugi's pincer which was engaging Agnold's left flank.

Elsewhere, Modri and Wilifrid's two-part confusion/fumbles spell swept through a widening corridor through the attacking forces closest to the pair of wizards. Ulrich Hairynose grinned vastly in his wild black beard when his diarrhea spell disabled the men facing him. His bodyguards went joyously to work, felling one after another miserably afflicted warrior. He laughed a short barking laugh, and began casting that same spell at another group of attackers.

Piotr's spell dulled the weapons of the force attacking his bodyguard, but even blunt swords have some heft to them, and what with good shieldwork and sweeping blows, the attackers didn't seem unduly disconcerted by the fact that they were now swinging dull slats of metal which couldn't cut a thing. Those with axes used them like maces, smashing faces and denting helms as they bore in on the wizard.

Finally, Little Theodoric's tempest spell brought screaming winds laden with hail sweeping over friend and foe alike.

Gorm Erik's son, Sugi's shortest warrior, stood as tall as a seven-year-old child. That didn't prevent him from burrowing on hands and knees under the press of men protecting Mikal *wigilaz*. The latter was busy controlling his demon, and paid no attention to the activity near his feet. Gorm's child-sized broadsword stabbed straight up between the wizard's legs. Needless to say, that instantly broke the wizard's concentration. Mikal screamed as the sword's point rammed upward through soft tissues until it split his heart. The demon, now uncontrolled, grabbed a double handful of men at random, lifted them high, and swallowed them whole before reaching down for more. Panicked men from both sides fled in terror, as Gorm recovered his sword and crawled away from the bloody corpse through the forest of stamping, thrashing legs, snaking his unobserved way toward the next wizard.

Muha was still in the clear. None of the enemy spells had touched him yet. He continued to stand motionless, directing the land's defenses.

Agnold had counted on the local *vettir* being taken out at the beginning of the battle. It was clear, by the suddenly-entangling vines and the gopher holes which always seemed to be right where one of the horses would step, that the land and the *vettir* were very much still in the fight It was the *vettir* who, en masse, chased the demon back to its otherworld plane of existence, and it was the *vettir* who blunted or deflected so many of the enemy wizards' spells.

At the very rear of Agnold's column, ten giant dogs burst through the forest, leaping at the men and horses comprising Agnold's supply train. The rangers, following the dogs, used their bows to good advantage as the panicked draft animals scattered in all directions. The supply-laden wagons bumped and lurched on the rough ground, tipping over or smashing against trees and boulders in their way, scattering their contents all over the place.

Hrof, left behind with his boat, didn't want to be left out of the action. After tying his bow line to a tree, he hopped ashore and followed his passengers. The swampy area gave him an idea, and he slowed and stopped beside a huge mossy stump on the edge of the misty water. He let his senses roam, and it wasn't long at all before he found the Moss Folk, those reclusive marsh dwellers so feared by those who live on dry land.

The Moss Folk usually kept to themselves, but when Hrof described the dangers to them posed by Agnold's forces, they arose from their soggy abode in great numbers to defend their homeland. They drifted toward the edge of solid land, following the dogs and men. Any of Agnold's troops who made the mistake of running into the swamp—or even placing one foot in marshy ground—would not greet another dawn.

Agnold got control of his horse just in time to take advantage of the openings that his wizards had provided. His hoarse shouted commands spurred his troops into action, and they poured through the weak spots, hacking and slashing at the confused, discomfited, and horribly ill men facing his warriors.

Sugi Jarl's army was now on the defensive, and was just about to lose the battle. Agnold's warriors fanned forward and out, pushing as hard as they could. Little Theodoric's tempest winds whipped the branches of the forest trees about, and blew sleety gusts of gale-force winds throughout the entire battlefield.

Ulrich Hairynose began to launch his fourth diarrhea spell, but Gorm Erik's son spoiled his concentration just in time, and the spell ricocheted back upon the caster. Gorm had to move off to the side very quickly in order to avoid the result.

Over toward Ulrich's right, Piotr *wigilaz* was paralyzed by a sneaky little spell cast by one of Sugi's Talents, a Healing Woman named Hedwy, who usually used it to immobilize and anaesthetize patients requiring surgery. The Slavic wizard toppled like a tree, falling limply on the ground, his empty eyes staring fixedly straight in front of him. His bodyguard quickly grabbed him and trotted him back to safety through the press of men.

Sugi Jarl, magnificent in his mail shirt and antique Roman plumed helmet, rallied his faltering troops. He seemed to be everywhere, pulling men from one area which was seeing no action to another, where there was plenty of action. He seemed to instinctively know what had to be done where. The grieving would come later. He'd seen two cousins and a brother lying broken and dead in the field, as well as the sons of his friends and his countrymen. Now was the time for vengeance.

Diccon finally made it to the battle proper. Armed men flashed and flickered in the foggy clouds of flying spume and rain. The tempest's hurricane force winds whipped leaves from wildy thrashing tree branches, and howled above their heads as loudly as screamed the wildly battling men and thrashing, spooked horses. It was a surreal scene, something out of a bard's tale on a winter's night. The young smith was ready with his Spear, but he had to be sure to throw it over the bulk of the opposing force so that as many men as possible fell under its spell. The men following him swarmed forward, eager to attack the enemy. Diccon paused, praying to Týr that his aim would be true. More of Sugi's warriors crowded in. Diccon knew that he'd better focus and throw before they got close enough to the enemy to also be affected by the Spear's flight.

There! The main body of Agnold's men was thrusting its way through Sugi's weakened defenses. Diccon's right arm swept back; then he launched the Spear, shouting Týr's name thrice as his smith-strong arm lofted the Spear into the teeth of the gale.

It flew true, high over the heads of a hundred or more men. There was a tearing sound in the air as the Spear's spell fell onto the enemy host, stripping them of any magical protection that they might have had. This allowed the local *vettir* to double and triple their efforts, and the land itself to fight the now vulnerable intruders.

Sugi's men charged, wreaking bloody havoc on the disconcerted warriors facing them, blasting through the enemy lines to meet their compatriots on the far side of the enemy lines. It was a no-holds-barred dogfight. No possible control could be held over the knots of fighting men. Agnold tried again and again to marshal his forces into some kind of weighted attack, but even he couldn't get anyone's attention. It was man to man, sword against sword and axe against axe. Men of both sides fell as if under the reaper's scythe.

Diccon spotted Agnold, recognizing him instantly even though he'd never seen the man before. Here was the Enemy. No matter the cost to himself, Diccon knew that he *had* to act. His left hand fumbled at the small pouch at his neck, tipping the thunderbolt amulet into his palm. The Power drew in and swelled within him as the metal heated to white-hot agony in his hand. The young smith gritted his teeth as he raised his hand, index finger out-thrust, in the direction of the man on the wild-eyed stallion.

The blue-white lightning flared forth, sending an incandescent bolt directly to Agnold's chest. It picked him off his horse, exploding him in mid-air. The horse, thoroughly spooked, flailed out with shod hooves and bolted, knocking men spinning out of his way. The Power built again, and the half-conscious Diccon aimed at the largest knot of men he could find. The crashing sky-fire struck again, scattering half-burnt corpses in all directions. Then the Power built up again . . . Diccon could no longer control the amulet or feel his hand, the pain was so great . . . and another streak of lightning struck a desperately fighting group of men who were trying to attack the warriors who'd followed Diccon into battle. And another. And another.

The lightning lashed out yet again. Diccon, barely conscious at this point, was reeling where he stood braced against a tree. His left hand, holding the white-hot amulet, still pointed at the enemy, willing the lightning to strike more of the foe. Smoke curled from the clenched fingers, and the smell of burnt flesh choked the air. The lightnings kept pouring out, lashing at Agnold's men. Diccon had wanted to take out as many of the enemy as he could, and in his battle-madness paid no heed to his burning hand. Once more, the blue-white river of fire reached out, slagging the foemen down where they stood. Diccon could no longer sense the spells of Muha and Sugi's other Talents; his whole being was focused on his amulet and the lightning. He could no longer feel his left arm, just the terrible, repeated indrawings and releasings of the amulet's Power.

One, then several, then groups of Agnold's men turned to flee. Agnold was dead, and with him died the dream of conquest. The mercenaries were the first to bail out. A dead chieftain didn't have a payroll, and they weren't about to risk their lives for nothing.

Diccon fainted at that point, his charred, smoking left fist still pointing toward the enemy. His thunderbolt amulet had done what it was designed to do before slumping into a shapeless mass, fusing to the bones of Diccon's hand. Sugi's men, greatly heartened, cheered and threw themselves into the fray. More and more of Agnold's troops fled, and before long, the battlefield belonged to the victors, the dead, the wounded, and the ravens.

One of Agnold's deserting men chanced upon the Spear where it lay on the ground. The Spear's head had fallen free of the shaft, its work done. The man scooped it up, recognizing that here lay great magic. He didn't have time to grab the shaft; Sugi Jarl's men were coming for him with thirsty swords. He ran like a scared rabbit, grasping his prize close to his chest. He eventually made it home, but somewhere along the way, the Spearhead fell out of his pack and was lost. All the man wound up with was a good story and a few scars, but no actual souvenirs.

Agnold's army had lost well over a half of their own. Sugi's forces fared slightly better, but many wives and sweethearts would never see their men again. The ravens picked over the reeking, bloody battlefield, sating themselves. Surely Wod would be pleased with so many newcomers in Val Halla!

Far away, standing in front of a forester's hut, an orphaned boy child raised his head and looked to the southwest, from whence that mysterious shaft of Release from some fated destiny had come. Biornulf, later to be known as Biw-wulf or Beo-Wulf, suddenly felt the hands of the Norns upon him, weaving his future into new patterns.

# CHAPTER 28

It was all over except for the looting of bodies and recovery of the wounded. Agnold's men had to fare for themselves, since Sugi Jarl's warriors looked after their own first. Two men happened across Diccon, who lay senseless on the ground. They carried him off, but neither dared touch the young smith's charred hand. They didn't want any residual lightning to nail them, too.

Muha was among the many missing. More than a few of Sugi's Talents had perished in the battle, slain either by magic or by the sword. The tempest blew itself out, and a soft rain fell, splashing on the upturned, unseeing eyes of the dead. Sven came through unhurt, but stone sober. He'd used a great deal of ale-magic, and that sobered a man quickly. He staggered wearily back toward Sugi Jarl's headquarters, badly in need of a drink.

Diccon struggled to semi-consciousness as he was carried into Sugi's longhouse and laid on a bench next to the firepit. He moaned and writhed in terrible agony, eyes clenched shut, teeth gritted as his head rolled from one side to the other. Hedwy, Sugi's most Talented Healer, examined the raw, blackened mess that was the young man's hand. Buffeted by Diccon's pain which was blasting at her senses, she cast her Stun spell for the second time that day. When the young man lay quietly, she and two helpers managed to pull Diccon's mail shirt up over his head and toss it into a heap off to the side in a corner of the room. The Healer then cut his padded tunic sleeve off to the shoulder and, with ointment-smeared hands, carefully began to uncurl the terribly burnt fingers. The thunderbolt amulet was now merely a shapeless blob of metal, half-fused to the charred bones of Diccon's palm. Delicately, Hedwy daubed a numbing ointment on the burnt flesh and bones, praying under her breath that she would get the job finished before Diccon regained consciousness. There were many wounded who needed her aid, so she simply had to stabilize as many patients as she could before beginning the actual Healing. She managed to pry the metal loose, and then she curled the remains of Diccon's fingers around an ointment-smeared wad of soft carded wool. Finally, she bandaged the hand and arm halfway up to the elbow with clean linen strips. Hedwy knew that, in spite of the good *valurt* and *groblad* in her salve, this young man would never have the use of that hand again.

Hrof, who'd recovered the weary dogs and rangers, turned the bow of his boat back to Sugi's main harbor. He didn't worry about having to make a break for it, since the Moss Folk had told him that the invaders were defeated and were running home as fast as they could scuttle. Just to make sure, Hrof had sent an illusion chasing the fleeing men, that of a terrible huge ship with torn sails billowing in a ghost wind, corposant flickering in its rigging, and manned by rotting skeletons. The ghost hulk silently loomed over the terrified remains of Agnold's élite corps of berserkers, sailing eerily through the air dead at them. Of the few berserkers who managed to make it home, none would ever voluntarily set foot on a boat again. They would tell their children and grandchildren of the ghastly ship, warning them to avoid it like the plague. Some said that Wod himself was at the tiller, eternally scouring the seas for souls.

It took the better part of two days for Svarting to find his way back out of the woods. None of the battle had come near him, but the tempest had disoriented him and he'd wandered hither and yon, plaintively calling for his human. Eventually, the kitten stumbled on a trail which had Sven's scent on it, and he followed it back to Sugi Jarl's longhouse, where he could also smell his human. The kitten leaped up, following his nose, onto the unconscious Diccon's stomach. But the young smith just lay inert; there was no welcoming head-skritch and a snack. Svarting tried his best, but he couldn't wake his human, who smelled so oddly of herbs and medicine. Finally, he gave up and trotted out to the kitchen area, where he begged the six meals that he'd missed. His hunger finally sated, he hopped up on Diccon's cot, curled into a ball next to Diccon's head, and purred himself to sleep.

Sugi's men gathered huge piles of enemy weapons and shields. These were carried back to the brink of Nerthus' Bog, where they were heaped high. Occasionally, a half-dead or unconscious foe was found lying on the battlefield, and Sugi's men wasted no time in sending him off to Val Halla. Some of Agnold's wizards had managed to escape, but a few remained for the attentions of Sugi's mopping-up squads. Unconscious, they could not resist the purely physical blows that sent them to Wod's grim hall.

A week passed, during which Sugi Jarl's community buried their dead and dug great trenches for the enemy slain. The latter, after everything of value had been stripped from their bodies, were unceremoniously tossed into the pits and burned. Hedwy kept Diccon unconscious for this entire time, only arousing him to semi-consciousness long enough to get some food and water into him. She didn't want him to thrash about in pain and injure himself even worse. Sven and Hrof shared a biggish keg of mead, and stayed rip-roaring drunk for three days straight. Neither wanted to see such carnage again in his lifetime, and each vowed to live a simple, quiet, peaceful life in the future.

Toward the end of the week, Hedwy came to the conclusion that Diccon's hand was not going to heal, and that it would have to come off. She had tried her best and used her most powerful Healing spells and ointments, but the signs were clear that the flesh was dead or dying, and that soon it would poison Diccon's blood. She asked Sven to magically distill as much pure alcohol as he could get from a keg of mead. Sven screwed up his eyes, fortified himself liberally from the keg . . . he claimed that he had to test it for suitability . . . and went to work. Before long, water-clear drops of alcohol began to fall out of the air directly above a narrow, deep bowl which Hedwy had placed on top of the keg. The drip-drip became a trickle became a flow pouring into the bowl. Sven managed to suck all the alcohol out of the keg in short order, yielding about three and a half quarts.

"Now comes the hard part," she said, after fine-chopping a handful of fresh *valurt* leaves, grinding them into a green paste, and then stirring them into the alcohol. "Sven, would you fetch two or three strong men? I will also need a bucket and a mallet."

"Would a shmith's hammer do? Hic? I know where Dicconnn's Great Hammer got put."

"No, a metal hammer would be too hard to control. And a Great Hammer can only be wielded by the smith who made it. What I need is a wooden mallet. That way, I can do delicate taps, rather than a heavy blow."

Sven trotted out on his mission, and Hedwy began assembling her surgical tools. First, several small knives and a wide chisel had to be honed to a razor edge. Then she set out small packets containing forearm-long pieces of linen thread strung on sharp curved bone needles. The knives were dipped into the alcohol and laid upon a clean linen towel, upon which was set a bowl filled with lint balls, clean linen bandages and a jar of salve. The lint balls and bandages, which were wrapped in clean linen towels, had been steamed over herb-scented boiling water for almost an hour that morning. The linen-threaded needles had been steamed in separate packages, and were only waxed when they were laid out for use. Hedwy was a skilled Healer, and had learned from experience as well as her training that anything which touched a wound or penetrated the body had to be treated so, lest the Red Wolf come and bring infection. Some of her tools had been custom-made for her, such as the smallest knives and the needles. She took pride in her work, and in her high survival rate.

Sven returned with three men, another keg, some rope, a smallish mallet, and a fistful of tankards. Amputations, in his experience, required lots of strong men to tie down and hold down the patient. He'd up until now managed to be elsewhere when something like this was going to happen. Now his luck and timing had run out. What was worse, this patient was his friend.

Hedwy reinforced her Stun spell, backed up by Sven, who trotted out his pet Inebriation spell. Diccon was out like a light, and would not feel the knife. Just before beginning, Hedwy rinsed the mallet, chisel, and then her hands in the alcohol. For some reason, the Red Wolf abhorred strong alcohol, so anything that would come in contact with the wound got an alcoholic bath. Then, she unwrapped the bandages on Diccon's hand. Leaning close, she examined the wrist and hand carefully in order to determine where the separation would take place. The blackened, shriveled fingers and most of the palm would have to go, but Diccon's thumb was pink and showed signs of healing. Now . . . to leave as much tissue as possible to support the thumb . . . she lifted her small knife and began the operation.

It turned out that the men weren't needed to hold the youth down, so Sven and his three companions wasted no time in accompanying the keg and tankards back outside into the fresh air. Diccon didn't stir at all, even when Hedwy poured what was left of the alcohol over her completed work. There had been enough of the skin left on the back of the hand so that Hedwy could fold it over the wound and stitch its edge to the healthy skin in front. This left a neat, clean seam which curved from just above the thumb down to the wrist. The alcohol was let air dry; then, Hedwy thickly smeared a salve containing *valurt*, ground white willow cambium, crushed juniper leaves, and ground white oak bark on the wound before bandaging it with fresh bruised *groblad* leaves, undersides to the wound, tied in place with a long, soft strip of linen.

Sven came in at that point to grab the bucket containing the excised parts of Diccon's hand, used bandage, bloody bits of cloth, and spent lint balls, to take it outside to be buried. The three men and Sven then picked up the unconscious youth and laid him in a clean bed, tucking a down coverlet loosely around him. Then they and Hedwy sat down next to the firepit for a flagon or two (or in Sven's case, six or seven) of mead.

Two days later, Diccon was finally allowed to awaken. His whole left arm hurt, but the pain was bearable if he didn't move his arm around much. Hedwy arranged a sling for him so that he could sit up and eat something. He'd been dismayed to learn how badly he'd been injured, but what was done was done. There was no turning back. He'd have to learn how to function with only one sound hand. But the smith's trade was now effectively closed to him; a smith needed two good hands. He'd have to follow another Path.

Sugi Jarl praised him at length for his courage and magical skills in using the amulet against Agnold's forces. That amulet had been a decisive factor in his victory, and the jarl offered the young man a position in his community as a Wise Man. Muha was dead; they'd found his body huddled on the ground bristling with arrows. Diccon was unsure about accepting the offer. Muha had known so much more than Diccon did, and now he was gone, along with all that knowledge. Sugi suggested that Diccon think about it; there was no rush to commit.

A few days later, the great sacrificial rite was to be held honoring Tiw, Nerthus, and Thunor for their aid in the battle. The *vettir* weren't forgotten either; mead, cream and honey were poured over their home-stone, and snippets of cloth and brightly colored yarn laid at its base. Diccon was recovering nicely, and was able to walk to Nerthus' bog, where the rite was to be held for the gods.

Three of Agnold's dead berserkers were dragged over to the bog. Their hands had been roughly tied behind them, and they were thrown into the bog and weighted down with heavy flat stones. Next, most of the enemy swords and spears were bent and twisted into uselessness by inserting them into the coals of a hot fire, waiting until the metal glowed orange-white, then pushing them point-first against boulders so that they bent like strips of belt leather. When the weapons had cooled, Sugi's surviving warriors reached for them, raised them high, and dedicated them to the memory of their fallen comrades so that they could now use those weapons in the Land of the Dead. Then the bent swords and spears were pitched into the bog, as well as the more damaged of the enemy shields, helms, and chain shirts. The bog would take all.

The sacrificial rite was an all-day affair, with *lur* players, acrobats, and a sun-chariot procession, followed by a great feast. Sven cut Diccon's meat for him, and drank three tankards of mead to Diccon's one. In the evening, the bards took turns reciting newly-composed epics describing the battle. Sugi Jarl, of course, got lavish verses extolling his feats, for which he rewarded the bards with golden rings, items looted from the enemy, coins from the south, and fine woolen cloaks. Diccon was embarrassed by the verses describing his heroic stand, especially the parts comparing him to Týr when the god bound the wolf Fenris. Sven, too, came in for praise, but in his case, it was a sprightly drinking song with lots of pauses so that folks could raise their tankards high, swig a great draft, and get a refill. Fortunately, that song was performed toward the end of the feast, since after it ended, more than a few revelers lay passed out on the ground.

During the next few days, Hedwy spent some time convincing Sven, who missed the conversation and good ale at Jan Sverre's son's brewery, and Diccon, who missed Marit, to stay until Diccon's hand was healed. The two had been invited to guest at the jarl's house, and were treated to every luxury that the generous household could provide. Every morning, Hedwy chanted Power-songs over Diccon's hand to speed the healing and keep the Red Wolf at bay.

Hrof had made out very well. He'd been presented with a biggish sack of hack-silver and gold, so he bought a piece of land down near the harbor and was in the process of building a snug house and capacious boathouse. The fishing was good in those parts, and before long, he had racks and racks of fat silvery herring in his new smoke-house. Smoked herring was a great treat, and Hrof was a master at turning them out. He traded for tangy round yellow cheeses, honey, apples, bread, and ale; and before long, had picked out a likely lad to be his new apprentice. One of the cheese-makers, a short, buxom lass named Lillemor, chased him until he caught her. They were married within the month.

The days fled, and Diccon's stitches came out easily and smoothly. He could move his thumb a little, but Hedwy told him to take it easy until the wound had completely healed over. He was impatient, though, and every so often when he thought nobody was looking, he'd twitch his thumb, easing the stiffness out of it. The Red Wolf stayed away, to Hedwy's and Diccon's great relief. Before long, the final bandages came off, and Diccon could exercise his thumb openly. It wasn't easy being effectively one-handed, but gradually he learned to manipulate his belt and legging-thongs after a fashion. He talked to Ragnar, the local smith, who fitted him with a leather wristlet which had a short, protruding iron finger, so that Diccon could pinch an object between that finger and his thumb. This permitted him to finally be able to cut his own meat, which was a great joy to him. He valued his independence, and having to have someone else cut his meat had wounded his manly pride.

Weeks passed, and both Diccon and Sven got more and more restless. Sugi Jarl repeated his offer to Diccon, but the latter's thoughts continually centered on Marit, and of that incredible last time he'd seen her. He wanted to get home to her, even though he was half-scared that she'd refuse his offer of marriage because of his hand. Sven, although he enjoyed Sugi's ale and mead, wanted to get back to his own land, where folks spoke in his own dialect and didn't have to repeat what they said to him all the time. He also missed Helga, his wife, even though he didn't say so out loud.

# Chapter 29

Autumn came to Marit's northern home a lot earlier than to that of Sugi Jarl. Marit and Inga brought their herds back down to the village pasturage from the high mountains. They and the young men of the village had also ferried down wagon loads of various kinds of cheese, tubs of butter, innumerable great sheaves of hay, crocks of berries stirred in honey, dried berries and mushrooms threaded on linen strings, sacks full of reindeer moss and thistledown, heavy jars of honey, tawny ingots of beeswax, dried herbs, and a whole raft of other edibles and useful items. These were carefully stowed in various barns and sheds, placed in soapstone tubs set in a nearby spring, hung in rafters, and lined up on shelves in Marit's large storeroom. Marit and Inga weren't the only herdsfolk of the village, but they were by far the most successful. They would trade for grain, dried fish, smoked and salted meat, eggs, yarn and woven cloth, leather, rendered lard, cut and seasoned firewood, charcoal, and a myriad of other things that they didn't manufacture or gather themselves. The last of the trading ships which plied the coast offloaded bar iron, walrus teeth, ice-bear hides, and coal for their share of the villagers' products, and headed home before the fall storms would come barreling in eastwards across the sea.

Gytha worked on Berit throughout the fall, coaxing the encapsulated tumor away from the spine and down under the ribs so that it could approach the skin. When it had formed a large lump on Berit's side, Gytha again gave her patient a dose of poppy syrup, and then she made a long cut over the top of the bulge. It was an easy matter then to slide the skin down the sides of the white-ish hard globule and edge the mass out of Berit's body. Twenty stitches closed the nearly bloodless gash, accompanied by the Power chants to keep the Red Wolf away.

When the fall gales began beating at the coast, one after the other in three-day intervals, Marit realized that Diccon wouldn't be returning until Spring. They'd been apart for months now, and Marit sincerely hoped that Diccon hadn't forgotten her. She'd hoped that he'd given her a child, but such was not the case. Now he was so far away . . . could he have met someone else, another woman, where he was now residing? Could he have forgotten her? The smith, who knew Diccon well, did his best to reassure her when she came to the smithy with her wonderful bread, cheese, butter, and honeycomb. Sometimes it was Inga who came, and the smith noticed that she spent more and more time watching Ulfgeir, whose muscles had firmed and hardened. That young man, now recognized by all as a journeyman smith, was learning the finer skills and spellcraft of the forge-Master. The smith had long since dispelled the geas binding Odd and Ulfgeir to the forge. In Ulfgeir's case, it was no longer needed, and Odd was obviously not cut out to be a smith. One of the brothers had to become chieftain after Soti, and Ulfgeir no longer had any interest in the job. The smith didn't envy Soti Jarl. Whipping Odd into shape would be a major task.

The snows came early to Sugi Jarl's lands that year. There was no question of Diccon and Sven returning home until the spring, when the fury of the winter gales would be over and Hrof could safely ferry them back to the northlands. Diccon's hand was still quite tender, so he couldn't do much in the way of heavy work. Fortunately, Sugi Jarl's hospitality allowed them to stay in his longhouse and, since his supply of ale and mead seemed endless, Sven wasn't averse to that idea at all.

In spite of Sugi Jarl's generosity, Diccon felt more and more useless. He was shy about his hand, and dreaded the thought that Marit would spurn his advances because of it. He was now a cripple; he could no longer do much of the smith's work. There wasn't much a one-handed man could do to support himself and, even though Sugi Jarl had given him a biggish chest of gold and silver coins, hack-silver, and strange jewels and ornaments from the south, the young man wanted to be able to earn his own way in the world. There had to be *something* that he could do.

It was Hedwy who, remembering what Muha had said of the youth, came up with the idea that Diccon train in earnest as an *erilaz* during the winter season. There was nothing wrong with his Talent, and his hand certainly wouldn't stand in the way of his spellcraft. Sugi Jarl approved heartily. Now that Muha was gone, he had no *erilaz*. If Sugi were very lucky, and if it was clear to Diccon that the jarl was obviously helping with this training, the jarl might be able to induce the young man to stay. At least, he certainly hoped so.

Diccon was already half-trained. His command of smithcraft and metals was superior even to Muha's, and Gytha had given him a head start on the Healer's Way. Muha had begun the youth's training, but had barely finished with some of the basics when he left Diccon's village to return home. Hedwy, a member of the Bear-Star Clan, recognized that Diccon was definitely a potential candidate for that élite company.

Those men and women who had won the title *erilaz* grew fewer and fewer each year. This meant that training a new crop of would-be wizards now forced the candidates to travel from specialist to specialist, training themselves, as it were, under the guidance of a whole series of mentors. Normally, one *erilaz* mentored a given candidate, much as a craftmaster would take on an apprentice. Agnold's forces had eradicated the greater part of Sugi's Talented people, especially the battle-wizards. By default, Hedwy assumed the mantle of mentor, with Sugi Jarl helping out on what he knew of the Warrior Way parts. Neither were accorded the title of *erilaz*. That was reserved for the high adepts, the ones who had intensive cross-class training and who could create effective spells as needed.

To start with, Hedwy focused on what she knew best. If Diccon thought that he'd learned a lot about Healing from Gytha, this soft-spoken woman soon disabused him of that notion. She made him memorize the names, appearances, find-spots, harvesting charms, storage, and uses of hundreds of herbs, barks, roots, seeds, nuts, mosses, berries, and leaves. Plants, fungi, lichens, algae, even insects and their products were of use in the healer's art. He dissected pigs, birds, fish, and rabbits (which were later put into the stew pot) to learn anatomy.

Hedwy had several scrolls, some written in strange characters which she said were used in an ancient southern land called Hellas, and others in the script used by the fabled Romans. This meant that Diccon had to learn those various alphabets and tongues in order to read them. Sugi contracted a deal with an itinerant Greek trader who happened by, for that purpose. This suited the trader just fine; he didn't like having to haul his goods around northern Europe in the snow.

The chieftain made sure that the news went out that the Greek merchant was staying there. This meant that folks from far and wide came to see the man's display, which was eye-catchingly set up in a barn. Sugi's wife was thrilled to have such a wonderful shop in her back yard, and she took frequent advantage of the opportunity of buying lengths of Egyptian cotton cloth dyed with rare colors, kohl, spices, and a dizzying variety of other hard-to-find exotic items from the southlands. The merchant was equally thrilled with the idea of having a stationary store in an easily-guarded location. Sure beat sailing from port to port, hoping to unload a bolt of cloth here and statuary and luxury goods there. He was able to trade silk cloth, ivory, wine, spices, and cowries for beeswax, honey, dyed wool, amber, salt, and unicorn horn . . . the twisted horn of the narwhal . . . and he grew sleek and fat at Sugi's table.

The three weeks originally contracted for Diccon's Greek education stretched well into the winter. The trader, Milo Pappadopoulis by name, knew that he had a Good Thing going. Free food, a snug seat by the firepit, and free housing weren't things to be scorned. He spent long hours with Diccon, teaching him Greek letters and, more importantly, the Greek language. It was sort of an immersion course; Milo's command of Sugi's tongue was essentially nonexistent, and any serious communication had to be made either in Latin or Greek. Sugi Jarl, who vastly admired the vanished warrior-Empire to the south, had learned some Latin, and so he acted to the best of his abilities as interpreter.

Before long, Diccon was able to converse haltingly in Greek. Milo despaired of his barbarous accent and tried his best to eradicate it, but Diccon's tongue simply wouldn't obey. As Diccon gained fluency, he learned of the spells and superstitions of Milo's homeland, and also of the sophisticated thaumaturgy used by the Jewish and Christian adepts in the far south. True, some of the spells such as those used to fix chariot races had few applications in the north, but demon-traps, word pyramids, the famous *sator-rotas* word-square, and other such esoterica were of interest, and could be adapted for situations found in Diccon's world.

As the winter progressed, Milo also began teaching Diccon Latin. Hedwy's texts were painstakingly translated, and Diccon learned even more from the trader about some of the simples and techniques described therein. Hedwy's scrolls were terse descriptions; Milo was able to supply a lot of extraneous information and various insider's insights which had not been recorded.

Sven, meanwhile, had discovered the joys of Greek wine. He'd never tasted it before, and Milo had easily fifty amphorae of thick red wine stashed in the barn. Sven spent a goodly portion of his share of Sugi's largesse on Milo's wine, which pleased Milo no end. Sugi Jarl was experienced enough to haggle for goods, but since Sven was willing to pay top price, Sven got the Greek's wine and Sugi lost out. Most of it tasted like pine trees, but the kick was good, and after a few cups, Sven was able to ignore the strong resinous flavor.

By Yule, Diccon could converse quite easily with Milo in the latter's tongue, and his Latin was now better than that of Sugi Jarl. He spent many days copying Hedwy's medical texts onto clean vellum, translating them into his own tongue and writing them in the friendly runes he'd learned as a child. Svarting had to be shooed away from the ink and vellum now and again, but even so, there were a few cat prints here and there on the pages.

Diccon finally got to practice surgery for real when Lars Harald's son, one of Sugi's berserkers, fell ill with the belly-stone. This was a sudden illness, accompanied by excruciating pain. Diccon had to use his smith's strength to hold the man down while Hedwy cast her Stun spell on him. When the man lay quiet, the two used their special senses to feel where the stone lay, wedged close to the end of the delicate urine-tube leading outward from the bladder. Using a razor-sharp obsidian knife, Diccon carefully cut into the man's flesh, working along the muscle rather than across it, trying not to damage anything more than he had to.

When the knife tip grated on the stone, Diccon edged the knife tip under it so that he could flick it out. Then he bathed the wound in alcohol and pulled the flesh together again, stitching it with Hedwy's help. He smeared *valurt* salve on the incision and bandaged it with a bruised *groblad* leaf and clean linen strips, chanting the Power songs to keep the Red Wolf at bay. This operation was a major eye-opener for Diccon; usually, sufferers from the stone either passed the stone in agony, or died in agony.

When she was finally satisfied with Diccon's mastery of the Healer's Art, Hedwy released him into Hrof's care. It was time to learn the lore of the sea. Hrof and Sven, by now fast friends, helped each other empty the amphorae, and Sven learned a new repertoire of sailorly curses. There was a lot for Diccon to master, from netmaking and splicing rope to learning the fishes of the deep sea and the Powers that ruled the waters. Among other things, he memorized the cantrips to call fish into nets, whistle up the wind, and ward off storms, gales, and rogue waves. It was Sven who taught him how to get mead from the mast by sticking his knife into it and milking it, much as Marit could distance-milk her cows. Sven always did have a practical approach to things.

Diccon's winter was more than busy. He went from craftmaster to craftmaster, from the falconer to the musicians and skalds, from woodsman to weaver to cook, soaking up the lore and as much of the skills and magics peculiar to each one that his maimed hand would allow. As he cross-trained, he discovered certain aspects that cut across the trades, certain Laws which all obeyed. Things like the Law of Similarity, in which one item or being that resembles another may be magically acted on (or magically act) in a similar manner. It was like a kind of mental thunderbolt, this sudden realization that by knowing and understanding these Laws, he could devise spells on his own, and that he didn't have to rely on memorized material which had been created by others. It was then that Diccon truly grew up as a wizard.

The only thing remaining for his education was for him to be tested by the Bear-Star Clan. In the old days, a candidate was examined by a panel of the Clan members and the *erilaz*, but with Muha's passing, only three high-level adepts remained in Sugi Jarl's domain. It was pretty much impossible to hunt down and assemble enough members of the Clan in order to undertake this testing. Hrof, Hedwy, and Ragnar, the local smith, were members, but three weren't enough to conduct an examination at this level . . . or hadn't been, before the recent battle. Now, it would have to do. In addition, Diccon still had to make his scramasax, which meant a stint at the forge. Ragnar agreed to part with a chunk of his prized star-metal for this, and Diccon began shaping a piece of amber for its hilt.

The familiar smells of the forge caressed Diccon's nostrils as he set out his tools and asked the forge fire and anvil to help him with his task. He'd gotten skilled in the use of his artificial finger, but he was woefully clumsy compared with what he'd been able to do before, and his smith's muscles had softened during the winter. He'd have to practice his forgecraft again, learning how to adjust to his new physical limitations. Ragnar suggested that he work back up to his former strength by pounding metal for the village for a while. He would be helped at first by the smith's apprentice, a placid fellow named Thorarin Arnulf's son, known far and wide as "Squirrel" because, unlike that chattering rodent, he rarely said more than two words at one time. Squirrel was to hold the hot metal on the anvil with his pliers while Diccon did the hammer work. One of the first things Diccon made was a short bar with weights on each end, which he would lift repetitively with one and then with what remained of the other hand, so as to bring back his arm muscles. The second thing that he made was a cupped thumbless mitt, which was attached to another leather wristlet. That way, he could handle light pliers after a fashion. He wanted to be able to use his left hand as much as possible in his forge work.

Yule was now long past, with its feasting, bright lights, baking, and evergreens brought into the longhouse for decoration. Sven, to his great joy, learned how to brew Yule-ale, which was much stronger than the usual variety. Now, it was the season of slow, snowy days leading up to spring, when the seaman begins to think about his boat, and the farmer his fields.

Out in the woods, in a hole under a half-rotted oak tree, four week-old fox cubs began to explore their den, venturing away from the immediate vicinity of their mother's teats. One cub discovered a brick-shaped metal box off to the side of the den. He was curious about it, but his mother announced lunch, and he forgot about it again in the dash to beat his brother and sisters to the best teat. The strange box could be investigated at another time.

# Chapter 30

One beautiful early spring day, just as the willow buds were beginning to show yellow and the long-legged storks were returning from the far lands of the south, Diccon finally felt confident enough to make his scramasax. The blade and tang had to be made during one forging, which meant that he couldn't leave the smithy for any reason until the job was done. Sugi Jarl's wife made sure that the young man would get fed, and that there was a bucket for other necessities. She also made very sure that a trusted thrall, not Old Sven, would be responsible for bringing the occasional pitcher of ale to the smithy.

Some things were done differently here in the south. There was no coal; Sugi's smith fired his forge using charcoal alone. Out of respect for his host, Diccon used the traditions of this particular smithy if they differed from those he'd learned at home during his apprenticeship. For one thing, the libation to the forge fire and Thor was ale, not rowan mead. For another thing, before awakening the anvil, Ragnar would remove his apron, which had been laid on the anvil like a coverlet the night before, and greet the anvil as if it were a live human. Thus warned, the anvil wouldn't be surprised by the three hammer-strokes that would set it to ringing like a bell, rousing the magic of the smithy from its slumber. For a third thing, the anvil and the tools to be used that day got a drink of ale, too. But most things were the same as back at home.

Star-metal required special care. It was an iron-nickel alloy, and first had to be heated and beaten a number of times in order to coax out any stony impurities, and to test the metal for suitability. Diccon had to do all his work himself, and he thanked his lucky stars that he'd made that cupped wide mitt for his left hand. The smith worked the bellows and fetched things, telling Squirrel to pay close attention to everything that was done. Since not a word was to be uttered during the forging, only the bellows, Diccon's Great Hammer, and the forge fire would speak that day.

Diccon raised his head, closed his eyes, and awoke the anvil with his Great Hammer, telling it what it was going to be called on to do that day. He asked for its especial aid in the forging of this so-important Tool, and then gave ale before feeding the forge fire its breakfast. Among the lumps of charcoal, there were bits of mistletoe, which grew profusely in Sugi's land. At home, mistletoe was rare, and was only used for the most advanced work or for things like Gytha's arrow paste.

Svarting checked out the room, making sure that there were no evil spirits lurking about. He would remain on watch during the entire process, as sort of a feline security system. It would be up to him to drive off anything malign which might dare enter the smithy.

The young smith cradled the two-something pound nugget of star-metal in his right hand, muttering under his breath the Making charms taught to him by his master back home. Then he placed it on the lip of the forge-box and took up his long-handled pliers. Oblivious to Squirrel, Svarting, and Sugi's smith, he began his work, focusing his entire being on the star-metal. It was as if he were the Cosmic Smith who forged the bright stars and set them in the sky-dome, who knew the inner secrets of the earth's metals. Diccon was more than half in trance, Voyaging to the beat of his Great Hammer on the metal on the anvil. It wasn't easy working with a crippled left hand, but somehow the young smith transcended that limitation and soared with the forge fire sparks as the star-metal was heated, shaped, and returned to the fire to re-heat. He didn't even notice his left hand; he just followed the beat and flowed with the metal as he worked the star-metal with the help of the sacred earth-born flame and his Hammer.

The day sped quickly, and both Ragnar and Squirrel ate, drank, and used the bucket. Diccon was in another plane of awareness; he never left the forge, never swallowed a drop or ate a crumb. He was the metal, and the metal was him. He drew in the Powers of Earth, wedding them to the Sky-Powers inherent in the metal which the gods had thrown from their home beyond the starry dome to the world of Man.

The sun touched the western horizon as Diccon was shaping the tang, and he had to set the runes on the blade by the light of the forge fire and an oil lamp held close by a weary Squirrel. The celestial Power shuddered and sang through his body as he engraved the runes on the blade, which accepted them eagerly. Finally the Work was done, and the finished blade thrust into the barrel of thunder-water. When the bubbling, hissing, and clouds of steam had subsided, Diccon retrieved the blade, holding it for the first time in his ungloved right hand. The raw Power sang in it so strongly that Diccon had to quickly place the blade on the edge of the forge box and re-glove his hand. Now he realized why his master only handled his scramasax by its amber hilt, and never touched the blade. It was a direct conduit to the Power beyond the celestial sphere, the naked sky-fire that the gods alone could seize.

Diccon was still partially in trance as he fastened the amber hilt on the tang and sharpened the blade, using a series of files and grind-stones. He polished the bright blade with ashes from the forge, bringing the metal to a mirror-like sheen. When at last the scramasax was truly finished, Diccon held it high, saluting the heavens from whence the metal had come. The blade shone brightly in the firelight like a silver beam of unearthly light.

It was then that the young man emerged from trance, reeling from fatigue and the shock of returning to the here-and-now. Ragnar supported the young man's suddenly weak body, guiding him to a bench where he could sit and relax. Diccon's head hung down, his eyes drooping in weariness, and his right hand shook as the incredible forge-Power sank back into the earth, to be roused again only when another such Tool would be made.

"That was very well done!" The smith smiled approvingly at Diccon and continued, "I couldn't do any better myself, and I've been pounding metal for twenty years! Here, have some ale! You must be parched!"

Diccon suddenly realized that he was terribly thirsty and hungry, and he emptied the proffered tankard as quickly as Sven might have done. Ragnar then handed him a bearskin scabbard, which was just large enough to take the entire length of the blade. Diccon looked at him curiously and the smith nodded, a toothy smile spreading in his brown beard.

"It's a great honor to host another smith in the making of one of his most sacred Tools," he said quietly, "Please take this scabbard as my gift. The Power of the bear is more than most folks realize. May it be with you now and in the future as you use this blade!" The smith, a member of the Bear-Star Clan, recognized that his temporary protégé would soon be invited to join that secretive confederation of Master-grade Talents.

Diccon thanked the smith, and then rose to thank the anvil, the forge fire, his Great Hammer, and the other tools which he'd used in the making of the scramasax. Only then was he able to sit and eat, devouring huge chunks of cold roast pork and chicken laid on good oat bread. Squirrel went out for more ale. Then he and Ragnar joined Diccon in the late-night meal. The smith laid Diccon's leather apron over the anvil, bidding the anvil to sleep until the next day, when it would be called upon once again to work.

Diccon was bone-tired. He'd been at his Work from just after sunrise to late at night. He finally rose, thanked Ragnar and Squirrel once again, and then wearily staggered off to his bed in Sugi Jarl's longhouse. Svarting, who'd curled himself into a ball next to the warm stones of the forge box, was already asleep, and he spent the night there in comfort, dreaming catly dreams.

The clatter of the usual household chores woke Diccon early the next morning. He was still exhausted, so he rolled over and tried to get back to sleep. He lay there, but sleep wouldn't come. It wasn't until Svarting, who'd begged a perfectly delightful breakfast from the kitchen crew, jumped up on the bed and snuggled into the crook behind Diccon's legs, purring his sleepy-time spell, that Diccon slid back into a doze. That doze led into deep sleep, and Svarting kept a faint purr going as long as he could. He was comfortable and fed, so he soon joined his human in dreamland.

After a while, Ragnar spoke to Sugi Jarl, and the clatter ceased. The members of the household found other things to do outside while Diccon and Svarting slept on, waking only when the sun was halfway down to the western horizon. The young man stretched and yawned vastly, feeling the good ache of muscles well-used, and then he slowly struggled to a seated position. This woke Svarting, who immediately chirruped, hopped off the bed, and headed off for a much-belated lunch. Still half-dazed with sleep, Diccon got to his feet and readied himself for the day. He was surprised that he'd slept as long as he had, but he'd really needed it.

After a quick bite to eat, he pulled out the bearskin scabbard and held it in his hands. Forging his scramasax had been an incredible experience, and he re-lived portions of that process as he sat there staring at the long black furry sheath which had a smooth amber hilt sticking out of one end, half-unbelieving that now he, too, had made the second of a Master Smith's major Tools, and that the work was good. Ragnar came into the room at that point, carrying two horns and a pitcher of ale. The two smiths sat there, silently sipping the good ale and admiring the rune-inscribed bright star-metal blade.

Several days later, when Diccon had fully recovered from his Work, he went down to the docks to visit Hrof. He hadn't seen much of the Master Seaman of late, and he didn't want to seem standoffish. He brought a medium-sized keg of mead with him, and wasn't at all surprised to see Old Sven there, helping Hrof eat golden smoked herring and exchanging tall stories. When Sven saw the keg, he stopped mid-story, and filled his tankard to the brim. Diccon was glad that Hrof was obviously pleased to see him, and he told his two companions about his Work at the forge. This called for more mead, and before long, the keg was dry.

Hrof mentioned that these past few days he'd been feeling faintly uneasy about something. He couldn't put his finger on it, but there was something not quite right. The *vettir* were restless, and were moving uncomfortably about from place to place. Diccon tried to sense what the disturbance was, but all he got was a very weak unsettled feeling. Nothing strong, nothing that he could identify.

Deep in the foxhole, the cubs were getting stronger and more playful. They had wonderful games, chasing each other about and gnawing on their mother's ears and tail. The largest male, eager to test his teeth on something harder, had begun gnawing on the brick-shaped box, worrying one corner and loosening the wax seal slightly. After a while, he tired of that game and went over to get a snack from his long-suffering mother.

It was a small hole, but it was just large enough to let a whisper of Froðuwarða's Terror spell begin to leak out.

# CHAPTER 31

The uneasy feeling was getting stronger. It was still impossible to track down from whence it came. It was a faint "off" whiff in the magical environment, still only detectible if one really concentrated on it. Sugi Jarl, who as chieftain was linked to the land-*vettir*, felt their unease and began prowling around, trying to get a bead on whatever it was that was spooking them.

Then unlucky things started happening. Stupid accidents and unforseen phenomena, such as Sven dropping a half-full amphora of Milo's best wine. Sven had *never* dropped anything that had booze in it. He got a mouthful of pottery shards and sand from the floor when he tried to suck up what he could. One of the pottery shards cut his lip, and suddenly Milo started learning how fluently and eloquently a Northman could swear.

Then there was the curious case of Groa Harald's dottir and the weasel; folks were laughing about that one for days. But it was when all the milk, cream, and ale in the village suddenly soured that things came to a head. Sugi Jarl went out to the rounded standing stone which the *vettir* called home, with a horn of mead to gift them. When he got there, it was clear to him that they had fled. He raised his head, sniffing the air, letting his land-senses roam . . . and yes, the good *vettir* were nowhere within his lands or ken. Something had spooked them, and they no longer watched over Sugi's lands, no longer warded off bad luck, no longer protected everyone from any magical attack. Sugi's lands now lay naked and vulnerable.

One of the responsibilities of a Jarl was to maintain and protect his lands, crops, herds, and people. He was also supposed to be a prosperity and luck-bringer. Only with the good will and active participation of the *vettir* was this possible. Now it was as if they had never existed. It was up to Sugi Jarl to figure out what had driven them away, and how to bring them back home.

The first thing he did was to summon Diccon, Hedwy, Hrof, Sven, Ragnar, and any others with Talent to his longhouse for an urgent meeting. He hoped that one or several of them might have some hints or clues to follow up, but so far, there was no point source that could be identified for whatever it was that had chased off the *vettir*. Hrof came the closest to identifying a direction; his navigation magic suggested that yes, this evil seemed to emanate from a single source, and that this source was not in the settlement proper.

Toki Orm's son, who was a skilled hunter and tracker, tried linking with Hrof, since he had the land-navigation Talent. The two men weren't meshing well until Diccon joined in. Diccon's cross-training permitted him to bring all of the Talented, one by one, into a kind of mental fusion where they could, as a single gestalt being, begin to sniff out the alien magic that was causing the problem. With so many Talents in the Unit, the Power's sensitivity was stepped up so that what was to each single Talent an impalpable, inchoate unease became a definite taint of black magic flowing into Sugi's lands from a relatively close-by nexus. Diccon, who had been in a similar Unit before, spearheaded the search, and it was he who identified the Terror spell for what it was. He'd faced its like before.

The flow of Dark magic came from the southeast, from the direction of the great battle with Agnold the Black. It wasn't a strong flow; just a tiny trickle, but what was coming through was nauseatingly evil. There was just enough of it for the Talents to determine a likely vector, somewhere within a cone of about 45 degrees fanning outwards to the southeast from Sugi Jarl's longhouse. Two of the younger, more inexperienced apprentice mages became ill and disoriented, and suddenly dropped out of the Unit. Before others could be similarly affected, Diccon dropped the linkage and suggested that he and three or four of the strongest Talents set out at once in search of the source. Sugi Jarl agreed, with the stipulation that the seekers be accompanied by a group of scouts, archers, and armed men just in case. Agnold was dead, but it was entirely possible that one or several of his followers had remained behind in hiding, biding their time and waiting for their chance to swoop down on the last of Sugi's Wise Ones in order to clear the decks for a final revenge attack. Almost seven months had passed since the great battle, and Sugi's people had begun to relax. Tactician that he was, Sugi knew that a trap like this, if it worked, would render his lands totally unprotected by any magic whatsoever, and would make it easy meat for a daring foe.

Sven fortified himself liberally with some of Milo's strongest wine. Then he carefully poured the rest of the amphora into a large beeswaxed wineskin which was nestled in his backpack. He put the heavy pack on backwards, so that it hung on his chest with the straps crossing his back. The skin had a spout, into which the canny old lush inserted a long hollow reed so that he could suck up the wine without dropping or spilling it. This arrangement also left his hands free. He didn't mind looking foolish; this was business, and he wanted to be prepared.

Diccon thrust the handle of his Great Hammer in the belt which held his scabbarded scramasax, and Hedwy snatched up her "ready-pack" of healing herbs, bandages, and potions. Hrof slung a coil of rope over his left shoulder; one end of it was attached to a wickedly barbed harpoon he'd used for catching sharks. His lumpy canvas ditty bag, smelling ferociously of sailor's tar, dangled from the hand not holding the harpoon, and a short white rune-carved whalebone whistle hung from a tarred linen cord around his neck. Toki Orm's son, the hunter, packed various items in a leather backpack, including flint, striker, and tinder. His long scabbarded gutting-knife swung at his hip, and he had his "mission face" on. Five brawny swordsmen came forth, clad in mail byrnies and helmets, along with two leather-clad archers and three scouts wearing their forest green-grey-brown-white mottled tunics. Svarting, who had not been invited to go with the expedition, lurked invisibly in the shadow of one of the out-buildings, waiting for the party to set out on their mission. He had absolutely no intention of being left behind. He wanted to be where the action was.

Sugi Jarl pronounced a blessing on the group, calling on Thunor, Tiw, and Freij to watch over them as they went into harm's way. He would continue to call on the gods until either the menace was abated or the expeditionary force was slain to a man or woman. If the latter case happened, his men would arm themselves and prepare to defend their homes as best they could. Sugi fervently hoped that this would not be necessary. Swords and shields were no match for a magical attack.

The scouts went first, fanning out in front of the archers. If they spotted anything suspicious, they would alert the archers as to the nature of the opposition by means of bird and animal cries. They were also alert to any tracks left in the scattered patches of late-spring snow. The armed men, who were a lot noisier due to their mail shirts and heavy feet, surrounded the Talents, relying on them to use their Powers to get in a first shot at any enemy in their way. When the last man disappeared into the scrubby woods, Svarting darted out from his hiding place to bring up the rear. He could already feel the evil. Cats have a certain inborn Talent which permits them to see the Unseen. This particular Unseen had a familiar flavor about it. He tried to remember, but all he could think of was being lost and something about a rat.

It was a tacit agreement among the scouts that they take the central axis. That approach had the best probability of finding the source of whatever it was that drove off the *vettir*. They couldn't detect any evil yet; they were not Talented. They moved silently, with only the occasional "all-clear" chirp in the way of communication. The warriors looked about as they walked, carefully scanning under evergreen trees and at large boulders which might hide a man. Sven took an occasional drag on his reed as he formulated one of his famous curses, something that he could let fly in the wink of an eye. Svarting closed up behind, and soon was hopping along in front of Diccon, his eyes wide and whiskers a-tremble. The young smith was glad to see his friend, but he was also concerned that if things got rough, Svarting might go through several or all of his nine lives in one fell swoop.

Svarting began to angle slightly to the north, and his fur began to bush out. Toki noticed the young tom's actions and appearance, and voiced two crow-calls followed by the chitter of a squirrel. This told the archers and scouts that they were heading too far to the south, and that they should reorient their path of march. The hunter knew full well about the special senses of various animals, and he realized that Svarting was homing in on the source of the evil spell. Three blue jay calls answered him, telling him that the scouts and archers had heard his signal.

The scouts paused, letting the archers and then the main body of the group catch up with them. The forest was silent . . . no bird calls, no rustle of animals startled by the group's progress through the woods. Any tracks were old, and all were headed towards them. This was highly unusual; it seemed as if the local wildlife had also been routed by the evil whatever-it-was. It would be obvious to an enemy lurker if suddenly there were animal and bird cries where there should be none, so a different means of communication would have to be used.

The scouts, now following Svarting, headed out again, keeping one eye alert to the world about them, and the other on the cat, whose black and white pelt was easily seen in the early-spring landscape. Svarting's ears were flattened back on his head, and every hair on his body was fluffed out as far as it could fluff. He scooted from budding bush to stump to rock to dark hollow under a fir tree, darting and pausing like a veteran woodsman. The armed men loosened their swords in their scabbards, and Diccon grasped the hilt of his scramasax in his good right hand. Sven took three mighty swallows of his wine, as Hrof hooked his ditty bag to his belt and lifted his whalebone whistle to his lips.

But all was still; hardly a twig moved. The scouts, using hand signals now, stayed within sight of the archers, who in turn were within sight of the Talents and warriors. They drifted through the woods silently, with only the occasional muted jingle of a byrnie or rustle of dead leaves under a heavy boot.

Svarting gradually slowed down. He looked as if he were fighting his way forward against a heavy wind, but the air was still. He, of all of them, most strongly felt the dark Power streaming toward the group from someplace just ahead. He tried not to gag or spit as he slowly put one paw in front of the other, almost creeping, his belly-fur brushing the ground.

Suddenly, the scouts raised their hands simultaneously in the "stop!" signal. When everyone had halted and the small sounds of human movement had ceased, the scouts turned their heads back and forth, listening as hard as they could.

Silence.

Toki, in the main body of the party, had unusually keen hearing, and he, too, could hear nothing besides the breathing sounds made by his companions. The scouts signaled again, this time for a cautious, slow, silent advance. The archers nocked arrows, and the warriors slowly drew their swords. Whatever they were hunting was close by, and everybody was tense and incredibly alert. Danger sang silently in the air. The Talented could all sense the source just ahead of them, and even some of the warriors were now picking up on it.

Svarting paused at the brushy edge of a small clearing. In the center stood a huge old oak tree, one that Svarting suddenly remembered that he had seen before. He also suddenly remembered catching the rat, climbing the tree, the rat's escape, the tussle inside the hollow of the tree, and the heavy metal box that he'd guided down the fox hole. He crouched low, trying to link with Diccon to tell him what he remembered. Diccon couldn't hear him clearly; all he got was a sense of heightened danger and that the oak tree was where the spell was coming from. Diccon nudged Toki and pointed to the tree, and Toki risked a mouse-squeak to get the scouts' and archers' attention.

The archers split up, moving as silently as a cloud of smoke, and took up positions behind tree trunks, their arrows trained on the oak tree. If anyone emerged from the hole at the base of the tree, he or she would be full of arrows in a trice. Svarting eased back to Diccon, looking up at him with huge yellow eyes, willing Diccon to reach down and touch his head so that maybe he could punch his message through that way. Diccon, alert to his feline companion's hint, squatted down, taking his right hand off the hilt of his scramasax, and touched the young tom's head between the ears as he'd seen the smith at home do with Svarting's mother.

A blurred vision of the sequence of events got through. Diccon could judge the approximate size of the metal box, and he signalled this information to the others. He then pointed to the hole in the tree and pantomimed digging, followed by the motions of pulling something out of the ground. The others nodded agreement. Then Diccon stood and beckoned to Hedwy. When she came over, Diccon mouthed the word "salt," and then made as if he were strewing something in a circle. Hedwy nodded; first they had to wall off the spell so that when they tried to disarm and destroy it, it wouldn't flare up in a lethal burst of Power and affect every living thing within its originally specified sphere of influence.

The scouts and Toki heard no human or animal movement, which meant that there probably wasn't a sentient enemy ambush waiting for them. At least not there. Toki suggested in a low whisper that they scout around the clearing, and that the armed men station themselves so that the Talents wouldn't be taken by surprise. He'd realized that this was going to be a wizard's task, and that the pumped-up warriors would need something useful to do and think about while the Talents worked.

The warriors nodded grimly and spaced themselves around the clearing, just inside the tree line. Their heads swivelled from left to right and back again as they searched for any incoming threats. The scouts kept circling slowly and silently, alert to any sounds, no matter how minuscule, that might indicate an enemy approaching them.

Hrof let the whistle fall from his lips; it wouldn't be effective on an inanimate object. Hedwy moved slowly around the clearing's edge sunwise, scattering salt and chanting under her breath, followed by Diccon, who erected a nail fence similar to the one set by his master that had corralled the Dark spell which had hit him back in his home village.

The Master Seaman then sat down on a low rock and pulled a wooden jar out of his ditty bag. He uncapped it and carefully began smearing some of the greasy yellowish contents on the head of his harpoon. His magic was that of the sea, but maybe this charm would work on a land-thing.

Sven swayed gently, his Adam's apple bobbing up and down as he drained the last of the wine from the skin in his pack. He burped loudly, burped again, and pulled out his stubby mistletoe wand, the one he'd used to contain the demon serpent in the abandoned village. With that as a scriber, he set certain runes and sigils, which glowed faintly with a greenish-golden color, around the outside of Diccon and Hedwy's circle. When he got back to where he'd started from, he put his wand away (it took him some time to do so, since he was as tight as a tick) and got out his stone-thrower and a few pellets which looked a lot like acorn-sized hailstones.

While all this was going on, Toki dug around in his leather backpack and brought out his fire-making tools. He and two of the warriors then hacked out a biggish hole in the ground just inside the circle, heaping the dug chunks of earth in a berm around the outside of the hole. They gathered bits of dead wood and laid a bonfire, and Diccon, in his role of smith, kindled it. Fire was a good way to destroy a magical artifact, and he wanted a nice hot roaring fire handy for that purpose.

The Dark spell emanating from the base of the tree was unwavering, and seemed to take no notice of all the preparations. Diccon made sure that nobody was standing within the circle. He didn't want a messy death or three when he finally went in after the metal box.

It would be up to him and Svarting to actually retrieve the box from its hiding place inside the tree. Hrof would be standing just outside the circle, harpoon at the ready. Hedwy, also standing outside the circle, would make sure that it stood firm when the evil Power was unleashed: and Toki was in charge of the fire, which was close enough to the edge of the circle so that he could tend it from outside.

It was time. Diccon once again placed one finger on Svarting's head, asking him if he really wanted to do this thing. The young cat shivered, blinked, and then gave Diccon a quick purr, saying yes. He was a wizard's cat, the companion of an *erilaz* in the making, and he couldn't turn tail and run when the going got tough. He then turned toward the tree. Slowly he advanced with Diccon right behind him, bright-bladed scramasax in his right hand. Behind them, the other Talents sealed the narrow gate in the circle, magically walling Diccon and Svarting inside.

As they neared the hole, the evil exuding from it made Svarting gag and spit. Diccon felt increasingly queasy and disoriented, but he knew that it was up to him to get the box out into the open. He muttered a quick prayer to Thor as Svarting, hissing and spitting, entered the hole.

# CHAPTER 32

Back home, the villagers had celebrated Yule in a variety of moods. Inga, head-over-heels in the throes of puppy love, was gaga over Ulfgeir, who was now regarded as quite a competent smith. Ulfgeir was more than happy to return her affection, and the smith kept on having to separate them and shoo her home, so that the young man could get some work done.

Marit mourned Diccon's absence, and prayed every night to Freyja that he'd soon come home to her. Odd had managed to get Hilda, one of Aun's "sisters," with child. Upon hearing the news, Hilda's sister Ragny, she who was the *seiðkona*, insisted that Odd and Hilda get married as soon as possible. Since nobody in their right mind would dare challenge a *seið* witch, the date was set on the spot. The chieftain and his wife were thrilled; a grandson at last! Gytha had determined the sex of the unborn child, and Grandpa and Grandma started sifting through baby names even before the wedding.

Once married, Odd seemed to settle down and began applying himself to learning the duties and responsibilities of a jarl's heir. Berit's health and strength returned, to Halfdan's great joy, and Gytha pronounced the soon-to-be-born Solfinna healthy and strong. Arngrim the Lucky had gotten used to having ten daughters and no sons. The birth of their tenth daughter had been easy, but Sigyn had nursed for barely three months when Gytha told her that yes, she was pregnant again. Arngrim nearly fainted when the Wise Woman told him that this time it was a boy.

Helga, Sven Bluemouth's wife, missed her husband dreadfully, though she'd never admit it even to Mussi, her young grey tabby tomcat. Thord the Clumsy's leg finally healed, although it would never be straight again and he would walk with a limp. Arni and Thorstein, along with Gufi Gylfi's son and Dagfinn Thord's son, spent days at a time in the woods hunting for game, and they kept fresh meat on the table for everyone in the village. For some reason, game was unusually plentiful that year, and the men had no problems bagging all they could carry and drag back home.

None of them had any idea that Diccon was facing the deadliest danger yet.

The hole under the oak tree was empty. The fox family had fled a week before, and had taken up residence in a hollow log a mile away. Svarting eeled down into the depths of the den, and had almost reached the lead box when Diccon reached in with his cupped iron mitt, hooked him around his middle, and tossed him backward out of the hole and into the clearing. This wasn't the time for half-measures, and Diccon's mitt was much better at digging than the cat's paws. Svarting was miffed at being shoved aside, but what was done was done, and all he could do now was to send strength to Diccon, linking with him in the hopes that this augmented Power would guide Diccon's hands and that the box could be brought into the open, where the evil spell pent within could be dealt with.

Diccon wormed his way deeper into the hole, effectively blocking out the light. A faint gloom was afforded by the rat's-girth hole 'way above his head, but essentially, the young man had to probe his way forward with his good hand, which held the bright-bladed scramasax gripped tightly in its fingers. Svarting had visualized a big brick-shaped object, but what appeared to be a large object to a cat would be smaller in scale to a human. Bits of fluff and mold spores filled the air as Diccon pawed at the fox hole, making him sneeze. Sneezing while trying not to vomit is a difficult feat, so the young smith gritted his teeth, swallowed hard, and dug on.

Every so often, Diccon had to back out of the hole in order to get a clean breath of air, and to pull heaps of dug earth, rotten wood, and fluff out of the hole. After about three repeats of this exercise, Diccon used his cupped metal mitt to enlarge the opening of the hole so that he could scoop up dirt and fling it out behind him in one motion, like how a dog digs. A larger hole also permitted fresh, clean air to enter the hole where Diccon was working.

Just outside the perimeter of the faintly-glowing circle, the four Talents readied themselves for instantaneous action. Hrof's right arm, holding the harpoon, swept high and back, ready to begin the forward throw. Toki tossed pieces of broken dry branches and fir cones through the wall of the circle . . . items could pass from outside in, but not from the inside out . . . and into the medium-sized bonfire. He wanted a hearty blaze for destroying the item carrying the Terror spell.

Hedwy concentrated on maintaining the circle, and Sven leaned against a nearby tree, his eyes fixed on Diccon's rear end as the young man dug. He had one of the "hailstones" in his stone-thrower, which he cocked back into the "launch" position. The swordsmen, blades drawn, were at top alert, and the archers drew their bowstrings back.

Svarting, inside the circle and standing just behind Diccon, was the first to realize that Diccon's iron mitt had contacted the spell box. The thrusting mitt jarred the box enough to crack off more of the wax, releasing more of the Terror spell's power. The outwelling of sheer evil made the cat, and then Diccon, want to turn tail and run away as fast as possible. Svarting made it as far as the curving wall of the magical circle, but he fetched up there, unable to flee. Diccon, flailing out with his left arm, desperately scooped at the heavy box, trying to pull it towards him so that he could get it out of the hole and into the open where the other Talents could deal with it.

The box seemed to resist its eviction from the fox hole. Waves of stark Terror sheeted out of it, pouring over Diccon like a fetid, viscous flood of gibbering madness. Diccon's right hand, still clutching the bright-bladed scramasax, split some of the spell's impact, shunting it away from striking the young man directly with its full strength. But even the side-lobes were bad enough. Screaming, Diccon dug harder, desperately seeking to cup his iron hand around the box so that he could back out of the hole, dragging it free of the tree.

Svarting screamed, too. A sudden heartfelt cat scream can be amazingly loud and unnerving. One of the archers, startled by Svarting's outburst, loosed an arrow at the tree; fortunately, it missed Diccon's furiously moving rear end by a whisker and struck the tree trunk, sinking half its length deep into the rotting wood.

The tip of Diccon's iron mitt finally snagged the far corner of the box, and the young man began to wiggle his way backward out of the hole, his left arm outstretched to haul on the box, and his right hand, clutching the glowing scramasax, in front of his face. This meant that he had to rely on his right elbow, his knees, and his booted feet to grip the ground in order to caterpillar his way backward. Slowly, ever so slowly, the box began to move, and Diccon was able to cup more and more of his mitt around it. The box moved more and more quickly, and the watchers outside the circle saw Diccon finally pulling himself backwards out of the enlarged hole in the tree.

Diccon's shoulders cleared the opening. Screaming, the young man made a huge swiping motion with his left hand, scooping the box clear of the hole and throwing it a man's height behind him on to the ground. When the box hit, the last of the beeswax seal pulled free, and the top spun off the box. The full fury of the Terror spell unleashed itself within the confines of the circle. Svarting desperately tried to scrabble out of the circle. No sanity rode in his eyes now; the young tom was gripped in a world of absolute madness. He screamed again, shuddered, and fell to the ground, his rigid body twitching and vibrating on the earth.

Diccon wasn't in much better shape. His body was now between the box and his star-metal scramasax. He slumped to the ground, mewling in terror, and tried to draw his knees up to his chest in the fetal position. His Great Hammer, which was thrust in his belt, probably saved his life at this point; one of its peens had dug into the earth, and the Hammer began bleeding off the Terror spell from Diccon's body into the earth. But the people outside of the circle had no way of knowing whether Diccon was alive or dead.

The spell-box lay on its side, its opening facing Hrof. The Master Seaman's raised arm blurred into motion, launching the harpoon at the opening.

Simultaneously, Sven launched his pellet and spat out a highly consonantal phrase. His curse followed the butt end of the harpoon, riding the rapidly uncoiling rope. The harpoon struck true, its sharp barbed tip piercing the contents of the box and then the bottom of the box itself. Sven's curse roiled forward on the harpoon, vanishing into the maw of the box. The pellet followed the curse into the velvet inkiness of the box.

Hrof, who'd quickly placed the bonfire between himself and the box, began hauling his catch toward him as quickly as possible. The box was beginning to make horrifying screeching noises as the salve-smeared harpoon, Sven's curse, and the "hailstone" pellet mixed it up with the original contents. Hrof hauled even faster on his rope, hand-over-hand. The box, transfixed by the harpoon, bounced hard on the ground two times, and then bounced into the fire. Hedwy, Hrof, and Toki hastened to stiffen the walls of the circle as much as they could. Given the choice of having the contents of that box (and Sven's curse) loose on the land, or sacrificing two lives, there was no choice. Diccon and Svarting would have to take their chances.

The box sat in the fire for only the time it takes a man to take one quick breath before it exploded violently. Scraps of burning wood, melted droplets of lead, and a huge yellow-white fireball instantly filled the entire hemisphere of the circle, churning and battering at its walls. The armed men had spun around to see what was happening when Svarting screamed, and now they lunged a few steps forward, shields high. They stopped short of the brilliantly-flaring dome of light, eyes wide as they saw the utter chaos within.

Slowly the light faded and died away. The oak tree, which had housed the box for a while, was now a smoking, ragged stump. It and all the ground within the circle's perimeter was battered and blackened. Just in front of the stump lay a human-shaped black lump. Sven darted up to the dome, hands out in front of him. Diccon was a friend, and here he was burnt to a crisp! The old lush ran right through the walls of the circle, which admitted him as easily as it had Toki's bits of firewood. Sobbing, he collapsed by Diccon's side, half-fearing to touch him. Small bits of ash swirled up around Sven's knees . . .

. . . . and . . .

. . . Diccon . . .

. . . sneezed!

Sven gasped, and then grabbed the young man's shoulder, shaking it gently. Black ash cascaded off Diccon's body as he sneezed again. His belt, tunic, boots, and every hair on his body were ash, but his Great Hammer and scramasax were intact and untouched. It was these two Tools which had saved the young smith's life. The leather wristlet supporting Diccon's cupped metal mitt was ash, and the mitt itself was now a slowly-cooling puddle of metal. Fortunately, Diccon hadn't been wearing his mail shirt, which would have melted and fused to his body. Sven yelped the good news to the others, then grabbed Diccon's ankles to haul him out of the circle.

Hedwy released her part of the circle then, and Hrof and Toki went in to help Sven. Between the three of them, they got the unconscious Diccon over to the nail fence that he'd set. Hrof, thinking quickly, grabbed Diccon's right hand, which was still clutching the scramasax, and manipulated the blade so that it was the Tool of the smith who had set the nails which extracted enough of them in order to make an opening in the circle. Sven dashed back to retrieve what was left of Svarting, as Hrof and Toki carried Diccon to Hedwy, who had opened her medical kit.

"You've got two patients," said a now-sober Sven, "I think Svarting is still breathing. He was on the far side of the circle from the firepit, and he'd fallen behind a rock. Now, who has a jug?"

Nobody answered Sven's question, so he asked it again. And again. And again. When he opened his mouth to ask a fifth time, Hrof grabbed him by the arm, led him off to the side, and suggested that maybe he ought to find Milo. Milo had wine.

"By the way, let's both of us go and ask Sugi Jarl to send men with a stretcher. I'll make sure that we get home OK. I'm sure that Hedwy has things under control now, and she won't miss us."

By the time the two men reached Sugi Jarl's longhouse, the *vettir* had begun streaming back to their homes. The jarl had felt their return, and so he took a loaf of newly baked bread, a horn of his best mead, and a lump of butter as big as his fist out to the standing stone. He made a welcoming speech to the stone (and through it, to the *vettir*), explaining what had happened and why they had been forced into exile. Hrof and Sven, who arrived part way through the speech, filled in more details, and the good *vettir* let Sugi Jarl know that they understood, and that they would be more diligent in the future as far as their duties in protecting the land went. Sugi thanked them, and then he escorted Sven and Hrof back to his longhouse, wherein lay the kegs of Sugi's best mead.

Two weeks later, Diccon was finally permitted out of bed. He was as weak as a kitten, but he was sane. His hair and beard were beginning to grow back in, forming blond stubble which scraped against his skin if he brushed against them. Svarting had also survived, but he had to regrow several patches of skin, a whole new pelt, and his whiskers. He'd lost the very tip of his tail, too.

Two weeks after that, Diccon was back at the forge, working on a new cupped mitt. Sugi Jarl's household had been generous with clothes, and the smith gave Diccon a new bearskin sheath for his scramasax. Svarting, who looked horrible after his ordeal . . . any naked cat looks strange . . . milked his situation for all it was worth. Ten meals a day, a warm eiderdown cushion by the firepit, cream whenever he wanted it . . . yes, life was good.

Diccon's strength returned with the exercise, good food, and the knowledge that Agnold's forces were truly defeated and that the *vettir* would take singular pains to ensure that no enemy would ever again set foot over the jarl's borders.

One balmy summer night when the moon was full, Ragnar came to Diccon's bed where he slept. The smith gently awoke the young man, cautioning him not to make a sound. He whispered to Diccon to get his Tools, and to follow him. Puzzled, the young man pulled on his boots, tucked his Great Hammer in his belt, and made sure that his scramasax was snug in its new sheath. He padded as quietly as he could out of the hall, but Svarting heard him and felt that he had to be in on this mystery, too.

Curiosity seems to be inbred in the cat family. The young tom followed the two men outside, and then north to the standing stone. Hedwy and Hrof awaited them there. Svarting, who knew full well that he hadn't been invited, tucked himself into a tussock of grass where he couldn't be seen . . . but where he could see and hear everything that went on.

Hedwy asked the smith to stand watch. Then she and Hrof drew Diccon over to the stone, calling on the *vettir* to witness the short ceremony making Diccon a full member of the Bear-Star Clan. In low voices, they told him of the traditions of the Clan, how to contact his fellow members, recognition patterns, and certain other bits of information that must remain hidden from non-Clan folk. Svarting strained to hear, but the voices were too low. There wasn't much to see, either. Before the induction ceremony was completed, Svarting had fallen asleep, and so he missed the best parts. The *vettir* welcomed Diccon as an *erilaz* and Bear-Star Clan member, and added their blessings to those of the Healing Woman, the Master Seaman, and the smith.

When Diccon returned to his bed, the false dawn was brightening the eastern sky. The young smith-*erilaz* crawled under the cover, boots and all, and slept soundly until noon, when Sven woke him for lunch and a tankard of ale. The Dark was truly fled, and Sugi Jarl's lands were safe. With a light heart, Diccon tackled a large meal, and then he went down to Hrof's snug house to discuss travel plans. It was time to return home.

# CHAPTER 33

Marit was the first to learn that Diccon, Sven, and a stranger were sailing up the river. The seagulls had told the crows, who passed the word far and wide as only crows can. This meant that the girls ran to Soti Jarl's house with the news, and he sent runners out in all directions so that the far-travelers would have an appropriate welcome. Thorgrim and Ulfgeir hurried to bank the forge fire, and Gytha put on her best apron, the one with the wide embroidered hem that she'd inherited from her mother. Sigrun, the chieftain's wife, ordered the thralls to slaughter a sheep and four of the roosters for the feast that night. Odd took the opportunity to trot over to Aun's place to tell her the news, but somehow he got distracted while there, and none of them made it to the harbor in time to greet Wave-Cleaver and her passengers.

Diccon was surprised to see Berit among the welcoming committee. She'd been so ill when he left . . . but there she was, standing close to the idiotically-grinning Halfdan, and even Sven could tell that she was happy, healthy, and very pregnant. Halfdan laughed as he hugged his wife, delighting in life in general. Jan Sverre's son, the brewer, had brought his one-horse wagon down to the water's edge, with a keg of his finest nut-brown ale all tapped and ready for Sven's expert opinion. Thorgrim and Ulfgeir, still clad in their leather aprons, stood next to Jan's wagon, hinting broadly that yes, they would really *really* like to make sure that the ale was worthy of Sven's finely-tuned taste buds, and that they would gladly undertake the preliminary testing of same. Jan laughed heartily as he filled two brimming-full horns for them.

Wave-Cleaver's bow slid up on the beach, and Sven hopped out first. His eagle eyes had spotted Jan pouring out the ale, and he didn't want to miss out. As he loped toward the brewery wagon, Helga intercepted him, hugged him tight, and started scolding him among her kisses and tears. Diccon, shy about his left hand, hid it behind his back as he swung himself over the gunwale and onto the beach. Svarting casually hopped off after him, pretending a blasé indifference to the cold water he met upon landing. The smith started toward his erstwhile apprentice, but a leggy blonde blur passed him and leaped onto Diccon with open arms, covering his face with tear-wet kisses. The young man instinctively braced himself and reached out with both arms to catch her, clasping her around her waist. The smith, who'd hung back in the face of this greeting, saw what was left of Diccon's left hand and the clever cupped iron mitt which replaced it, and his smile momentarily went away. Then he grinned wide, nudging Ulfgeir to do likewise. Diccon and Marit clung to each other, and it was hard to say who was crying the most, or who was kissing whom the most. Gytha's sharp eyes instantly noticed Diccon's maimed hand, and her professional curiosity awoke, joining her gladness at seeing both Sven and Diccon return home safely.

The last to debark was Hrof, who was greeted effusively by the village seamen, all of whom wanted to look Wave-Cleaver over and exchange information on the weather and sea conditions. Hrof learned where the cod were running, three new knots, and who could fix nets if need be, all within the space of five minutes. The village seamen were singularly interested in Hrof's anchor, a four-pronged affair on a long wrought iron shank which had a massive holed chunk of soapstone reminiscent of a bulbous drop-spindle weight threaded on the shank. There was a loop at each end of the shank; a small one below the crossed prongs with a slender linen rope spliced to it, and a large loop at the far end of the shank, with the anchor line spliced to that. This anchor, when dropped, would fall so that the prongs would dig into the bottom. If they snagged, all Hrof would have to do was to haul in on the thin rope, which would lever the business end of the anchor upwards and pull the anchor's prongs free. Then, the anchor could either be re-set or hauled aboard.

It was a grand party. Marit accepted Diccon's offer of marriage, and paid hardly any attention to his left hand. Diccon was otherwise healthy and whole, and what with the staggering reward given him by Sugi Jarl, was probably now the richest man in the village. The chieftain asked him to be the new *erilaz* for the village, heartily seconded by Gytha, Marit, Sven, and Thorgrim. Everybody cheered and clapped when Diccon accepted the chieftain's offer, almost as loudly as they had when Diccon proposed to Marit a few minutes earlier.

The chieftain and the smith suggested that they go ahead and hold the wedding that very night. Diccon and Marit were more than agreeable, and suddenly the "welcome home!" party became a boisterous wedding feast. Thord the Clumsy, Orn's son, he who had broken his leg at the funeral games held for Arinbjorn, broke that same leg again when he leaped on top of a rickety table to propose a wedding toast and the table had collapsed.

Magni Wrongfoot supplied a whole sackful of puffins that he'd caught; they were plucked, gutted, stuffed with sage and dill, and roasted in the coals at the edge of the firepit. The sheep carcass turned slowly on its spit, frequently basted with ale and a honey-garlic-thyme blend. The smell of yeasty rye and oat bread filled the air, and excited children ran amok. Eirik and Egill Tune's sons, the twins, managed to drink themselves under the table, along with Simple Grinulf, Dagfinn's thrall, and the hunters Thorstein and Arni. Tosti, the carpenter, was made of sterner stuff, and was still standing when Soti Jarl, in his capacity as *goði*, performed the ceremony uniting Diccon and Marit. The smith had held off much of his drinking until after the wedding vows were taken, since he would be standing in for Thor, whose mighty hammer hallowed oaths and marriages.

Fortunately for all concerned, the ceremony was brief. Everybody wanted to kiss the bride, who blushed and giggled and kissed everybody on the cheek in turn. The more serious kissing would come later.

Moth, Skogi, and Mist, the now-grown children of the tuxedo cat, greeted Svarting eagerly, asking for news about his wide travels. The four cats then conspired to drag off one of the roasted roosters, and were promptly joined by their siblings Tussi (who was linked to Marit) and Mussi (linked to Helga, Sven's wife). The tuxedo cat had remained at the forge, very much on duty, and so she missed out on the festivities.

# CHAPTER 34

Once again, it was Time. The tuxedo cat heard her yowling suitors serenading outside the smithy, all eager to gift her with new life. But she had something else to do that night. The suitors could wait. Tonight she had to sing new life into Marit's womb, sing the human kitten-to-come, bring the child's spirit from the Otherworld. She settled next to the warm stones of the forge, humming her song, calling, and knowing that as a mother herself, her call would be answered.